Praise for the stories in *Love in Thirds*

Missing Linc

"*Missing Linc* is heartwarming and heart stopping! The sex is off the charts amazing with a little something for everyone..."

— Heather Nestorick, *Just Erotic Romance Reviews*

"Readers looking for a hot and sexy love story that will have their emotions on edge will enjoy *Missing Linc*."

— Ley, *Joyfully Reviewed*

"I've read a lot of ménage a trois love stories, but none come as close to perfection as Kori Roberts's *Missing Linc* in terms of physical eroticism and emotional depth."

— Marame, *Rainbow Reviews*

Redesigning Adele

"*Redesigning Adele* radiates heat from the beginning to end. The interaction between the characters is amazingly hot..."

— Dawnie, *Fallen Angel Reviews*

"This is a beautiful story with the perfect blend of sizzle and love to make any reader happy."

— Kimberley Spinney, *eCataromance*

"Hands down *Redesigning Adele* will make you blush and stutter."

— Natasha Smith, *Romance Junkies*

Loose Id®

ISBN: 978-1-59632-942-3
LOVE IN THIRDS
Copyright © December 2009 by Loose Id LLC
Cover Art by Natalie Winters
Cover Layout and Design by April Martinez

Publisher acknowledges the authors and copyright holders of the individual works, as follows:
MISSING LINC
Copyright © January 2009 by Kori Roberts
REDESIGNING ADELE
Copyright © January 2009 by Talya Bosco

Printed in the U.S.A. by
Lightning Source, Inc.
1246 Heil Quaker Blvd
La Vergne TN 37086
www.lightningsource.com

Contents

Missing Linc
Kori Roberts
1

Redesigning Adele
Talya Bosco
179

MISSING LINC

Kori Roberts

Chapter One

Some days, Lincoln Castillo wondered why he even bothered to get out of bed. As he slammed on his brakes, he knew without a doubt that this was one of them. The sea of traffic on the expressway engulfed his limousine and made movement of any kind virtually impossible.

As the traffic came to a halt, Linc felt his irritation escalate. He cursed the name of his employee and cousin Miguel, who called off from work at the last minute for the third time in as many weeks. His other drivers were all booked solid, which forced him to scramble and rearrange his schedule once again in order to fill in as chauffeur for the day.

"Fuck!" Linc slammed his hand against the steering wheel in frustration. He didn't have time for this shit right now. When he'd moved to Puerto Rico from New York several years ago, Linc figured he'd left this kind of headache behind as well.

He snorted in disgust. Apparently not. Rush-hour traffic in Puerto Rico—particularly on a Friday evening—was a real bitch. It didn't help matters that it was the height of tourist season, and there were even more vehicles on the road than normal. Linc was certain that the traffic jams here rivaled any he'd experienced during his entire thirty-two years growing up in New York City, and they made traveling around the island a complete fucking nightmare at times.

A glance at the clock on the dashboard made him swear again. His passengers' flight had arrived from New York more than thirty minutes ago. At the rate he was going, it would still be at least another twenty minutes before he reached the airport.

Linc hated being late, and everybody who worked for him knew it. Since he'd started his limousine company seven years ago, his drivers had always arrived on time for a scheduled pickup. And that was exactly how he liked it. Thanks to that little *pendejo* Miguel, his perfect track record was over.

Linc shook his head in disgust. Who needed enemies when you had family to make your life miserable?

His cell phone rang, and Linc glanced in the direction where he'd mounted it to the dashboard. He groaned when he saw the familiar number on the display. He reached out and pressed the Speaker button.

"*Hola*, baby. You miss me?" His secretary, Lorna, practically purred over the phone.

"What is it, Lorna?" Linc tried not to sound annoyed. He'd known Lorna for years. Extremely bold and outrageously flirtatious, she'd been trying to get him to fuck her since her first day on the job. That she was married and had three kids never deterred her from offering herself to him on a regular basis. Luckily for her, Lorna also happened to be the best assistant he'd ever had; otherwise, he would have let her ass go a long time ago.

"Your passengers called. Where are you?"

In hell. "I'm almost there," Linc lied. He stared out the window at the parking lot of vehicles around him. "I got caught in traffic. Call them back and tell them not to leave. I'll be there in a few minutes, okay?"

"*Sí*, baby, *anything* for you. I'll call them now."

Linc disconnected the call and fought the urge to yell. This was the last thing he needed. Not only was it bad for business, it had a tendency to really piss people off, especially when they were trying to enjoy their vacation.

With his luck, his passengers were some rich, old couple who would give him hell all the way to the hotel and demand a full refund once they got there. Shit.

Linc didn't give a damn if Miguel was family or not. Whenever he caught up with him, he was so fucking fired.

Convinced that he would have an episode of road rage if he sat in the same spot for another second, Linc released a small sigh of relief when traffic finally started to move, inching forward slowly for several minutes before progressing more rapidly. After a few miles, vehicles began to flow at a normal pace, and Linc allowed himself to feel a small glimmer of hope that he would get to the airport sometime before nightfall.

Fifteen minutes later, Linc arrived at his destination. He quickly navigated his limo into an available parking space alongside the curb, ignoring the honking of several angry motorists he cut off in the process.

Picking up the sign off the seat next to him, Linc read the names of his passengers. MR. AND MRS. MITCHELL ELLIOTT.

That's just great. Even their names sounded uptight. With a sigh, he opened the driver's door and climbed out of the limo. Linc paused long enough to straighten his hat and adjust his uniform before he joined the throng of people standing outside the terminal.

Holding up the sign in front of him, Linc searched through the crowd for his passengers, hoping they hadn't gotten too tired of waiting for him and taken a cab instead.

"Are you here for Elliott?"

Linc turned at the sound of the voice behind him. "Yes, ma'am, I…" His voice died in his throat at the sight in front of him.

Whoa. This definitely was *not* what he'd anticipated. Calling her beautiful seemed so inadequate. She was much more than that. Nevertheless, Linc couldn't think of a single word that was powerful enough, perfect enough, to describe her.

She wasn't tall; even with wedge-heeled sandals on, she only reached his shoulder. A strapless, baby-doll sundress with a colorful tie-dyed print covered her petite frame and provided the perfect contrast to her smooth brown skin.

Large, dark sunglasses held ink black hair away from a face that was an exotic blend of African and Asian ancestry. The long tresses hung in thick waves well past her shoulders. Almond-shaped eyes the color of cognac stared back at him from underneath the longest lashes Linc had ever seen. Her only makeup was a thin coating of gloss on full, sensuous lips that many women paid a fortune to emulate.

Linc stood there, frozen in place, staring at her with his mouth open, incapable of speaking a coherent word or having a logical thought. He watched in silence as the look of confusion on her face turned into one of understanding, and her mouth curved into a sexy smile.

It took a moment for Linc to realize that she'd spoken again. He'd been captivated by the sight of her; he hadn't heard a single word she said.

"Sorry, I didn't...what..." Linc paused and closed his eyes. Jesus, he sounded like a fucking idiot.

His eyes flew open at the sound of her soft chuckle. Linc didn't know if he felt relieved or horrified when he saw the amused look on her face.

"Elliott." She pointed to the sign that he still held in front of him. "That's us." She motioned between herself and the man next to her.

How in the hell did I overlook him? Linc found men to be just as attractive as women. He always enjoyed the unique types of pleasure he found in both sexes. And if someone asked him to describe the ideal man, Linc was certain that his description would match the one standing in front of him.

Only slightly shorter than Linc's own height of six feet, he had the physique of a man well acquainted with the inside of a gym. Strong and hard, he made a simple gray T-shirt and tan shorts look spectacular on his ripped and well-defined frame.

Sunglasses prevented Linc from seeing his eyes, but he felt certain that they were as amazing as the rest of him. His short, sandy brown hair and lightly tanned skin were the perfect complement to her darker coloring.

Physically, he was as handsome as she was beautiful, as masculine as she was feminine. Together, they made a stunning and gorgeous pair. He'd never met a woman or man who attracted him as much—or as quickly—as them.

With effort, Linc forced himself to focus on his job. "Hi, I'm Lincoln." He reached out to shake the woman's hand. "I'm very sorry for the delay." Her small hand was soft inside of his larger one. Linc felt his groin tighten as a sudden image of it wrapped around his hard dick came to mind.

"Hi, Lincoln. I'm Tomi." The smile she gave him was warm and genuine. "Don't worry about it. The secretary at your company called and explained that you would pick us up because the original driver had a death in his family."

Linc wanted to tell her that nobody was dead, but that would all change as soon as he got his hands on Miguel. In the meantime, he'd have to thank Lorna for her ability to think fast and lie well.

"Besides," she continued, "we've been enjoying the warm air and beautiful view." Their gazes locked for a long heartbeat before her hand eased from his.

Linc cleared his throat. "Well, thanks again for being so understanding and patient." He smiled. "I wish I had more customers like you."

He turned his attention to the man. His sunglasses no longer covered his eyes and now hung casually from the neckline of his T-shirt. As Linc predicted, his eyes were as impressive as the rest of the man.

Eyes the color of the clearest blue sky stared back at him as Linc reached for the man's outstretched hand. His strong, firm grip was in complete contrast to Tomi's gentler touch, but it was no less appealing.

"I'm Mitch." Damn, even his voice was sexy.

"It's nice to meet you both." Linc returned his smile. "And please, call me Linc." Reluctantly, he released Mitch's hand. "Is this your first time in Puerto Rico?" At their nods, his smile broadened. "Well, welcome to San Juan, the most beautiful city on the island."

He opened the door and helped Tomi into the limo. Linc tried not to stare at her toned legs and the sexy silhouette of her shapely ass when she climbed inside, but he failed miserably.

Linc glanced in Mitch's direction. He frowned when he saw the other man loading the luggage into the trunk.

"You don't need to do that. I'll take care of it." He reached for the bag in Mitch's hand. "Why don't you relax with Tomi in the limo? There's some cold champagne on ice waiting for you."

"It's cool, man. I don't mind." Mitch smiled and winked. "Besides, I've always liked two sets of hands better than one anyway."

Linc paused. He'd made—and received—far too many suggestive comments and sexual innuendos over the years for him not to be able to recognize a flirtatious remark when it came his way. And, that was *definitely* flirting.

Not that Linc was complaining. Mitch was a fine-ass man, and Tomi was the sexiest woman he'd ever met. So many responses came to mind, and normally, Linc would share each and every one of them in vivid detail. Instead, he kept them to himself. As tempting and alluring as he found Tomi and Mitch, they were still his customers, and the thoughts he had for them were slipping further and further away from being anywhere near appropriate. Slowly, he removed the hand covering Mitch's on the suitcase handle.

"Thanks. I appreciate it." He reached for one of the two remaining bags sitting by the curb. "Looks like you two are going to be here for a while."

"Yep, we'll be here through the Fourth of July holiday."

Linc calculated the time. This was early June. The Fourth of July was still a month away.

He whistled. "That's a nice, long vacation."

Mitch's expression sobered. "It's long overdue." Something flashed in his eyes, but he looked away before Linc could decipher it.

Once the last piece of luggage was loaded into the trunk, Linc waited for Mitch to climb inside the limo before he closed the door and walked around to the driver's side. He got in and started the limo.

"You're staying at the El San Juan Resort, right?" Linc turned around in time to see them locked in a kiss; their bodies practically entwined together, their mouths moving hungrily, as if they couldn't get enough of each other.

Seeing that simple act of intimacy between them made his cock throb. They were creating so much heat that Linc felt it from where he sat.

Slowly, they pulled apart, and Mitch met his gaze. "Sorry about that." He smiled. "And yeah, that's where we're staying."

Linc chuckled. The only thing Mitch looked sorry about was stopping. Linc couldn't blame him. He could imagine how incredible it felt to kiss a woman like Tomi.

Linc glanced at the sign he'd placed back onto the seat next to him. "You two must be on your honeymoon." He saw them share a look, a silent communication that he wasn't privy to.

"I guess we jumped the gun with that sign." Tomi's eyes met his. "We aren't married yet." Her gaze found Mitch's again. "But we will be soon." Her voice was soft and tender, the love she felt for Mitch evident in her tone.

"Well, sit back and relax. We'll be at the hotel soon." Linc raised the privacy glass and pulled away from the curb. He drove for a few minutes before he pressed the intercom to check on them.

"How's everything? Is it cool enough for you, or do you need more air?" When they didn't respond, he tried again. After several long seconds passed without a response, he lowered the privacy glass. What he saw almost caused him to have an accident.

Mitch sat with his head against the back of the seat, his eyes closed, and his shorts around his ankles. Tomi's head was in his lap; Mitch had his hands wrapped in her long hair, holding the thick strands away from her face. Linc saw Mitch's cock sliding in and out of her mouth.

In an instant, Linc was as hard as a brick. His mind practically screamed at him to look away, close the privacy glass right now, and pretend as if he'd never seen anything. He needed to haul ass to their hotel, drop them off, and forget he'd ever met them.

Yep, that's what his mind said. But his rock-hard cock thought that idea completely sucked—and not in a pleasurable sort of way, either. Instead, Linc sat mesmerized as he watched Tomi's full lips work the mushroom head of Mitch's cock, her pink tongue teasing at the opening before she swallowed Mitch's thick length inside her mouth.

Linc alternated his attention between the road in front of him and the view behind him. His mouth watered as he stared at Mitch's swollen cock, wet and glistening from Tomi's saliva, and he imagined that they were his own lips wrapped around Mitch's dick, giving him the pleasure that Linc saw written all over his face.

"Oh, baby. Yeah…just like that." Mitch's moan rang out, filled with equal parts need and desire. The sound was so desperate and raw that Linc couldn't help the groan that fell from his lips in response.

Mitch's eyes blinked open, and he looked at Linc in the mirror. Linc expected to see anger in his eyes at the invasion of their privacy; he waited to hear the irritation in Mitch's voice at the disruption of their personal moment together.

But it never happened.

Instead, those blue eyes held an unmistakable request to watch, an undeniable invitation to participate—even if only from a distance. He held Linc's gaze as he thrust into Tomi's mouth, his expression hot and feverish.

With one hand still on the steering wheel, Linc slid his other hand between his legs, massaging his aching erection through his pants as he drove aimlessly. He'd lost track of where he was a long time ago, knowing without a doubt that he was nowhere near his intended destination. He tried to focus on his surroundings, but the sights and sounds coming from the backseat affected his ability to think about anything other than what would happen next.

For some unknown reason, limos brought out the freak in people. This wasn't the first time Linc witnessed a couple getting busy in the backseat, and he'd received and turned down more than his fair share of offers to join in on the fun.

But this time—with this couple—he was certain that, if asked, he wouldn't have the strength to say no.

Movement in his rearview mirror drew his attention to the backseat once again.

"*Jesús.*" Linc didn't think he'd ever seen anything sexier than what he saw now. They'd switched places, and Tomi now leaned against the back of the seat with her dress bunched around her waist. Mitch pushed her legs back, holding them open with his large hands. He kneeled on the floor of the limo in front of her with his face buried in her pussy. Tomi's fingers gripped the back of the seat behind her head, and her face contorted in pleasure as her cries of ecstasy echoed in the air.

"Oh, yes." Her hips gyrated, as if she were trying to force more of herself into his mouth. Mitch groaned in response, and his efforts increased.

"God, baby...gonna make me come."

"Uh-huh." Mitch's voice sounded husky, his words slightly muffled. "Wanna taste you."

Tomi's sudden cries filled the limo, and her body bucked wildly against the seat.

As he watched, Linc had a death grip on his cock, knowing that if he let go, he'd come in his pants.

Mitch raised his upper body off the seat until he was eye level with Tomi. Leaning forward, he kissed her, whispering words against her lips that he spoke too quietly for Linc to understand.

In one easy movement, Mitch lifted Tomi off the seat and onto his lap. With his hands wrapped around her waist, Mitch positioned her so that she straddled his legs with her back against his chest. When their eyes met in the rearview mirror, Tomi looked at Linc with the same hunger he'd seen in Mitch's expression. And Linc was certain that it matched the one burning in his own gaze.

Linc didn't give himself time to think about the consequences as he unzipped his pants, reached inside, and pulled his cock free. As he stroked up and down his shaft, he stared at Tomi's pussy. Smooth and hairless, it was wet with her arousal; the cream that coated the lips was visible, even in the darkened interior of the limo.

Mitch lowered Tomi onto his waiting dick, and the sound of three distinct moans rang out as he pushed inside her. Once he was fully seated, Mitch began fucking Tomi hard and deep, his big dick stretching her wide. Each time he thrust, Linc reciprocated the move, his cock, hot and leaking, fucking into his hand as he imagined it was Tomi's warm, wet heat instead.

"Oh...fuck me, baby." Tomi's eyes closed, and her head fell back against Mitch's shoulder as she rode him.

Mitch kept one hand wrapped around her waist and used the other hand to pull the top of her dress down, exposing her perfect breasts for Linc to view. Mitch massaged each breast, pausing to play with her nipples, rubbing and rolling the darkened berries between his thumb and forefinger.

Their voices became a constant chorus of moans and groans, begging and pleading, their bodies came together frantically, the movements filled with urgency and desperation.

"*Goddamn*...you feel good." Mitch pounded into Tomi; her body vibrated from the force of his thrusts.

"Yes." Linc saw Tomi's body begin to shake. "Gonna come again."

"Ride me, baby." Mitch encouraged her. The hand around her waist moved between her legs and played with her clit. "Come on my cock."

Tomi began to wail even before Mitch finished speaking, her body trembling uncontrollably on top of him, fluids squirting from her as she came. Mitch was right behind her, shouting her name while slamming inside her.

The sight of Mitch's cock sliding in and out of Tomi's pussy, covered in a mixture of his cum and her cream, was more than Linc could take. He shot so hard, his ears rang and vision blurred. It was through sheer willpower that he managed to stay on the road; his hands were shaking, and he barely maintained control of the steering wheel.

The sounds of their combined breathing floated through the limo, and it took several minutes before Linc could finally think clearly. The clock on the dashboard confirmed that less than an hour had passed since he'd picked them up from the airport, but it felt like an eternity.

He looked down at his cum-covered hand and grimaced. Linc leaned over, opened the glove compartment, and removed a small box of Kleenex. He pulled several out of the box and cleaned his hand as much as possible while he continued to drive. Glancing in the back of the limo, he saw Mitch and Tomi pulling tissue from the built-in dispenser as they tried to do the same thing.

"Sorry, we made a mess back here," Mitch called out as he helped Tomi adjust her dress.

Linc shrugged. "Don't worry about it. Leather cleans easily." A smile spread across his face. "Besides, the privilege of witnessing the two of you together in the back of my limo more than made up for anything you leave in it."

Tomi met his eyes in the mirror and smiled. Running her fingers through her hair, she said, "I guess you see this kind of thing all the time, huh?"

"Occasionally," he admitted. "But I've never seen anything as incredible as the two of you." It was true. The chemistry between them was amazing.

"We haven't done anything like this is a long time," she confessed. "I guess the atmosphere"—she gave him a sultry look—"and the audience brought our wild sides to the surface."

Afterward, they settled into a comfortable silence. Mitch and Tomi cuddled together in the backseat, sharing whispered words and gentle kisses, and Linc drove on autopilot, his thoughts still focused on the events of the past hour. What he'd done was completely out of the realm of professionalism, yet Linc didn't feel an ounce of guilt about it. Tomi and Mitch had a certain magnetism that he found irresistible. Linc hadn't been this attracted to one person—let alone two people—since...well...in a very long time.

Before he knew it, Linc was pulling into the circular drive of the hotel. He parked the limo and turned off the ignition before turning around to look at his passengers.

"Well, we made it to the hotel, and we're all still in one piece." Although Linc had no idea how he'd done it. With all the activity in the limo, his attention span was nonexistent. Sheer luck got them to their destination without him running over anyone in the process.

Linc got out of the limo and walked around to their door. He waited for them to climb out of the limo before he moved to the trunk and began unloading their luggage. He handed each piece to the hotel attendant, who loaded it onto a baggage cart. Once Linc removed the last piece from the trunk, he turned to Mitch and Tomi, who stood off to the side.

"It was nice to meet both of you." Linc smiled, ignoring the inexplicable disappointment he felt knowing that he wouldn't see these two people again. "Welcome again to San Juan. I hope you have a great wedding and an even better honeymoon."

Smiling broadly, Mitch reached out to shake his hand. "Thanks, man. That was a hell of a ride and the best way to start a vacation." When Linc pulled his hand away, there was a fifty-dollar bill in his palm.

"I can't take this." Linc held the money out to him. Mitch tried to protest, but he insisted. "Trust me." He chuckled. "The pleasure was as much mine as it was yours."

"Well, there has to be a way for us to thank you for making our trip enjoyable thus far," Tomi spoke up. She glanced at Mitch, who nodded.

"Tomi's right," Mitch said. "Since you won't take our money, why don't you join us for dinner tonight? Maybe you can show us some nice places to get a good Puerto Rican meal."

Linc thought about all the reasons why he didn't need to mix business with pleasure any more than he already had with these two. But when he looked into their faces, it was impossible for him to say no to either of them.

"I'd love to." The smile Tomi gave him erased any doubts he had and made his decision to say yes worth it.

He glanced at his watch. It was almost seven o'clock in the evening. "Does eight thirty work for you?" At their nods, he smiled. "Cool. I'll meet you back here at that time. I know a good place not too far from here that I think you'll like."

"That sounds good," Mitch told him. "We'll see you then." Linc watched Mitch lead Tomi into the hotel by the hand before he returned to the limo.

As he drove away, a huge grin spread across Linc's face. He made a mental note to thank Miguel for not coming in to work for the day. Hell, maybe he'd even give him a raise.

Chapter Two

"This is beautiful." Tomi stood on the balcony of their hotel suite, watching the sun set over the ocean and enjoying the warm evening breeze.

Mitch's strong arms slid around her waist, and he pulled her tightly against him. "It's nowhere near as beautiful as you," he whispered in her ear.

Her eyes fluttered closed as Mitch's lips moved along the column of her neck. Leaning back, she offered him a kiss, moaning softly when his mouth covered hers. Immediately, her lips opened, her tongue automatically sought his, and she poured everything she felt for him into her kiss before their lips parted.

As they continued to watch the sunset in silence, Tomi's thoughts shifted to their limo ride. She'd forgotten how much it turned her on to have sex in front of another person. In fact, she still felt turned on. Linc was an extremely handsome man, his skin a beautiful shade of butterscotch, and he had the most amazing gray eyes she'd ever seen. Even in his uniform, it was obvious he was in great shape. Tomi found herself wondering what he looked like underneath all those clothes.

The thought of Linc naked had Tomi feeling grateful that Mitch couldn't see her face. If he could, he'd see the sudden guilt—and desire—she was certain shone plainly in her eyes.

She was here to marry this wonderful man. They'd gone through so much—their relationship had seen far more than its fair share of happiness and heartache during the three years they'd been together.

Through it all, they'd managed to not only survive but grow stronger, their love for each other becoming even deeper, leaving no doubt in Tomi's mind that she'd found her soul mate. With mere days to go before they were scheduled to say "I do", it seemed wrong somehow that she'd be distracted by thoughts of any man other than Mitch, let alone someone she'd only met a little more than an hour ago.

Still, she couldn't deny the way she felt. There was no way to pretend she didn't notice the way her body responded to Linc when his heated gaze moved over her in the limo. It was impossible to forget the look in his eyes, burning with need and passion, touching and caressing her as sensuously, as seductively, as if he were using his own hands while promising that the real thing would be even better than the fantasy.

Her eyes slid closed as a shiver of pleasure raced down her spine, forcing her to bite her bottom lip to stifle the moan attempting to escape.

"You're trembling." Mitch's strong arms tightened around her. "Are you cold?"

"No." She turned in his arms. "I'm fine." Tomi was far from cold. And that was the problem. "So...that was some limo ride, huh?" Her words were spoken quietly, almost hesitantly, as she stared into his handsome face. Tomi needed to see whether their earlier activities had affected her fiancé as much as they did her. She wanted to make sure that he had no regrets about what they'd done, knowing that she'd rather die before she did anything that would cause him any more pain than he'd already endured.

"Oh, yeah, that was one ride I won't forget anytime in the near future." Mitch chuckled before he paused, and his expression suddenly turned serious as his blue-eyed gaze searched hers. "Are you okay with what happened?"

"Yes." Tomi nodded. "I am." She was more than okay with it, but she had to know that he felt the same way. "Lincoln seems nice."

Mitch continued to study her; the look on his face told her that he shared her concerns. Tomi smiled at him, wanting to ease his worries—and her own. As long as he was okay, she was fine.

Several long moments passed before Mitch's face relaxed, and Tomi felt her fears begin to evaporate. "So, you think he's nice?" His voice sounded playful once again, and the smile returned to his eyes when he looked down at her.

"Yes, I do." She continued, "He's really gorgeous too."

"He's okay." His words were nonchalant, but the smile tugging at the corners of his mouth gave him away.

Tomi leaned her head against his chest to hide her own smile. "Just okay, huh?"

"Yeah, he's not bad, if you like the strong, sexy, Latino-stud type."

Tomi leaned back and looked up at him again. "Oh, and you don't?" His dismissive tone didn't fool her at all. She knew him as well as she knew herself. They had so many things in common; their wants, needs, and desires were so similar, they often mirrored each other. Whenever she saw him, it felt as if she were looking at a male version of herself.

Like her, Mitch didn't discriminate between genders. He loved both women and men, and so did she. Their tastes in members of the male sex were the same as well.

"Don't get me wrong, he's definitely my type." Mitch laughed. "I was simply making an observation."

"Uh-huh, that's what I thought." Tomi's laughter joined his. From his words, it was apparent that Mitch liked Linc as much as she did.

It would bother many people to hear their future spouse admit to an attraction to another person. Fortunately, Tomi wasn't one of those people. Mitch's comments didn't bother her at all. Instead, they thrilled her and reminded her once again why he was the perfect match for her.

They had a relationship that was far from orthodox. It was uninhibited and filled with adventure. Those things that most people frowned upon—even condemned—when it came to sex were the same things they found exciting and arousing. Having multiple partners was something that many would view as an exception in a relationship, but for them, it had been the norm during the years they'd been together.

Until recently.

Tomi's joy left her in a sudden rush as thoughts of the last time Mitch and she shared pleasure with another person raced through her mind and left her ready to scream and sob at the same time.

The bitter betrayal of that experience had changed them. The months they'd spent recovering left them hardened, feeling wary and unwilling to risk ruining their relationship after spending so much time repairing it.

Since then, their sex life consisted of just the two of them. Tomi never imagined they'd even consider including another person in their relationship again.

Until Linc.

With effort, Tomi pushed her negative thoughts to the side, refusing to allow them to disrupt her happiness.

"I'm glad you invited Linc to dinner," she said to Mitch. "I know we just met him, but I like him. There's something about him that feels right…" She paused and looked away, unable to find the right words to describe the immediate attraction she'd felt, the instantaneous connection she made whenever she met someone special. It was the kind of reaction that was hard for her to explain—and even harder for others to understand, unless they'd experienced it before.

Mitch's hand caressed her cheek, and Tomi met his eyes again, taking comfort in the look on his face that told her an explanation wasn't necessary. He understood what she meant; he'd experienced what she felt. It'd been that way between them when they first met.

"I know." Those two words confirmed her thoughts. Mitch leaned down and kissed her on the lips. "I think it'll be nice getting to know someone new, like we used to."

"I think so too." She smiled up at him. "We haven't let another person into our life since…" Her voice trailed off as the memories of an unhappy time, the images of an unwelcome face, intruded into her thoughts once again.

"Hey." Mitch cupped her face. "Don't do that to yourself. We're over that part of our life. We're over *him*. We've wasted enough of our time, enough of our lives, wanting and wishing for someone who neither of us even needed." The kiss he gave her was gentle and filled with so much love. Leaning forward, he rested his head against hers.

"This is about *us*, Tomi. It's been too long since we enjoyed ourselves, too long since we enjoyed being around another person like that." His lips met hers again. "If this thing with Linc turns into something more, that's great. We'll have a lot of fun while we're here, and great memories to take with us when we leave. But if nothing happens and we never see him again after tonight, that's fine too. We'll still have each other, and that will never change."

"You're right." Tomi practically melted into Mitch's tight embrace. She loved the feel of his strong body pressed against hers.

"I'm so happy." Tomi put a voice to her feelings. "I'm so glad we're finally doing this."

"Good." She felt Mitch's lips against her hair. "You deserve to be happy, and I'll do whatever it takes to make sure that you are."

"As long as I have you, I'll always be happy." Tomi held his gaze, wanting him to know without question that she meant every word.

"Prepare yourself to be happy for a very long time then." His mouth covered hers again, the kiss equal parts love and lust. His hands touched her body, moving downward until he reached her ass. With their lips still connected, Mitch lifted her and carried her back into their suite. Gently, he laid her on the bed, his hard body coming down on top of her. With his weight resting on one elbow, Mitch stared down at her.

"I should have married you a long time ago. I can't wait until you're truly and officially mine in every way."

"Me too." She reached up and stroked his face. "I love you so much, Mitch."

"Love you more." Mitch grabbed her hand and placed a kiss against her palm.

Tomi leaned up and kissed him. "Prove it," she whispered against his lips as she pulled him even tighter against her.

Chapter Three

Linc hadn't felt this good in a long time. He couldn't remember the last time he'd looked forward to a night out as much as he did this one. Not even Miguel's ridiculously pathetic excuses for missing work or Lorna's incessant and irritating flirting were enough to dampen his mood.

After he dropped off Tomi and Mitch, Linc returned his limo to his company's garage and hurried home to take a shower and change clothes before he went to pick them up.

While he drove to their hotel, Linc kept reminding himself that this wasn't a date; it wasn't the start of some new and lasting relationship between the three of them. Despite what happened in the limo, Linc had no idea whether Mitch and Tomi were even into the whole threesome thing. Although it seemed as if they were genuinely attracted to him, maybe it was wishful thinking on his part. For all he knew, they were just a friendly heterosexual couple who got off on other people watching them while they fucked.

Not that it mattered anyway. Linc had gotten over the need for full-time commitments a long time ago. When it came to relationships, he was all about instant gratification, immediate satisfaction. And he'd made it a point to have plenty of it over the years. He'd learned the hard and painful way that it wasn't worth the risk of losing his head—or his heart—over anything more substantial than that.

Even if he did want more—which he adamantly told himself he didn't—it couldn't be with Mitch and Tomi. Hell, the only reason they were even in Puerto Rico at all was so they could get married. They wanted to enjoy themselves and each other before they headed back home to New York. As appealing as the thought was, Linc suspected that having a fling with a stranger wasn't on their list of things to do during their honeymoon.

Nope, Tomi and Mitch definitely weren't the couple for him. They were just some nice customers he was joining for dinner and would probably never see again after tonight.

Yeah, right. Linc snorted. Tell that to his racing heart and throbbing dick. The thought of seeing them again made him more excited than he had any right to be.

They were already waiting for him in the hotel lobby when he arrived. Linc watched as they walked in his direction, his arousal increasing with every step they made toward his car. He got out and met them at the curb. Reaching out, he tried to shake Tomi's hand, but she ignored his outstretched hand and pulled him into a brief embrace instead.

Linc wanted to groan. God, she felt so damn good in his arms. Her body was soft and warm, and the sweet, seductive scent of her perfume teased his nose and made him ache. With effort, Linc released her and reached out to shake Mitch's hand.

"I hope we're dressed okay," Tomi said, glancing at Mitch and back to him. "We weren't sure what kind of restaurant we were going to."

From where Linc stood, they looked a hell of a lot better than okay. Tomi wore a short-sleeved dress with a colorful paisley print. It was short enough to show off her beautiful legs, and the neckline plunged deep enough to display her incredible cleavage. Mitch looked equally as good in a pair of loose-fitting, cream-colored linen cargo pants and a white linen shirt.

"Trust me, you're fine." Linc held the car door open for her while Mitch opened the rear door and had a seat in the back. "You both look great."

"Thanks." She smiled up at him as she got into the car. "You do too. The color of that shirt looks good against your skin. It reminds me of Mitch's eyes."

Linc glanced down at his shirt. Tomi was right. The different shades of blue were similar to Mitch's eyes. And he'd admit—if only to himself—that it was the reason he'd chosen to wear this particular shirt tonight.

"Nice car," Mitch commented from the backseat once Linc climbed into the car.

"Thanks." He smiled at Mitch through the rearview mirror as he started the engine. "It was one of the few luxuries that I brought with me when I moved here." Linc lovingly caressed the steering wheel of his Mercedes-Benz. It cost him a fortune when he'd purchased it eight years ago, and it was ridiculously expensive to maintain, but it was worth every penny. Although he'd bought other cars over the years, this one still ranked as his favorite, and it was one of the few possessions he'd kept from his previous life.

"So, you're not originally from Puerto Rico?" Mitch asked.

"No," Linc said as he pulled away from the hotel. "I was born and raised in Brooklyn. But my parents are from here, and I have a lot of family here as well."

"Well, that explains it." Tomi laughed. "I thought I detected an East Coast accent in your voice."

Shaking his head, Linc smiled. "No matter how hard I try, I can't seem to get rid of it."

"Don't bother. I like it. It sounds sexy."

Linc laughed hard. "I think that's the first time anyone has ever told me that." Inside, he hoped that his voice wasn't the only thing about him that Tomi found sexy. "What about you two? Are you both originally from New York as well?"

"I grew up in Greenwich, Connecticut." Linc glanced up at the sound of Mitch's voice. From his tone, it was clear that he was less than impressed with his birthplace.

"Good area," Linc said carefully. "You must have had a nice upper-class upbringing."

"I guess that's one way to describe it." A ghost of a smile passed across Mitch's face. "Although I'm sure my life is nowhere near what my parents planned for me growing up." Linc saw Mitch's gaze lock on the back of Tomi's head. "But I wouldn't change it for anything in the world."

When Mitch didn't offer any more information, Linc took the hint and left the subject alone. It didn't take a genius to understand that was a sensitive topic for Mitch, and the last thing Linc wanted was to remind him of unpleasant memories that he clearly didn't want to discuss.

"What about you?" He shifted his attention to Tomi.

"Oh, I'm an army brat. I was born in Hawaii, but I grew up wherever my father was stationed."

"So, I have to ask how a beautiful, feminine woman ended up with such a masculine name."

Tomi's soft laughter filled the car. "My actual name is Tomiko," she explained. "In Japanese, it means 'child of Tommy,' which is my father's name. Growing up, everyone called me Tomi, and it just stuck with me."

Linc looked into her exotic face. "I take it you're part Japanese."

Tomi nodded. "My mother is Japanese." She didn't specify her father's nationality, but it wasn't necessary. Everything from her face to her hair to her skin made it apparent that her father was black.

Linc's conversation had him so distracted that he almost passed the red, glowing sign of the Ajili Mojili restaurant. He slowed in time to grab one of the few parking spaces out front.

"Oohhh, I read about this place!" Tomi stared out the window. "I hear their food is delicious."

"It is." Linc smiled at the excitement in her voice. "My cousin is the chef tonight. They have some of the best Puerto Rican food in the area." They got out of the car and headed toward the restaurant. Linc reached the door first and held it open for them.

"*Buenas noches.*" The smiling hostess greeted them at the door.

"Hola, Selena." Linc returned her smile. "We have an eight forty-five dinner reservation."

"Sí." She grabbed three menus. "Right this way." She led them to a quiet table in the corner of the restaurant. Linc waited until Tomi and Mitch sat down before he took a seat.

"Would you please let Alejandro know that we're here?"

"*Sí, Señor* Castillo. I'll tell him." Once she walked away, he turned to Mitch and Tomi. They sat studying the menu.

"I have no idea what to order." Mitch stared blankly at his menu.

"You should try the *mofongo relleno de camarones o langosta*," Linc recommended.

Mitch glanced up at him. "What's that?"

"It's stuffed plantain. You can get it with shrimp or lobster inside. Mofongo is common in Puerto Rican cuisine, and it's one of the specialties here. The *arroz con pollo* is chicken with rice. It's excellent as well."

"Why don't I get that, and you get the mofongo." Tomi looked at Mitch. "We'll share."

Mitch closed his menu and placed it on the table. "Sounds good to me."

Once the waiter arrived and took their orders, they settled into an easy conversation.

"Thanks again for inviting me to dinner," Linc told them. "I don't think I've ever had customers extend an invitation like this before." He'd had plenty of customers offer to let him eat something, but none of it ever involved food.

"It was the least we could do after subjecting you to our impromptu show earlier." Mitch's words brought back images of him and Tomi fucking in the backseat of the limo. The memory made Linc's groin tighten.

"Like I said, it was definitely no hardship on my part. The two of you are incredible together."

Tomi smiled. "Well, I'm just glad that you were able to join us on such short notice." Her expression suddenly became concerned. "I hope you didn't cancel any plans you already had in order to be here with us."

"Not at all." Linc shook his head dismissively. "I didn't have any particular plans for tonight. Before your invitation, I was going to have an unexciting evening at home alone."

"I guess it was our lucky night," Tomi said softly, a suggestive smile on her lips. "I suspect it's very rare that you're alone, especially on a Friday evening."

"You give me too much credit." Linc laughed. In truth, she was correct. Linc typically had something—and someone—to do most weekends. Tonight was no different. When the day began, he'd promised to attend a hotel party with a hot young thing that he'd met at another hotel party a couple of weeks before.

Somewhere between breakfast and lunch, he'd lost all interest in going, willing to risk missing out on a guaranteed piece of ass if it meant not having to suffer through another party filled with pretentious people walking around trying to be seen, when they weren't in the restroom getting high. As far as Linc was concerned, he couldn't have picked a better night to cancel his plans.

"So, do you live here in San Juan or one of the surrounding cities?" Mitch asked him.

"San Juan," he confirmed. "I stay in Punta Las Marias. It's about twenty minutes from the hotel where you're staying."

The waiter arrived with their food, and their conversation slowed some as they focused on their meals.

A full dinner plus dessert, a pitcher of sangria, and several beers later, they sat back laughing and talking. Linc noticed how comfortable, how good it felt to be in their company. Their conversation flowed easily and naturally, as if they'd known each other for years instead of hours.

Tomi sighed. "That was one of the best meals I've had in a long time."

"I'm glad you enjoyed it." Linc looked up as his cousin Alejandro approached their table. "Here comes the person responsible for it now." He stood and embraced Alejandro before he introduced him to Tomi and Mitch.

"*Gracias por una cena maravillosa*, Alejandro." Linc looked at Tomi in surprise. He had no idea she spoke Spanish.

Alejandro brought Tomi's hand to his lips. "*Es un honor a cocinar para una señora tan hermosa*." Alejandro released her hand and shook Mitch's. "I trust your dinner was enjoyable as well?"

"Oh, yeah." Mitch smiled. "This place is great. It more than lived up to its reputation."

"I'm happy to hear that. Any friend of my cousin is always welcome here. Enjoy the rest of your evening."

Once Alejandro left, Linc looked at Tomi. "Your Spanish is perfect."

"It should be." Mitch chuckled and rested his arm around the back of Tomi's chair. "She makes a living teaching it to others."

"Oh, you're a teacher?"

Tomi nodded. "A professor. I teach foreign languages at New York University."

"NYU is my alma mater." Linc smiled. "I completed undergrad and grad school there." He paused. "Although I'm certain that none of my finance and economics professors ever looked anything like you."

"That's what I told her." Mitch looked down at Tomi. "But she doesn't believe me. You should see all those young kids in her classes, watching her with hopeful eyes, hanging on to her every word."

The picture Mitch painted made Linc laugh. Looking at Tomi, he understood their reaction.

"I can't blame them. You look young enough to still be in college yourself." He looked at Mitch. "You both do."

"Not so young." Tomi smiled, glancing at Mitch. "We're both thirty."

Linc laughed. "Compared to me, that's young."

"Like you're so old." It was Mitch's turn to chuckle. "What are you, thirty-two, thirty-three?"

"Try thirty-nine." Linc tried to pretend that Mitch's words didn't flatter him, but he couldn't hold back the grin that spread across his face.

"Damn." Mitch looked at him appraisingly. "I would never have guessed that. I just hope I look as good as you when I get that age."

"Something tells me that you won't have anything to worry about," Linc murmured. He looked at Tomi. "Neither of you." He decided to change the subject and stick to safer, less suggestive topics. "So, do you only teach Spanish?"

She shook her head. "I alternate between Spanish, French, Japanese, and Russian."

"So you speak five languages, including English?" At her nod, he said, "Damn, that's impressive."

"Thanks." Her smile was tinged with the embarrassment of a person who knew she was incredible, but wasn't all that comfortable with the knowledge. Mitch, on the other hand, had a look of absolute pride on his face—and all of it was directed at Tomi.

"Do you teach as well?" Linc asked him.

"Only if it involves sweating and grunting." Linc's confusion must have shown on his face, because Mitch began to laugh. "I'm a personal trainer," he explained. "I have about twenty regular clients who I work with, and I teach classes for Equinox gyms."

Linc was familiar with the upscale chain of gyms dedicated to the buff and the beautiful. It also explained Mitch's amazing physique. And from the look of her, it was obvious that Tomi was one of his clients.

"What about you?" Tomi asked. "Were you always in the limousine business?"

Linc paused. Tomi's question caught him off guard and triggered so many memories; memories he'd spent years trying to forget. He didn't respond immediately, still trying to figure out what to say, how much to share. He rarely discussed his past life with anyone, even his family. Yet as he looked at the couple sitting across from him, Linc suddenly felt the need to share it with them.

"I used to own a brokerage firm when I lived in New York City. It wasn't huge—I had close to a dozen employees—but we did well. We had a solid client base, and we made good money for them and ourselves." Linc glanced at Mitch and Tomi to find them watching him intently. Their focus seemed centered on every word he spoke.

"I lived with my two lovers, Ava and Paul. Ava was the office manager for my firm, and Paul was a firefighter." Linc met their eyes again, unsure of how they'd react once they knew about his lifestyle, but unwilling to hide who he was.

"We'd been together for a couple of years, and everything was great. But after a while, things just…changed. It was gradual at first, and one day we looked up and realized that two years had gone by, and we still didn't seem to know each other. We all wanted different things, each of us was moving in different directions. Deep down, I think we all knew that it was over between us, but none of us had the guts to say it. One night, we had this big argument, and we said a lot of fucked-up things to each other. It was clear that our relationship couldn't be anything but over, and I remember wishing that they would just disappear, go away and leave me alone." He shook his head at the memory, still as fresh as if it'd just happened.

"Anyway, Paul spent the night at his firehouse, and Ava slept in the guest bedroom. The next day, I slept late. I *never* did that. I was always the first one in the office at seven o'clock in the morning, and Ava usually rode to work with me. But I was still feeling pissy about our fight from the previous night, and I didn't want to be bothered with her. She must have felt the same way, because she went to work without saying a word to me." He met their gaze. "That day was September eleventh. My brokerage firm was on the twenty-seventh floor of Tower Two."

Linc heard Tomi's soft gasp. "My God..."

"Well...you know how that story ended." Linc cleared his throat and continued. "Ava and two other employees got trapped inside the building and never made it out. Later, I learned that Paul and members of his fire engine company were in Tower Two as well when it collapsed."

"Damn, man. That's..." Mitch shook his head, his expression sympathetic. "I'm so sorry."

"That's why you moved here, isn't it?" Tomi's softly spoken words pulled Linc from the past, and he looked down to see her smaller, darker hand covering his. His fingers automatically entwined with hers, and he held on for several long moments.

Finally, he nodded. "I sorta fell apart for a while after that. Guilt ate me alive. I locked myself in my condo for weeks, wouldn't talk to anybody and wouldn't see anybody. I'd convinced myself that if I'd given Paul and Ava the kind of love and commitment that they wanted and deserved, they'd still be alive. My family was terrified that I was going to do something crazy. Finally, my cousin Pedro came to see me. He practically kicked my door in and dragged my ass here to Puerto Rico for some R and R."

Linc sighed. Time was a funny thing. Some days, it seemed as if a million years had passed since his life had taken such a sudden, dramatic change. Other days, it felt like it happened yesterday.

"I never went back to New York City, never tried to reopen the firm. I'd made good investments over the years, so money wasn't an issue for me. I already owned a house here, so I spent a few months trying to regroup and get my shit together. Once I felt sane again, I worked through my attorney to provide settlements to all my employees, including those who died. I was the beneficiary on Paul and Ava's life insurance policies, and when I received the money, I gave it to their families, along with whatever personal items they wanted. Everything else I either sold or gave away. After that, I started the limousine company."

Linc gave them a small smile. "That was seven years ago. Now things are great. I've got a good, solid business going, I live on this beautiful island, and I'm having dinner with two amazing people." They both smiled in return, but it never reached their eyes.

Oh, hell. He just had to screw up the mood by telling them his depressing life story. Because of him, the relaxed, laid-back couple of a few minutes ago was gone, and in their place sat two people whose expressions held a mixture of emotions—none of them happy.

"Listen," Linc began, hating the sudden change in direction the evening was taking, "it's obvious that my story bothered you. I'm sorry. I didn't mean to upset either of you."

"No," Tomi spoke quickly, trying to reassure him. "You didn't do anything wrong. I think we just realized that we have more in common with each other than any of us knew."

Linc frowned as he looked back and forth between the two of them. "What do you mean?"

They both seemed to hesitate before Mitch said, "Tomi and I used to be part of a triad relationship too." Linc stared at him in shock. He didn't know what he'd expected the other man to say, but that wasn't it.

"His name was Alec," Mitch continued. "He was my lover as well as my business partner when I first started my personal training business several years ago. Alec handled the sales and marketing part of the business, while I focused on the daily operations. We'd been together for three years when he started hinting that he thought it would be fun to add a third person to our relationship. At first, I was hesitant. I was worried that the wrong person would disrupt our life together."

Mitch's gaze shifted from him to Tomi. Linc watched him stare into her eyes, his expression filled with worship.

"Then, Alec met Tomi. She was looking for a personal trainer and came by for a consultation. When Alec told me about her, I was still skeptical. But when I met her, I knew right away that she was the one."

Tomi nodded. "It was mutual. The connection between us was so immediate, so…right. I'd never felt anything like it before." She paused for a moment before shaking her head and chuckling. "I wish I knew the right words to describe the feeling to you."

Her words weren't necessary. Linc already knew the feeling. He suspected that it was similar to what he'd felt when he first met them.

"You don't have to," Linc murmured. "I think I know exactly what you mean." Their eyes locked, and from the look on her face, it was obvious that Linc's eyes reflected what he felt for her.

"Yes." Her voice was soft. "I think you do."

Linc slowly dragged his eyes away from Tomi and glanced at Mitch, who sat watching their exchange with a knowing look on his face.

"Anyway," Mitch continued, "it didn't take long before our threesome became a lot more than physical—at least for Tomi and me. I think the novelty of it wore off for Alec after the first few months we were together. I don't think any of us could have guessed that Tomi and I would bond the way we did. Within weeks, we had feelings for each other that would have taken most people years to develop. The love that I felt for her was deeper and stronger than I'd experienced with anyone else before—including Alec, even though I'd known him longer."

"I think Alec knew that, and he felt threatened," Tomi spoke up. "He was used to being the center of attention, and for a while, he was the center of our relationship. When we realized that we shared a special connection that didn't exist between Alec and us, we felt guilty. We never meant for it to happen, but we couldn't deny that it existed. That didn't mean we loved Alec any less, because we didn't. We loved him differently. We went out of our way to make sure that Alec knew how much we loved him, and how important he was to us, but it seemed that the harder we tried, the more he resented us. He went out of his way to let us know as often—and as cruelly as possible—that his biggest mistake was bringing the three of us together."

The sadness on Tomi's beautiful face, the pain in her words, was almost too much for Linc to bear.

The conversation stopped for a moment when the waiter came by and refilled their water glasses. When he walked away, Mitch spoke again.

"Finally, we decided to do something symbolic to show our love for Alec—and each other. We approached him about having a commitment ceremony. Frankly, I was surprised when he said yes, considering how distant and combative he'd become lately. But he really seemed excited about it, even made most of the arrangements, and I remember thinking that we were finally on the right path to getting our relationship back on track."

Mitch grew quiet for a moment, as if lost in a distant memory. Based on what he'd heard so far, Linc suspected that the worst of the story was to come. He waited patiently for Mitch to continue.

"On the day of the ceremony, we were all set to leave when Alec said that he'd left something back at the apartment, and he'd meet us there. When he was a few minutes late, we weren't worried. After a half hour, we were calling his cell phone. Once nearly two hours passed and he still hadn't shown up or called, we knew he wasn't coming. By the time we got back home, all his things—and quite a lot of ours—were gone. He'd even emptied out the accounts that we had together." Mitch paused, his jaw muscles clenched tightly, and his face showed the disgust he felt.

"Five years together, and he wasn't man enough to say good-bye. He didn't even have the courage or the decency to leave a note or anything. He just disappeared like a fucking coward, and we never saw him, never heard from him again."

The lingering anger and resentment in Mitch's voice was evident. Reaching out, Tomi grasped Mitch's hand; her impressive diamond solitaire engagement ring sparkled brightly in the dimly lit room as she brought his hand to her lips for a kiss. He placed a kiss against her temple, and Tomi rested her head against his shoulder as she looked at Linc.

"That happened over a year ago, and for a while, things were difficult for us. We were both so bitter; we felt so betrayed by Alec. He started as the anchor in our relationship, the one who brought us together. Then he became our adversary, the one determined to tear us apart. And he almost succeeded. When Alec left, it was as if he took a part of us with him. We felt like we had a void in our relationship, and we couldn't figure out how to fill it. One day, we realized that we didn't need to fill it. We had more than enough love between us to make up for the loss of Alec in our lives."

Linc remained quiet as he struggled to gain control of the inexplicable anger that boiled inside him. He'd only known Mitch and Tomi for a few hours, but that was more than enough time for him to see their true character, to know that they were good, beautiful people—inside and out.

"Pathetic bastard." Linc looked up to find both Mitch and Tomi staring at him. He hadn't meant to speak out loud, but now that he'd said it, he refused to take it back. He'd love the chance to be a part of their lives, to be included in the love they had for each other—even if it was only for a little while. It was unfathomable to him how a person could deliberately try to destroy them, would voluntarily walk away from them. He didn't know who the fuck this Alec asshole was, but it was obvious that he was a sorry piece of shit.

"I know it's not my place to say this, but I can't imagine how anyone could give up the chance to be with the two of you. He didn't deserve you."

Tomi laughed. "I couldn't agree more." She sobered some. "Despite everything that happened, despite everything he did to us, I still can't bring myself to hate Alec. If it weren't for him, I would never have met Mitch."

"And now you're finally getting married, like you've always wanted." Linc changed the subject and tried to lighten the mood. "When's the big day?"

"Two weeks from tomorrow," Mitch told him. "It can't happen soon enough for me."

"Well, I think that deserves a toast." Linc lifted his glass. "To new beginnings."

"To new friendships." Mitch touched his glass against Linc's. Tomi raised hers as well.

"And to new possibilities," she added.

Linc took a sip from his glass before placing it on the table again. Glancing at his watch, he was surprised to see that it was after midnight. They'd been at the restaurant for hours. As he looked around the room, he saw that most of the other patrons were already gone.

"Wow, it's later than I realized. We probably should get ready to go before they kick us out." He meant for his words to be a joke, but inside, he hated the thought of leaving them.

"You're right." Tomi stood. "I'm going to use the ladies' room before we leave."

Both Linc and Mitch watched as she walked away from the table. Linc glanced at the remaining men in the room, and he noticed that their gazes followed her as well.

Turning to Mitch, he said, "You're a lucky man."

"Don't I know it," Mitch murmured. His gaze remained locked on Tomi's departing form.

Linc paused for a moment before he said, "I'm sure Tomi knows how lucky she is as well." Linc waited for him to meet his gaze, made sure Mitch saw the interest in his eyes, understood the meaning of his words.

Mitch gave him a slow, sexy smile and a slight nod. Understanding shone in his expression.

They both looked up as Tomi returned to the table. "Ready to go?" She smiled down at them, and Linc felt his heart skip a beat. He was blown away by how unbelievably stunning she was.

Damn, he wanted this woman. His gaze switched to Mitch, and he felt the same attraction, the same desire for him as well. God knew he had no right to feel the way he did about them, knew he was only making things worse for himself when the night was over and they walked out of his life for good. Nevertheless, he couldn't seem to help it.

"Yeah," Linc said. He and Mitch stood as the waiter arrived with their bill. Linc reached into his pocket for his wallet and pulled out his credit card.

"Uh-uh." Mitch stopped him. "We invited you, remember? This is on us." Before Linc could say anything else, Mitch handed the waiter his credit card along with the bill.

Smiling, he said, "You know, I really don't mind paying. I'm honored that you'd want to spend part of your evening with me."

Tomi laughed. "In that case, you can pick up the bill next time. How does that sound?"

Linc searched her face, trying to make certain he wasn't reading between the lines, wasn't jumping to conclusions.

But Tomi's expression confirmed her words. She wanted to see him again. One look at Mitch and it was obvious that he felt the same way.

"That sounds good." Linc spoke casually, trying not to sound too excited or appear too anxious. It was hard to do when that's exactly how he felt.

After the waiter returned with Mitch's credit card and receipt, they left the restaurant and got into the car. The ride back to their hotel seemed much shorter than the ride to the restaurant, and Linc was tempted to take a scenic route in order to stretch out their time together.

All too soon, he pulled up in front of the hotel. Linc got out of the car and met them around on the sidewalk. He forced a smile and prepared to thank them for dinner, say good night, and get the hell out of Dodge before either of them had a chance to see how deeply they'd affected him in such a short period of time. However, when he opened his mouth, what came out was nothing like he'd intended.

"I have to be honest with both of you. I'm not ready for this night to end. I don't want to say good-bye."

There. He'd said it. The looks on their faces left no doubt that they'd gotten his message loud and clear. It was too late to pretend that he hadn't said it, to act as if he didn't mean it. Besides, he wouldn't take it back even if he could. All he could do was hold his breath and hope that he hadn't gone too far, crossed too many boundaries.

He watched them share a brief look before they turned to him. Tomi held out her hand to him as she spoke two of the sweetest-sounding words he'd ever heard in his life.

"Then don't."

Reaching for Tomi's outstretched hand, Linc felt his heart begin to beat again. He handed the valet his car keys and then he followed her and Mitch inside the hotel.

Chapter Four

The elevator ride to Mitch and Tomi's room passed in silence. However, words really weren't necessary at that point. They all wanted the same thing; they knew what would happen once they reached the room. As far as Linc was concerned, they couldn't get there fast enough.

The elevator bell chimed softly as the doors slid open on their floor. Linc followed behind Tomi and Mitch, his cock growing harder and harder with every step he took. Mitch unlocked the door to their suite and held it open for Tomi and Linc to enter.

Linc barely managed to take in his surroundings; his thoughts focused solely on what would happen next. He watched as Tomi laid her purse on the table before she walked to the balcony and opened the doors, allowing the warm evening breeze to filter into the room.

"Make yourself comfortable." Mitch's hand landed on Linc's shoulder. "I'll grab us a drink." Mitch looked at Tomi. "Would you like something, babe?"

Tomi turned in their direction from where she stood on the balcony. "No." Her gaze moved slowly over each of them.

"I'm not thirsty." The expression on her face said it all. Tomi wanted many things, but a drink wasn't one of them.

Mitch chuckled. "Be right back."

Mitch's hand disappeared from his shoulder as he walked away. Linc's gaze remained on Tomi, admiring the way the wind gently moved through her hair, allowing the heavy locks to cover her face like a veil.

God, she's beautiful. Before he knew it, Linc was moving in her direction, not stopping until he was standing on the patio directly in front of her. Unable to resist, Linc reached out and brushed Tomi's hair away from her face. His fingers toyed with the soft strands.

"You're gorgeous." He put a voice to his thoughts. Tomi smiled back at him, the gesture a simple acknowledgment of the obvious.

Linc ached to kiss her, craved the feel of those full lips against his, desperate for a taste of her honeyed sweetness, but he didn't want to move too fast, go too far. Tomi belonged to Mitch, and he didn't have the right to touch her without Mitch's permission first. Tomi wasn't making it easy, though. Her passion-filled eyes were talking to him, silently telling him that she wanted him as much as he wanted her.

As if she'd read his thoughts, Tomi leaned in his direction. Her lips slowly moved toward his, and she made him an offer he didn't have the strength to refuse. Linc's fingers slid through her hair until they rested at the base of her neck, and his palms cupped her jaw. Tilting her head, he bent slightly. His lips met hers halfway, and he moaned as their lips made contact. The connection shot sparks of pleasure through him.

Tomi's lips parted, and Linc's tongue slipped inside, hungrily tasting her, savoring her as he deepened the kiss. One hand traveled eagerly over her body, feeling every supple curve, every sensuous contour, slowing only to knead her breasts before reaching the bottom of her dress. Easing the silken material upward, Linc caressed her soft skin until he reached her bare ass. He palmed the round globes in one large hand, lifting her off the floor and grinding his erection against her core.

He felt Tomi's arms wrap around his neck. The sounds of her whimpers raced through him and made his body shudder, his knees weak. The hand at her neck joined the one on her ass. Tomi's legs wrapped around his waist, and Linc gripped her tightly as he blindly stumbled backward until his legs bumped against the patio chair.

With their lips still connected, Linc sank down onto the seat, thrusting against her gyrating body, his dick throbbing and aching for release. When Tomi pulled away, he wanted to protest, but any words he was prepared to say instantly died on his lips when she slid off his lap to the floor and buried her face between his legs.

Tomi looked up at him again as she began to unzip his pants, and her hand disappeared inside. Linc watched as she pulled his dick free and pumped up and down the length of his shaft, her soft fingers making his already-hard cock even harder, pushing him closer to the point of no return.

Her eyes remained locked with his as she lowered her head, and her lips covered him, slowly taking him into the warm heat of her mouth, not stopping until the crown of his cock brushed against the back of her throat.

"*Dios...siente tan bueno.*" Linc's whispered words filled the night air. "You feel so good."

Tomi moaned in response as she increased her pace and sucked him even deeper into her mouth.

With his head back and eyes tightly shut, Linc gripped the chair for dear life, afraid that if he let go he'd lose the already-tenuous control he had on his emotions, throw her to the floor, and fuck her until neither of them could move.

He needed to tell her to stop. They needed to wait for Mitch to return. But *fuck*, she was making him feel good. Her teeth, lips, and tongue were driving him out of his mind, and he couldn't bring himself to say the words that would end the bliss she gave him.

A sound from the doorway made Linc look up, and he found Mitch standing there, watching them intently. As if she sensed his presence as well, Tomi stopped and glanced over her shoulder in Mitch's direction.

"Oh, don't stop on my account." Heat filled Mitch's words and made his voice deeper, raspier. "You two look amazing. In fact"—he set the two glasses he held in his hand on the patio table—"I think I'll join you."

He moved toward them until he stood next to Tomi's kneeling form. Bending, Mitch kissed her softly, languorously, on the lips before he slowly pulled away. His attention shifted to Linc, his intent obvious in his eyes as he leaned forward until their lips met.

His firm lips were a contrast to Tomi's softer ones, but just as pleasurable. His tongue, confident and sure, searched for Linc's, finding and mating with his, tasting and teasing him. Linc was helpless to stop the groan that poured from his lips when Tomi's mouth began to move on his cock again, and Mitch continued to kiss him so deeply and completely, it left them both breathless.

When their mouths parted, Linc leaned back and looked at Mitch, who stared back at him with eyes that were smoldering and filled with desperate need. Without a word, Mitch dropped to his knees next to Tomi, and his mouth joined hers on Linc's cock.

Reaching out with both hands, Linc cupped the backs of their heads, silently encouraging them, begging them for more.

"*Jesús...siente así que bueno...* Don't stop."

They didn't stop, didn't disappoint him one bit. Linc watched as their lips moved on his dick in perfect sync, licking, sucking, and tangling together, giving him pleasure that was so intense, so extreme, it made his toes curl, his hips rise out of the seat. The feeling was so incredible, it was almost too much to handle.

The sounds of cheers and whistles from below were the only thing that pulled them back to reality and reminded them that they were outside on the balcony. Even at night, it was still possible for anyone to see them.

Mitch leaned forward and gave him a lingering kiss on the lips. "I think it's time to move this party inside." He eased himself off the floor. Once he was standing, Mitch reached out and helped Tomi to her feet.

Linc stood on shaky legs. His cock jutted out from the opening of his pants, stiff as a metal pole, the tip wet and leaking as he followed them inside the room.

Linc closed the doors behind him and turned around to find Tomi standing by the bed wearing nothing more than a thin triangular piece of material over her pussy.

She was a picture of perfection. Linc stood transfixed as he committed every shape, every line, and every detail of her amazing body to memory. From her small, firm breasts, down to her narrow waist and flat stomach, all the way to her curvy hips, toned legs, and ample ass.

Linc smiled to himself at the thought of the latter. He'd take a woman with something to hold on to any day over those fake, anorexic-looking Barbie types who flooded televisions and magazine pages these days. As far as Linc was concerned, the only things they had to offer were pretty faces and smiles.

Tomi had all that and then some. Brains, beauty, body, she was his definition of a complete package, a petite powerhouse with the face of an angel and the body of an athlete. Just the thought of all the things he wanted to do to her made his dick swell even more.

When she smiled and reached out for him, Linc didn't hesitate. He immediately went to her and pulled her into his arms, his lips automatically seeking hers. As he kissed her, Linc was vaguely aware of the rustling of clothing behind him moments before Mitch's nude body pressed against his back.

Mitch's lips caressed the nape of Linc's neck. The warmth of his breath against Linc's skin made him shiver, and when Mitch slid one strong, callused hand between him and Tomi and wrapped it around his cock, it made him ache and tested the limits of his control.

Linc released a moan and thrust his hips forward as Mitch stroked his cock. With one hand still wrapped around Tomi, Linc reached behind him to grip Mitch's hip and pull him closer. He shuddered, and his cock throbbed when Mitch pressed his solid erection against his ass.

His lips separated from Tomi, and Linc leaned his head back until his lips pressed against Mitch's. Their kiss was eager and greedy, filled with the frantic need of two men who couldn't wait to fuck each other.

Linc felt Tomi's hands on him as she began to unbutton his shirt. Her lips trailed a path of heat down his chest and abdomen with each button she released. Mitch's hands joined hers, and their fingers moved quickly as they unbuttoned, unbuckled, and unzipped his clothes.

Within seconds, Linc was completely undressed, his clothes lying in a pile on the floor by his feet. He looked down at Tomi, who was kneeling in front of him again, her lips slightly parted, her attention focused entirely on his cock. Mitch positioned the head of Linc's stiff shaft directly in front of Tomi's waiting mouth, and Linc watched in amazement as she covered his length all the way to the root.

As Tomi sucked him, Mitch's hard dick slowly rubbed up and down the crease of his ass, a silent request that Linc heard loud and clear. He hadn't allowed another man to fuck him since he'd been in a steady relationship so many years ago. Even then, it rarely happened. It was as if there was an unwritten rule that said when it came to fucking, Linc was the designated man on top. Yet in this moment, with this man, he was suddenly willing to make an exception.

Linc pushed back against Mitch's probing cock, the gesture an unspoken message that communicated his permission to Mitch's request.

Mitch groaned and whispered, "Wanna fuck you so bad." His heated words excited and worried Linc at the same time.

"Uh-huh." He panted. "It's been a while." Linc tried to say more; he wanted to be sure that Mitch knew it'd been a long time since he'd been on the receiving end. However, Tomi made further speech next to impossible. Her amazing mouth worked him over so well that she had him ready to dissolve into a puddle on the floor.

Despite Linc's sudden inability to express himself, Mitch still seemed to understand the meaning of his words. "Don't worry." He placed kisses along Linc's neck. "I'm gonna make you feel real good."

Linc felt air against his back as Mitch stepped away. When he heard the rattling of paper behind him, Linc said a silent prayer of thanks for the twenty-four-hour gift shop inside the hotel that had an entire section dedicated to lubricants and condoms of every imaginable variety.

Reaching down, Linc eased Tomi off his dick and onto her feet. He laid her on the bed and followed her down. His mouth covered hers, and he kissed her slowly, deeply, before moving his lips down her body, kissing and caressing every inch along the way until he settled between her spread thighs.

His fingers worked her thong over her hips and down her legs, impatiently pulling at the thin straps, so tempted to rip the fragile scrap of material from her body instead. Once they were off, Linc threw them across the room before he buried his face in her pussy, tasting, teasing her, growing more and more excited with every cry, every moan he pulled from her.

With his mouth busy between her legs, Linc's hands made their way back up her body until they reached her breasts. He massaged one small globe in each hand, while his lips and tongue continued to lick and suck on her clit.

When Mitch's tongue pierced his hole, Linc released a groan of his own as pleasure rippled through him.

"Ahh, man. Feels good."

Mitch's hands palmed his ass and spread him wider as his tongue pushed even deeper inside. Mitch's tongue continued its sweet, torturous assault on his ass until Linc was convinced he'd shoot his load before he ever got the chance to get inside of Tomi.

As if he sensed Linc's need, Mitch's tongue disappeared, and seconds later, his cool, slippery fingers replaced it. The sensation was both foreign and familiar all at once, and Linc instinctively tensed when one thick finger eased inside, followed by another.

Mitch's lips against his spine were all Linc needed to relax and give in to the pleasure as Mitch's fingers slowly moved in and out of him. All too soon, he withdrew his fingers, and Linc felt Mitch's lips against his ear.

"You ready for me?" he whispered.

"Oh, hell yeah." Turning to the side, Linc's lips connected with Mitch's, and he pushed his tongue deep inside the other man's mouth as he shared Tomi's flavors with him.

Mitch was the first to pull away, and a few seconds later, a condom packet appeared in front of Linc's face. He sat back just long enough to rip the packet open and slide the condom over his erection. From the sounds coming from behind him, it was obvious that Mitch was doing the same thing.

He looked down into Tomi's face, and she stared back at him, her heavy-lidded eyes glazed with desire.

He leaned over her until their mouths almost touched. "*Dios, eres tan hermosa.*"

"You're beautiful too," Tomi whispered.

Linc smiled at that. He never imagined he'd like someone calling him beautiful, but coming from Tomi, it was the best compliment he'd ever heard.

"Can't wait any longer." He brushed his lips against hers. "Need to be inside you."

She nodded frantically, her eyes wide and pleading, her hands moving over his face, through his hair, and down his body. Her legs wrapped around Linc's waist as her hips gyrated against him, and her pussy rubbed along his hard shaft.

"Yes." That one word was all Linc needed to hear, and he didn't wait another second before he buried himself inside her wet heat.

"Ahh! Linc," Tomi cried out, her body trembled, and her back arched off the bed. Her snug pussy surrounded Linc like a cocoon and made his entire body shudder each time he thrust in and out of her.

He felt Mitch's hands on his ass, and he forced himself to hold still, knowing what would happen next and barely able to contain his excitement. Linc's teeth clenched tightly when Mitch's cock pushed inside, slow and sure, the pressure constant and showing no signs of letting up anytime soon.

The lubricant and condom helped to ease the way, but that didn't stop the burning sensation that flared through him as his rarely used hole stretched to accommodate Mitch's thick width.

As Mitch worked his length into Linc, Tomi provided the perfect diversion as her lips moved along his neck and chest, her vaginal muscles clenching tightly on his cock, giving him more than enough pleasure to distract him from the pain.

The more Linc's arousal increased, the more relaxed his body became, until it suddenly opened up, and Mitch's dick slid all the way in. Mitch released a shuddering groan, and his body covered Linc's back, forcing him to balance on his forearms to support Mitch's weight and to keep from leaning too heavily on Tomi.

"God*damn*." Mitch's warm breath feathered across his cheek and against his neck. "So fucking tight…feels so good."

Mitch gripped Linc's hips tightly and began to thrust inside him. Linc joined in, and they quickly settled into an easy rhythm together, as if they had been fucking each other forever. Their bodies gave and received pleasure in equal measures as their words of passion and desire poured from their lips.

Linc submerged himself in the sounds and sensations around him. Everything from Tomi's soft pussy and throaty sighs to Mitch's hard cock and heavy breathing had him in sensory overload. Somehow Linc had forgotten just how fucking fabulous it felt to be the man in the middle, and it left him wondering how he'd managed to live without it for so long.

He was clinging to his self-control and slipping fast when Tomi's body tensed, and she cried out.

"God, Linc! *Yes.*" Linc looked down at Tomi and saw all the emotions play over her face as she came. He covered her mouth with his and swallowed her screams and cries as her pussy pulsated around his cock.

He continued to stroke Tomi's sweet pussy as Mitch pounded his ass. Every thrust of Mitch's big dick made the heat build inside him, causing his belly to tighten, his balls to ache. One particularly powerful stroke across his prostate was all it took to shatter what little willpower he still had.

"Oh, *fuck.*" Linc groaned hoarsely, his voice barely recognizable. "I'm coming." His orgasm raced down his spine, setting off explosions throughout his body as his cock erupted.

"Uh-huh, that's it. Fuck, yeah." Mitch's fingers dug into Linc's hips, and his cock seemed to swell impossibly larger inside Linc's ass before his shout echoed in the room. Linc felt the pulses of Mitch's cock inside him as it filled the condom, his body shaking almost uncontrollably before he collapsed on top of Linc.

They lay there breathing heavily for several seconds, as if they all wanted to enjoy the feeling of their bodies connected together for just a little while longer.

Finally, Mitch sighed, the sound reluctant and tinged with regret, before kissing Linc on the shoulder and carefully easing out of him. As he rolled to the side, Mitch quickly removed his condom and tossed it into the nearby trash can. Linc groaned as he slid his still-semihard cock from Tomi's body and, following suit, threw his used condom into the garbage.

With a little maneuvering, they adjusted themselves on the bed so that Tomi lay between them. They wrapped around each other like puppies, their limbs entwined together, until it was difficult to tell where one person began and the other ended. Their lips met somewhere in the middle, and for several long and blissfully satisfying minutes, they fucked each other's mouths with the same passion, the same heat that they'd fucked each other's bodies. Their teeth nibbled, tongues tangled, mouths devoured each other in the most incredible three-way kiss that Linc had ever experienced.

Once the kiss ended, they continued to cuddle together in a comfortable silence, holding on to each other as if it were the most natural thing in the world. No one showed an interest in letting go anytime in the near future.

Linc's heavy eyelids warned him that he was only minutes from falling asleep. Tomi's deep, steady breathing and Mitch's light snoring signaled they were already gone. He contemplated the easiest way to slip out of the bed without disturbing them. Linc was in no hurry to leave, but he didn't want to wear out his welcome, either. Yet no matter how hard he tried, Linc couldn't bring his body to move, couldn't convince his feet to carry him out of the room and away from them. There was something special about this moment that Linc couldn't deny, a certain rightness that told him this was exactly where he was supposed to be.

"Do you have to go?"

Linc looked up at the sound of Mitch's voice and found the other man staring at him, those blue eyes watching him closely. From his words, it seemed as if Mitch read his mind and knew his plans.

Linc held his gaze for several long heartbeats before he slowly shook his head. "No," he whispered, reaching for the cover at the end of the bed and pulling it over them. "I don't."

"Good," Tomi mumbled sleepily before curling into Linc's side and burying her face against his shoulder. Mitch looked satisfied with Linc's answer, and he settled in on the other side of Tomi.

Long after Tomi and Mitch drifted off to sleep again, Linc still lay there, his thoughts focused on the events of the night, on the two people next to him, and the unshakable feeling that his life as he knew it had changed forever the moment they walked into his world.

Chapter Five

Linc woke the next morning to the sound of running water and the feel of a soft, warm body pressed against his. He opened his eyes and found Tomi fast asleep next to him. *Damn*. Even in slumber with her hair wild and spread across the pillow, her compact body curled around him, she was still completely breathtaking.

As he watched her, thoughts from the previous night came rushing back to him, and his cock was immediately as hard as stone again.

He dragged his eyes away from Tomi and glanced toward the bathroom. Linc imagined Mitch in there, his hard body wet and glistening from the spray of the water, and Linc almost came on the spot.

With another long look at Tomi's sleeping form and a quick kiss on those incredible lips, Linc carefully extracted his body from her embrace, eased from the bed, and made his way to the bathroom, his entire body still tingling from the previous night.

When he reached the bathroom, however, the sight in front of Linc brought him to an abrupt halt in the doorway.

A square, stand-alone shower sat in the middle of the room, enclosed by glass on three of the four sides. Mitch stood directly in the center, his back to the door as water rained down on him.

The actual sight was far better than anything Linc could have imagined. He licked his lips as he pictured sinking his cock into that perfectly round and muscular ass. Linc didn't wait another moment before he walked over to the shower and opened the door.

Without a word, Linc stepped inside the shower. His arms encircled Mitch's waist, and his dick pressed against his ass.

Mitch tensed for a brief second before his body relaxed and he groaned. Turning his head, he met Linc's lips; his mint-flavored tongue swept inside Linc's mouth, kissing him deeply.

"Good morning," Linc whispered, leaning in and kissing Mitch's soft, warm lips again. "Want some company?"

"Mmm," Mitch moaned low. "It is now." He stole another kiss, catching Linc's bottom lip between his teeth and sucking on it. "And I want a lot more than just company." To emphasize his point, Mitch pushed his ass against Linc's hard cock, and it was Linc's turn to groan.

That was all the incentive Linc needed. He ripped open the condom packet he'd grabbed off the dresser as he came into the bathroom and slid the latex down his stiff shaft. Then he pressed his body against Mitch's back, his hands covering Mitch's on the cool tiles. He thrust his cock along the crease of Mitch's ass as he trailed kisses down his neck, over his sculpted shoulders.

"Sexy motherfucker," Linc growled in his ear. He nipped at Mitch's lobe and made him jerk.

"Fuck." Mitch's voice shook, his hard body flushed with arousal. "Want some of that." He pushed his ass against Linc's thrusting cock.

"Just some?" Linc teased, ignoring the slight tremor in his own words. One hand traveled down Mitch's body and wrapped around his cock, slowly pumping up and down the thick shaft.

Mitch shuddered, groaned. His hips pressed forward as he fucked into Linc's hand. "All of it." He panted, his words laced with desperation. "I want all of it."

Linc couldn't wait any longer. He released Mitch's cock and grabbed his own, lined it up, and slowly sank it inside Mitch, using the soapy water rolling down Mitch's body to ease his way.

"Oh, shit!" Linc's head dropped back, a rough groan torn from his throat. That tight channel held Linc in a death grip, the muscles pulsating around his cock.

Linc's hand found Mitch's hard cock again and wrapped around it, his stroke firm and steady as he shoved his dick up Mitch's ass, driving hard and deep, in and out, their moans sounding loud in Linc's ears, even under the spray of the shower.

"Christ! So good." Mitch began to shake, his corded muscles straining beneath his skin. "Gonna come soon." One hand reached down and covered Linc's on his cock, and they moved in unison, their hands sliding together up and down Mitch's shaft.

The tip of Linc's cock brushed his prostate, and Mitch cried out. "Fuck! Again." He pushed back against Linc, fucking himself on Linc's dick. "Do it again."

Linc was more than happy to oblige him, nailing his prostate with every thrust until Mitch's entire body tensed, his back arched, and the muscles around Linc's cock rippled as liquid heat covered his hand. Linc was right behind him, roaring as his cock blew, and he pumped hard into Mitch.

He leaned against Mitch, his breathing labored as he struggled to right his world. Once the room stopped spinning and he was able to think clearly, Linc finally noticed Tomi in the room, sitting on the counter by the sink with her gaze locked on them, her fingers in her pussy and need burning in her eyes.

* * *

If someone had asked Tomi yesterday if she missed having sex with other people, if she missed having two sets of hands, two sets of mouths pleasuring her, if she missed sharing Mitch and being shared by him and another person, her response would have been a resounding, unequivocal, *hell, no.*

That was before they arrived in Puerto Rico, before they met Linc, and everything changed. Now, less than twenty-four hours later, here she sat, watching another man fuck her fiancé in the shower, hearing his grunts and groans of pleasure, and loving every single second of it, knowing firsthand just how amazing it felt to have her body filled with Linc's dick.

Tomi had no idea how long she watched them, first awakened by their absence in the bed, and then drawn by the sounds coming from the bathroom. It had been over a year since she'd seen Mitch with another man, but she couldn't recall ever witnessing a scene quite like this. The way their bodies moved together, so powerfully, so passionately, as if they were made to fuck each other. It was so erotic, so arousing, that Tomi was tempted to join in. But too mesmerized to move, she'd opted instead to pleasure herself to relieve her ache while she watched them.

When their bodies shuddered for the last time and they collapsed against each other, Tomi was ready to explode herself.

Linc was the first to notice her, his gray-eyed gaze so hot and stormy it made her shiver. Tomi watched as he slowly withdrew from Mitch's body and removed the used condom from his semierect cock.

Mitch finally lifted his head from the shower wall, and his gaze found hers. God, there was so much love in his eyes, Tomi felt it all the way across the room, touching her like the sweetest kiss, the softest caress. A moan burst unexpectedly from her lips as her orgasm rolled through her, catching her by surprise, stealing her breath, and leaving her gasping for air.

So distracted by her pleasure, Tomi never heard the shower stop or the door open. She didn't notice Mitch and Linc moving toward her until she felt their lips and hands moving on her skin, kissing, touching, teasing her, moving down her body until they settled on their knees between her spread legs, licking, sucking, and tonguing her pussy, setting her on fire once again, before she ever had a chance to completely cool down.

She was so close to coming, just a few more licks of those two incredible tongues was all she needed to push her over the edge. Suddenly, the only thing she felt between her legs was cool air. Tomi's eyes snapped open in time to see Mitch and Linc standing.

"Wait." Her voice bordered on panic, but she didn't care. Hell, she'd beg if she had to, as long as she got the release her body desperately needed. "Please don't—"

Mitch's lips interrupted her pleas. "Don't worry, baby, we're gonna take good care of you. By the time we're finished, you'll be begging us to stop." His lips covered hers again, and Tomi dissolved against him. As they kissed, she felt Mitch lift her from the counter, and she automatically wrapped her arms and legs around him as he carried her from the room.

When Mitch finally stopped and lowered Tomi down, she opened her eyes and found herself straddling Linc's lap on the chaise in the bedroom with her back pressed against his chest. His arms encircled her waist, and he held her tight. His dick pressed against her ass as his lips moved across her shoulder, up the column of her neck, and along her jaw, while his hands traveled over her breasts, down her stomach, and between her legs, where he slipped two fingers inside her pussy.

"Mmm, so wet," Linc groaned near her ear. His big fingers began to fuck in and out of her. She whimpered and thrust her hips forward.

Mitch leaned over, bracing his hands on the back of the chaise behind Linc's head, his face only inches from Tomi's. His lips hovered over hers, his blue eyes so dark they looked black.

"I love you," he whispered against her lips; then he kissed her until she felt like she was melting from the inside out. He finally dragged his lips away from hers, and his gaze shifted. Mitch leaned past Tomi until his mouth reached Linc's. They kissed each other for several long seconds, their tongues stroking deep inside each other's mouths before finally parting.

Mitch stood, and Tomi watched as he picked up the condom packet from the seat next to Linc, making quick work of opening it and sliding it down Linc's shaft. He grabbed the lubricant and coated Linc's latex-covered cock before tossing the tube to the side.

Once Mitch finished preparing him, Linc lifted Tomi, positioning her so that his dick pushed against the entrance of her anus. His hands gripped her ass, spreading the cheeks apart as he thrust upward, pushing his cock inside her.

Tomi's eyes rolled back, and her body relaxed as Linc entered her, inch by delicious inch, sending familiar heat racing up her spine. The sensation found its release in the form of a long, shuddering moan that emanated from her mouth.

Finally, she felt Linc's pelvis pressed snugly against her ass, his breath hot and labored at her throat. Linc held her steady as Mitch moved between their spread legs, using one hand to maintain his balance on the chaise and the other to guide his dick into Tomi's pussy.

A chorus of gasps and groans filled the room. Tomi could barely catch her breath as her body struggled to adjust to the sensations. She was no stranger to double penetration—she'd had sex with two men many times before—but she'd never felt so full, her body never stretched so wide, as it was right now.

They started to move, alternating their strokes inside her, and Tomi just held on, taking every ounce of pleasure they gave her. All too soon, she felt the pressure building, growing stronger with every thrust, zipping through her body, setting her nerve endings on fire, before settling in the pit of her stomach, where it exploded with enough force to dim her vision and make her ears ring.

"Oh, God... I'm coming again." She barely recognized the high-pitched wail that fell from her lips. As she rode out the waves of her orgasm, Tomi was distinctly aware of Linc's and Mitch's grunts of pleasure, felt the pressure of their cocks swell and erupt inside her as they came, one after the other, before they collapsed against each other on the chaise.

As she listened to their ragged breathing, felt the weight of their hard bodies pressed against hers, Tomi couldn't think of another place in the world that she'd rather be than sandwiched between these two amazing men.

Chapter Six

As Mitch buttoned his shirt, he studied his fiancée. From the look on her face, it was apparent that he'd more than lived up to his promise to Tomi. After another full round of sex, she threw in the towel, called it quits, and begged for a time-out.

Male pride and guilt warred within Mitch as he watched Tomi gingerly move around the room as she dressed. It was obvious she was sore. It'd been a while since she'd fucked two men at once. As much as he loved the idea of throwing her on the bed and burying himself balls-deep inside her once again, Mitch realized that she probably needed some time to recover from the workout they'd given her.

Tomi met his eyes, and Mitch instantly dismissed any thoughts he'd had of a reprieve as he watched her sensuous lips slowly curve into a smoldering smile, her gaze hungrily traveling over him. Her body might be sore, but it didn't appear to stop her from wanting him as much as he wanted her. Mitch stood there, grinning like a fool, feeling absurdly proud, knowing he was partially responsible for putting that well-satisfied look into those cognac eyes.

Without a word, she carefully walked up to him and rose to her tiptoes, planting a slow, hot kiss on his lips filled with promises of unimaginable pleasure before she pulled away and continued to put on her clothes. God, he loved her. If Mitch never had anything in his life but this woman, he would consider himself the luckiest fucking man in the world.

Movement drew his attention toward the bathroom, and Mitch looked at the other half of the reason why Tomi was so well satisfied. Linc stood in the doorway, fully dressed and completely mouthwatering. His short hair was still wet from the shower, and the inky curls appeared glossy under the lights in the room.

Memories of their time together in the shower made Mitch's groin tighten. Damn, it'd been too long since he'd fucked—or been fucked by—another man. After Alec, he figured his days of being with men were over—and that was fine by him. Mitch had had no idea how much he missed wrapping himself around a strong, masculine frame and sinking his dick deep inside a tight, muscular ass. He'd forgotten how much he loved having a solid body pressing against his and feeling a thick cock stretching him wide.

No man had ever done it for him—or to him—better than Linc. Mitch had the best sex during the last twelve hours than at any other time in his entire life with someone other than Tomi. Linc was definitely all man, giving twice as good as he got, making certain that the party didn't end until everyone was completely satisfied. Being with Linc and Tomi at the same time was Mitch's definition of having the best of both worlds.

He didn't even realize he was staring at Linc until Mitch saw the knowing smile on the other man's face; those smoky eyes stared back at him, holding his gaze like a laser, telling him without words that he was thinking the exact same things that were running through Mitch's mind.

"You know." Tomi's throaty laughter interrupted the moment. "If you two keep looking at each other like that, we're all going to end up horizontal again, and as much as the idea of being fucked by the two hottest men I've ever met turns me on, I don't think I'm quite ready for another round just yet."

There was no heat in Tomi's voice, no hint of jealousy in her tone. Her words were those of a woman who knew what—and who—she wanted. Mitch smiled to himself. The feeling was mutual.

Linc turned his sexy gaze toward Tomi. "Yeah, I can see your point." His voice rumbled, and it made Mitch's cock jump.

"So," Linc continued, "what are your plans for your first full day on the island?"

"I'm dying to see the El Yunque rain forest, but I don't think that's going to happen today." Tomi glanced at the clock on the dresser. "The last tour bus left nearly an hour ago."

"Oh, man, I haven't been to the rain forest since I was a kid. My cousins and I practically lived there when I visited during the summers. It became our personal kingdom. We'd get there first thing in the morning and spend our whole day running around, terrorizing the animals, each other, and any person unfortunate enough to encounter us on the trails." Linc chuckled, shaking his head, his voice slightly wistful.

"We were such a bunch of badass kids, causing havoc all over the place, but we had a good time."

"It sounds like it," Mitch commented, a smile spreading across his face at the image Linc painted and the way his eyes shined at the memory, despite his slightly embarrassed tone. "Too bad we missed the last bus for the day."

"You don't need to ride the tour bus in order to go." Linc looked in Tomi's direction, and Mitch watched him admire her bare legs as she sat on the edge of the bed and tied the laces of her Nikes. Mitch couldn't blame him. Tomi had amazing legs. Smooth and toned, they had just enough muscle definition without appearing too bulky. The tiny pair of shorts and tank top she wore emphasized the rest of her incredible body.

"The tour through the rain forest is self-directed," Linc continued. "It's quicker—and a lot more fun—if you drive on your own. You can stay as long as you want and leave when you're ready, not when someone tells you it's time to go."

"Cool!" Tomi's entire face lit up, and she bounced a little on the bed. "Let's do it." She paused, her face suddenly crestfallen. "Damn, we didn't rent a car, and I doubt there are any still available on a Saturday."

Linc laughed and sat down on the bed next to Tomi; his hand immediately reached out and touched her leg, as if he couldn't resist any longer.

"I just happen to know a limousine service, and I think I can convince them to provide you with a car for the day."

"Are you sure?" Mitch knew Tomi well enough to see that she was trying to hide her excitement, but the hopeful note in her tone was very evident. Her gaze shifted to Mitch and then back to Linc. "We really want to go, Linc, but we don't want to disrupt your business."

"For you, I'm sure I can work something out."

Tomi threw her arms around Linc and hugged him tightly before giving him a kiss on the lips. "Thank you," she whispered. "Although you won't admit it, I know that it's a big deal to change plans at the last minute when you already have schedules set for the day. I want you to know we really appreciate it."

Linc's eyes remained fastened on her lips. "It's more than worth it if it means getting a reaction like that." He dipped his head and kissed her again.

As Mitch watched, he felt his entire body tighten, his dick lengthen in his shorts. Jesus, they were so fucking hot together.

"I wish you could come with us," Tomi said when they finally came up for air. "I'd love to see the rain forest from your perspective."

"I don't think that's going to be a problem," Linc murmured against her lips. "Although I can provide a car, I don't have any drivers available today," he admitted. "So that means you're stuck with me again as your driver."

When their lips met again, Mitch found himself moving, no longer able to stand and watch from the sidelines any longer, needing to be part of the heat they generated.

He reached the bed and bent to kiss them both, and the kiss went from hot to fiery in an instant. Three sets of tongues played together, three sets of lips slipped, slid, and pressed against each other.

Linc was the first to pull away, his eyes filled with regret. "If we're going to make it to El Yunque anytime today, I think we need to stop now or we'll never leave this room. And we still need to stop by my house so I can change clothes, and then by the garage so I can pick up a car."

Linc was right. However, as much as Mitch wanted to see the rain forest, the urge to climb between the sheets with Linc and Tomi again was almost too strong to ignore.

With a sigh, Mitch reluctantly stood. "Linc's right." He reached for Tomi's hand and pulled her to her feet. "We need to go now." He was talking to himself as much as he was to them. They needed to put as much space between them and this bed as possible. Otherwise, he was going to start taking off clothes.

"You're both right," Tomi agreed. "But first, I need nourishment." As if on cue, her stomach rumbled loudly. "After the workout you two gave me, I could eat a small animal." She picked up her wallet and camera off the dresser and headed toward the door. Laughing, they followed her out the room.

* * *

"Oh, look at that!" Linc chuckled, following behind Tomi's rapidly moving form as she jogged down a trail. They'd started their tour of the rain forest nearly two hours ago with Tomi leading the way most of the time, her excitement infectious, increasing with every unique plant she discovered, every new animal she encountered. For the moment, her focus was on a tree with several small, colorful birds clustered together on a branch.

"That's a San Pedrito," Linc told her when Mitch and he finally caught up to her.

"Little Saint Peter."

Linc nodded at Tomi's translation as he stared at the tiny parrots in the tree. "They're very common in El Yunque."

"They're beautiful." She pulled out her camera and added another picture to the dozens she'd already taken for the afternoon. Something new caught her attention, and just that quickly, her interest shifted from the birds, and she was moving down the trail again toward a new target, her long, thick hair bouncing as she went.

Linc glanced at Mitch. "I take it she's having a good time," he told the other man as they followed behind Tomi at a slower pace.

Mitch snorted with laughter. "What gave it away: the constant shrieks of excitement, the mad dashes through the forest, or the nonstop picture taking?"

"I'd say it's a combination of all three," Linc said, laughing along with Mitch.

"In her defense, this place is pretty spectacular," Mitch admitted. "It's kinda hard to be surrounded by all this natural beauty and not have the same sort of reactions." He looked at Linc. "You truly live in paradise, man."

Linc slowed down and took a moment to look at his surroundings. He'd been to this place more times than he could remember, and after a while, it became easy to take it for granted. Sometimes it took a fresh pair of eyes or a new perspective to help him appreciate how fortunate he was.

"Yeah," he said to Mitch. "I think you're right about that." They continued down the path in search of Tomi, finding her just as she reached out toward a bush filled with bright, waxy-looking flowers in various shades of pink and rose.

"Wait!" Linc called out before her hand touched the plant. "Trust me; you don't want to touch that."

Tomi's hand paused in midair. "Why?" She looked over her shoulder at him with a confused expression on her face.

"That's an *alelí alhelí* plant. It's beautiful to look at, but don't let the pretty flowers fool you," he warned. "They're poisonous."

Tomi recoiled as if something had bit her, her eyes going wide with fear.

"Don't worry." Linc put a steadying hand on Tomi's shoulder when he reached her, and Mitch wrapped his arms around her midsection, pulling her against him. "They won't kill you if you touch them, but they're very toxic. They can cause some pretty nasty stomach viruses."

"It's a good thing you were here with us." Tomi smiled up at him. "Otherwise, I probably would have spent the rest of my vacation on my knees, praying to the porcelain god."

Before Linc had a chance to respond, the sudden sound of thunder filled the air. It was the only warning they got before the skies opened up, and rain poured down on them.

"Come on!" Linc yelled to them over the rain. "I know a place where we can stay until the rain stops." Linc veered off the trail, jogging through the forest with Tomi and Mitch behind him, trying to recall from memory where a small cave was that his cousins and he used to play in as kids, hoping that it was in the same spot as he remembered.

When the small entrance came into view a few minutes later, Linc released a sigh of relief, hoping that their luck would continue and they wouldn't find any other two- or four-legged occupants already residing inside the cave.

The interior of the cave seemed a lot smaller than Linc remembered. It was more of a small space really, with just enough room for them to walk around a few feet in any one direction. However, it would do for now.

"The rain should be over soon," Linc assured them, watching as Tomi squeezed water from her dripping hair. "Summer storms never last too long."

The light filtering in brightened the space just enough for Linc to make out Tomi's drenched form and the way her tank top clung to her body and emphasized the outline of her breasts.

Mitch pulled his T-shirt over his head and wiped his face before wringing the excess water from the material and laying it over a nearby rock.

Linc's mouth went dry, and his eyes alternated between the sight of Tomi's hardened nipples and Mitch's bare skin. God, there was just something about them that kept him as hot and horny as a fifteen-year-old virgin trying to get his first piece of ass. It didn't matter that they'd just finished a fucking frenzy only a few hours ago. The weight of Linc's cock, hard and heavy against his leg, told him that he was ready for them once again.

"So," Mitch said, his voice suddenly husky, his eyes trained on Tomi, his thoughts obviously headed in the same direction as Linc's. "Whatever shall we do while we wait for the storm to pass?" Pressing his chest against her back, Mitch slid his hands down to her hips and held her there as he gently thrust against her ass.

"Mmm," Tomi moaned softly, and her head fell against his chest. "I'm certain we'll come up with a thing"—her gaze shifted to Linc—"or two to keep us occupied while we wait."

As Mitch nuzzled along her neck from behind, Linc moved in front of her and kissed her lips. The temperature in the cave rose quickly, their mouths generating more heat than the weather outside.

Within minutes their damp clothes seemed to dissolve from their bodies, and Linc's attention immediately focused on Tomi's breasts. Unable to resist, he cupped the soft flesh. His thumb brushed over a nipple, and it went hard, growing so dark, so lovely. Leaning down, he sucked the tip into his mouth.

His cock was so hard, and he wanted to be inside Tomi so badly. Linc slipped one hand down her body, stroking her stomach and then her mound. Tomi spread her legs, and she wrapped one leg around his hip. Her pussy was wet and slick against his fingers, and his mouth covered hers again as he slipped two fingers inside, her body seeming to suck them right in. She cried out against his lips as one of Mitch's fingers slipped in with his. Together, they brought more cries from her until her body trembled and pleas fell from her lips.

"Please. I can't wait." Tomi panted, her voice shaking. "I need…"

"I didn't bring anything with me." Even as Linc said the words and heard the apology in his voice, he knew he was being ridiculous. Hell, how were they supposed to know that they would end up housed inside this cave instead of outside enjoying the rain forest as they had planned? Who could have guessed that the attraction between them would prove so strong, it would prevent them from keeping their hands off each other for longer than a couple of hours at a time?

Still, it didn't stop him from feeling guilty, especially at this moment, when he felt as if he'd spontaneously combust if he couldn't have them right now.

"Don't sweat it; none of us did." Mitch seemed to read his mind. He leaned over Tomi's head and kissed Linc. "We'll just have to improvise."

One moment they were standing, and the next Linc found himself lying on his back, his clothes a cushion between him and the hard ground. Tomi straddled him, her knees positioned on either side of his head, and her pussy poised over his face. Mitch stood above them with his dick in Tomi's mouth.

Linc didn't wait for an invitation. Instead, he jumped right in, his tongue flicking back and forth over Tomi's clit before delving inside and tasting her juices. Tomi began to moan, her gyrating body moving over him. Linc used one hand to hold her steady and the other wrapped around his cock, stroking up and down the shaft, using the fluid leaking from the tip to ease the friction.

Looking up, Linc watched Tomi suck Mitch's cock, watched the way those lips repeatedly slid over Mitch's thick length, leaving a glistening trail of her saliva.

"Damn, baby. Feels good." Mitch buried his fingers in Tomi's thick hair, holding her head as he slowly thrust in her mouth.

Tomi moaned in response. Her lips moved faster on Mitch's dick, drawing a hissing sound from him as his cock pumped faster between her lips.

She was close. Linc felt it in the way her body shook, the way her thighs trembled next to his head. He'd barely finished his thought when Tomi cried out around Mitch's cock, and her liquid heat flowed into Linc's mouth.

Mitch was right behind her, his bellow of pleasure echoing loudly off the cavern walls, his body jerking convulsively as he exploded, filling her mouth with his seed until it overflowed and dripped out, landing on Linc's cheek.

Mitch eased his dick from Tomi's mouth, and he leaned against a nearby rock, panting heavily. Linc continued to work his cock frantically, his own satisfaction only a few strokes away, when Tomi bent and licked the side of his face before she covered his lips with her own, the taste of Mitch still evident in her mouth. That was all it took to make Linc go off like a rocket, shooting jets of cum to splatter on his stomach and against Tomi's ass.

"Damn," Tomi spoke against his lips. "That was a hell of an improvisation."

Smiling, Linc said, "Yeah, it was." He took another long kiss, savoring the combined flavors of Tomi and Mitch on his tongue.

"It looks like we finished right on time." Mitch helped Tomi to her feet. "It stopped raining." He held out a hand to Linc, pulling him into his arms for a kiss as soon as Linc was standing.

Linc felt the spark of lust trying to reignite in his groin, felt his cock trying to lift its head again, and he reluctantly pulled away from Mitch before his body betrayed him.

Linc picked up his damp clothes off the ground. He searched through his pockets until he found a slightly wet handkerchief in the back pocket of his pants. It wasn't the ideal thing to use, but it was the best he could find under the circumstances. After quickly wiping himself off, he passed the handkerchief to Tomi and Mitch, who did the same thing before they began to put on their own clothes.

Linc busied himself with the simple task of getting dressed while desperately trying to ignore the sight of Tomi's soft curves and silky brown skin, frantically trying to concentrate on something other than Mitch's hard, chiseled body and big dick.

"Ready?" he asked once they were fully dressed.

"Yep." The darkened interior of the space did nothing to hide Tomi's bright smile.

Linc couldn't help but smile in return at the happiness in her tone. "Well, let's hit the trail, so you can get some more pictures." Linc paused, and his voice became teasing. "That is, if your camera can hold any more pictures."

"Trust me." Mitch laughed. "I don't think that's going to be a problem. She brought plenty of memory cards with her."

Linc's laughter joined theirs as he followed them outside. Inside, he tried to figure out how he would finish showing them the rain forest when all he really wanted to do was turn around and spend the rest of the day hidden inside this little cave with them, fucking until they all passed out from exhaustion.

God, it was going to be a long day.

Chapter Seven

Linc woke abruptly, swearing to himself as he shielded his eyes against the morning sunlight shining brightly through the open windows in his bedroom.

Movement drew his attention to the sleeping form next to him, and Linc smiled, suddenly remembering the reason why he'd been too preoccupied to remember to close the windows and lower the blinds the previous night.

Mitch lay next to him, his nude body spread out on display, his sun-kissed skin smooth and inviting, tempting Linc to explore every inch with his tongue. He quickly decided that a little irritating sunlight was a small price to pay in exchange for the immeasurable amounts of pleasure he'd indulged in the previous night.

After they'd left the rain forest the previous evening, Linc dropped Mitch and Tomi off at their hotel before going home, changing clothes, and returning to take them to a late dinner at Strip House, another of his favorite restaurants. Afterward, he surprised himself by asking them to spend the night with him at his home.

Linc couldn't remember the last time he'd invited someone to his home or awakened to find someone in his bed. Since moving back to Puerto Rico, he'd enjoyed plenty of sex with countless numbers of people, but never here.

This was more than just a house to Linc; this was his sanctuary, his private space, the place where he rediscovered his sanity at a time when he was convinced he'd lost his mind. Linc always found solitude and peace within these walls, no matter how crazy his life became, and he'd been unwilling to share it with strangers. In fact, he couldn't think of a single person other than relatives who even knew where he lived.

Yet he'd only known Mitch and Tomi for a couple of days, and he'd already let them into his personal world, welcoming them into his home and his bed, sharing the intimate details of his life with them about things he couldn't bring himself to discuss with his cousin and closest friend.

As he looked down at Mitch, Linc couldn't help but notice how right it felt to find the other man next to him first thing in the morning, how normal it seemed to be, lying here with him right now. In fact, the only thing better than waking up next to the sexiest man he'd ever met would be having the most beautiful woman he'd ever seen beside him as well.

He barely finished that thought when a familiar and distinctive splash outside his window caught his attention. Linc smiled. Tomi had obviously found the pool. Carefully, he eased from the bed, torn between staying with Mitch and joining Tomi by the pool. As he headed to the bathroom, Linc passed the window and caught a glimpse of Tomi, the sun beaming on her naked body as she slowly did the backstroke through the water.

Suddenly, Linc's decision became very simple. Ten minutes later, he was on his way to the pool.

* * *

Linc stood near the edge of the pool and watched Tomi. She was the picture of relaxation with her eyes closed, her arms slicing unhurriedly through the water, her legs pumping slowly and easily as she leisurely swam the length of the pool.

He walked to the end of the pool, quietly went down the stairs, and eased into the water. As Tomi approached him, he reached for her, provoking a startled screech from her.

"Sorry." Linc chuckled, pulling her into his arms. "I didn't mean to scare you."

"It's okay." She pushed her wet locks away from her face. "I hope you don't mind me using the pool." Tomi smiled up at him. "It's already so warm outside, and the water looked so cool and inviting that I couldn't resist getting in and going for a swim."

His hands moved along her back, over her ass, holding her a little tighter, making certain she felt his erection and understood how much he wanted her. "Don't worry about it." Linc stole a quick kiss. "My pool looks better with you in it." His head dipped lower, and he sucked one of her nipples between his lips, tasting the chlorine mixed with the natural flavor of her skin.

"You think so?" He loved the way she moaned. So soft and sexy. The sound always shot through him like a bolt of lightning, striking him right in the balls, making him want to come on the spot every time he heard it.

Reaching between her thighs, Linc lifted her legs and wrapped them around his waist. When his cock settled against her pussy, thoughts of coming almost became a reality, forcing Linc to close his eyes and take a deep breath in order to regain his composure before he embarrassed himself.

Fuck, he'd give his left arm for a condom right now. When he'd seen Tomi from the window earlier, he'd been in such a hurry to get to her that he'd forgotten to grab one on the way out the door. Now, here he stood with his hard dick pressed against Tomi's soft folds, and all he could think about was burying himself inside her as deeply as possible.

"It's okay," Tomi whispered, seeming to read his mind. "Mitch and I had to get blood tests in order to be married in Puerto Rico. We're good."

He cupped her face, his thumb gently stroking her cheek. "It's not Mitch and you I'm worried about. It's me."

She studied him for several moments before she smiled softly and reached out to stroke his face, her hand mirroring his caress against her cheek.

"You don't seem like the careless type, Linc, especially not about something as important as this."

"I'm not," Linc conceded. "I had a test less than a year ago, and I was clean. I try to be careful. I always use condoms, and I don't take any unnecessary risks when it comes to sex. But...what if I'm wrong? What if I slipped up somewhere along the way, and I don't even realize it yet? Are you sure you're willing to take that chance?"

"With you...yes, I am." Before he could utter a response, Tomi's hand wrapped around his shaft, and she guided him inside her.

"*Oh, mierda!*" Linc groaned, his entire body shuddering. "*Dios*, Tomi, we shouldn't...*cogida*." His eyes rolled back as her vaginal muscles clenched tightly around him. "*Que no debemos hacer esto.*" Even as he muttered the words, even as he tried to convince himself that it was the right thing to do because he wasn't wearing a condom, Linc knew he couldn't have stopped to save his life. He'd hit the point of no return as soon as his unsheathed dick slipped inside her warm, wet heat.

"*No preocuparte*," Tomi whispered, meeting his eyes, thrusting against him. "I trust you. I know you wouldn't do anything to intentionally hurt me or Mitch."

He groaned, moved by her words in ways he'd never thought possible. Linc buried his face against her neck, moving through the water until Tomi's back met the side of the pool. Gripping the globes of her ass, Linc began stroking hard and deep, the force of his thrusts making their bodies slap together, causing waves of water to splash against them. Linc ignored it all, his focus solely on Tomi and the pleasure he found within her arms, inside her body.

A second pair of hands touched him just before he heard Mitch's husky voice in his ear. "Is this a private party, or can I join in too?"

All he could do was nod, too lost in the moment to form words. He moved backward, giving Mitch enough space to slide in between Tomi and the pool wall. Gritting his teeth, Linc forced himself to stand still just long enough for Mitch to work himself inside Tomi.

They both held Tomi, alternating their strokes as they pumped inside her. He felt Mitch's cock rubbing against his through the thin membrane of skin separating them, causing so much friction that Linc felt overloaded by the sensation.

His body began to shake uncontrollably as his orgasm built inside him. If he was lucky, he had about a minute left before he imploded. Linc gripped Tomi even tighter, fucking her with everything he had. He met Mitch's gaze over her head, and those blue eyes held the same desperate need that drove Linc.

"Come on, baby." Mitch's words were tense, his voice strained. "Let us feel you come."

It was like a chain reaction. Tomi released a strangled scream, her teeth sinking into the place where his neck and shoulder met, her short nails digging into his back, her pussy pulsating around his cock as she came.

She was still screaming when Linc erupted, his back arching, his cum flowing from him as he shot hard and deep. He felt Mitch's cock jerking inside her, heard the other man bellowing Tomi's name as he filled her.

They leaned against each other, breathing heavily. "I swear," Linc said. "You two are trying to kill me. I'm not as young as I used to be."

"Yeah, right." Mitch chuckled breathlessly. "Most of the guys I train are at least fifteen years younger than you, and none of them are in nearly as good of shape as you are."

"I'll take your word for it." Linc tried to downplay Mitch's comment. Inside, he was smiling his ass off. To receive a compliment from someone who looked as hot as Mitch was a hell of an ego boost.

Changing the subject, he said, "We probably should get out of the pool and put some clothes on before the cleaning crew arrives."

Mitch smiled, his guilt evident on his face. "Actually, I think we're already too late. I sorta ran—literally—into a woman on the stairs when I was on my way out here to meet the two of you. From the look on her face, I obviously scared the shit out of her."

"That was Rosa," Linc finally managed to say. The scenario Mitch described made him laugh so hard, he could barely speak. He didn't doubt for a minute that Mitch's description of his longtime housekeeper's reaction was completely accurate. Rosa had taken care of his home since he'd purchased it over a decade ago. Aside from the other people responsible for the upkeep of his property, Linc was certain that she'd never encountered anyone else here besides him and his family.

"Well, I probably scarred the poor woman for life." Mitch laughed, shaking his head. "I'm sure the last thing she expected when she got to work today was to be nearly run down by some strange, butt-naked man."

They were still laughing when the sound of a throat clearing drew their attention toward the house.

"*Lo siento interrumpirte, Señor* Castillo." Rosa seemed to look everywhere but at the pool, as if she knew exactly what they'd been doing and couldn't bring herself to look in that direction. "*Hice el desayuno para ti y tus huéspedes. Está en el comedor.*"

She'd made breakfast. Linc's mouth began to water. Rosa was an excellent cook. "*Gracias*, Rosa," he called out. "*Estaremos adentro pronto.*"

When Rosa walked back inside the house, Tomi asked, "Did I hear something about breakfast?"

Linc nodded. "Although calling it breakfast is probably an understatement. Knowing Rosa, it's more like a feast. She's a damn good cook. Come on." He kissed Tomi, then Mitch. "Let's get some clothes on, so we can eat before the food gets cold."

* * *

Linc stared at the spread of food waiting for them when they walked into the dining room. This was way over the top, even by Rosa's standards. Three plates overflowed with fried *amarillos*, scrambled eggs, *tortilla de guineitos*, and thickly sliced bacon. A platter of freshly cut papaya, mango, and passion fruit sat in the center of the table alongside a basket filled with guava and cheese muffins. Steaming hot mugs of *café con leche* sat next to each of their plates.

"Wow, you weren't kidding when you said Rosa would make a feast," Tomi commented as she walked by Linc and had a seat. She'd already started eating and was moaning in approval with every bite of food she took in the short time it took for Mitch and him to find a chair and join her at the table

As he ate, Linc watched in amusement as Tomi steadily worked through the heaping pile of food on her plate, amazed that someone so small could put away so much food and not be twice her size.

Mitch and he were still eating when Tomi sat back with a sigh, the majority of the food gone from her plate.

"That was an amazing meal." She smiled at Linc. "I hope I get a chance to see Rosa before I leave, so I can tell her how much I enjoyed my breakfast."

"I told you Rosa's a great cook," Linc said, staring at Tomi's lips as she slid a piece of mango into her mouth. As he watched her suck the sweet, sticky juice from her fingers, Linc's groin tightened, and he wondered if she had any idea just how sexy she looked at that moment. He glanced in Mitch's direction and saw that he'd stopped eating, and his focus was on Tomi as well.

Looking at Mitch as she reached for another piece of fruit, Tomi said, "If I keep eating like this, we're going to have to do extra exercises just so I don't get as big as a house before we go home."

"You go ahead and enjoy your food, baby." Mitch's voice dropped a few octaves. "I got a special workout in mind just for you that's guaranteed to burn up all those extra calories."

"Don't think I won't hold you to it." Tomi chuckled softly. "That's one workout I'm definitely looking forward to."

Linc smiled, ignoring the twinge of envy he felt as he watched their easy flirting and gentle, back-and-forth bantering. It was obvious they were best friends. Their love for each other was so apparent. Despite living with two people for several years, he'd never experienced the kind of closeness in a relationship that he saw between Tomi and Mitch. He never imagined that he'd want the sort of connection they obviously shared. Yet as he watched them, Linc couldn't deny the yearning he felt to be a part of the link that bonded them together.

Tomi turned her attention to him. "You're lucky to have someone like Rosa around," she told him as she snatched another piece of fruit.

"I know," Linc murmured, picking up his coffee and taking a sip of the sweet, hot liquid. "Rosa has taken good care of me and my home for years. Occasionally, she even takes pity on me and cooks enough meals to last me all week, just so I don't starve to death."

"How long has she worked for you?" Mitch asked.

"Rosa's been with me since I bought this house. She's like family now, and the only person I trust to take care of things around here. Even when I lived in New York, I never worried, because I knew that Rosa would look after my home like it was her own."

"Well," Tomi spoke up, "I've only seen a few rooms, but it's obvious that you have a very beautiful home."

"That's right." Linc smiled apologetically. "You never got the full tour." When he'd brought them to his home the night before, he'd left his manners outside in the car. The only thing he wanted them to see was his California king-size bed. "Come on." He picked up his cup. "Let me show you around the place."

He waited for Tomi and Mitch to grab their coffee and stand up from the table before he led them through the house.

Twenty minutes later, they entered his office, the last room left to see. Linc sat in the overstuffed chair behind his desk, placing his feet on top of the walnut surface as he drank the remainder of his coffee.

"Man," Mitch began, as he had a seat on the leather couch, "you could fit at least five of our condo back in New York City inside this place."

"I remember that." Linc smiled sympathetically, thinking about the place he used to own when he'd lived there. The only thing big about it was the price tag. He suspected that Mitch and Tomi's condo probably cost nearly as much as he'd paid for this place when he first bought it. It was just one more thing that he didn't miss about the Big Apple.

He took a final drink from his coffee cup before setting it on the desk, his gaze on Tomi, who slowly walked around the room.

"I can tell you spend a lot of time in here." She glanced over her shoulder at him as she looked at various family pictures throughout the room. "Aside from your bedroom, you seem more comfortable here than in any other room in the house."

Linc couldn't argue that. He did spend quite a bit of time in this room, and not just working. His office was one of his favorite places to kick back and put his feet up, just as he was now. All the pictures in the room helped as well. Each one represented a special memory for Linc, a way for him to feel connected to his family, even when they weren't around.

"Is this Paul and Ava?"

Linc focused on the picture frame that Tomi held in her hand, immediately recognizing the couple in the photo.

"Yes," he confirmed, ignoring the sadness he always felt whenever he thought about his deceased lovers.

Mitch stood and walked over to Tomi, looking over her shoulder at the picture. "They're gorgeous," he murmured, looking back at Linc. "Where was this taken?"

"Rio de Janeiro," he said automatically, the memory still vivid in his mind, the picture capturing a moment of happier times between the three of them before everything went so terribly wrong.

Linc lifted his feet off the desk and dropped them to the floor, before standing and moving across the room to join Mitch and Tomi. Looking down, he stared into the faces that he knew so well. Paul was the serious one, a tough, strong firefighter with cinnamon skin and warm, chocolate eyes, and Ava with her blonde hair and smiling green eyes, always the peacemaker, always wanting everyone to be as happy as she always seemed to be.

"I bet the three of you had a lot of good times here," Mitch commented.

"Actually, we didn't," Linc admitted. "I originally bought this house as a place for us to get away, but Paul and Ava never saw it." When Mitch and Tomi looked at him in surprise, he shrugged. "We never could get our schedules to coincide long enough for all of us to be off at the same time."

"Do you miss them?" Tomi asked, her voice soft and gentle.

Linc thought about her question for a moment before he responded. "Yes," he finally said. "But not in the way you might think." He paused again before continuing. "I miss knowing that they're alive and well and living their lives with someone who loved them the way they deserved to be loved. I miss not having had the chance to say good-bye, and

I'm sorry; I wish things could have been different between us."

He felt Mitch's eyes on him. "So…do you think you'd ever want to be a part of a relationship like that again?"

He met Mitch's gaze. "You know, if you'd asked me that a few days ago, my answer would definitely have been no. Now"—he looked meaningfully between Mitch and Tomi—"I think I've had a change of heart on the subject."

Chapter Eight

Mitch lay in bed, leaning on his elbow with his head resting in his hand, quietly watching Tomi's sleeping form next to him.

He absently stroked her hair, his mind a million miles away as thoughts of their weekend with Linc raced through his mind.

Despite his intense attraction to Linc, the most that Mitch had allowed himself to hope for was a nice evening out with a man who, if they were lucky, Tomi and he would consider a friend once they returned home.

Somehow, their simple dinner had evolved somewhere along the way and turned into so much more. He'd never formed a connection so quickly, so deeply, with someone other than Tomi. Mitch felt drawn to Linc by an attraction that surpassed the mere physical.

The fact of the matter was that he liked Linc a hell of a lot more than he probably should, considering he'd only known the man for three days. Tomi's reaction to Linc, particularly the way she trusted him enough to share herself uninhibitedly with him, seemed to speak volumes about her feelings toward Linc as well.

"If you keep thinking so hard, you'll give yourself a headache." Tomi's sleepy voice brought him back to the present. Mitch smiled and leaned down, kissing her slowly, enjoying the feel of her soft, full lips against his.

"Good morning, sleepyhead," Mitch teased, kissing along her jawline and nuzzling her neck until she giggled.

"Well, I *am* on vacation." Tomi squirmed, trying to move away from his tickling caress. "Aren't vacations supposed to be about catching up on all the sleep and fun you missed during the rest of the year?"

"Speaking of fun." He raised his head to look into her face. "I enjoyed our weekend with Linc. I'm glad we met him. He's a good man."

Tomi seemed to sober. "Me too," she said quietly. She opened her mouth as if she was going to say more, but she remained silent, averting her eyes away from him instead.

"Hey." Mitch cupped her face, refusing to let her look away. "What is it?" He searched her face, his concern increasing by the second. "Do you regret what happened?" He suddenly worried that he'd somehow misread her attraction to Linc, misinterpreted her interest in being with him again. "If you do, it's okay. We don't have to see Linc again if it makes you uncomfortable."

Please say no. God, he felt like such a selfish asshole, but he couldn't help it. In a short period of time, he'd begun to have very strong, very real feelings for Linc. Mitch was willing to admit that the more time he spent with the other man, the more he wanted him.

Hell, Linc had just dropped them off at their hotel six hours ago, and Mitch could hardly wait to see him again, could barely contain thoughts of the three of them together as they'd been all weekend.

However, this wasn't just about him. Tomi was the most important person in his life, and he'd never do anything that made her unhappy. If she told him that she didn't want to see Linc again, he wouldn't try to change her mind.

"No," she finally said. Her cognac eyes stared back at him, her voice sure. "I do want to see him again...very much."

"Then what's wrong? Talk to me, baby," Mitch urged. "You know you can tell me anything, right?"

Tomi nodded. "I know." She paused again as a myriad of emotions flashed in her eyes. Her face filled with familiar expressions that said she was trying to gather her thoughts. Mitch remained silent, patiently waiting for her to continue.

Finally, Tomi sighed. "I had a really good time with Linc as well. In fact, it was almost...too good." She smiled slightly. "After this weekend, I realized just how special Linc is, and I...I think I could fall for him just as easily as I fell for you when we first met." Tomi looked at him guiltily. "The thought of that happening, the thought of doing anything that would hurt you or our relationship, scares the shit out of me." Her last words were barely above a whisper.

"Listen to me." Mitch cupped her face with both hands, his gaze locked with hers unwaveringly. "That will *never* happen. I trust you with my life. I know that you would never intentionally do anything to harm me, and I hope you know the same thing about me." When she nodded, he continued. "There is nothing and no one in this world or the next that could ever come between us, Tomi, or diminish the amount of love we have for each other. Okay?"

Tomi smiled. Her eyes were slightly watery. "Okay."

Mitch kissed her then, needing to reinforce his words, wanting to reassure her that things would never change between them.

He ended the kiss and looked into her beautiful face, his chest swelling with his love for her. "I won't lie to you. I don't know where this thing with Linc is headed, but regardless of what does or doesn't happen between him and us, the bottom line is, we came here to Puerto Rico together, and that's exactly how we'll leave…together."

* * *

"It looks like somebody had a good weekend." Linc looked up at the sound of his cousin and best friend's voice. Pedro stood in the doorway of his office, arms folded across his broad chest, watching Linc with a smirk on his face.

Linc had no idea how long the other man had been standing there. His mind had been solidly on a certain couple who'd occupied his every waking thought since he met them just a few days ago.

Pedro walked farther into the room and took a seat on the edge of Linc's desk. "It wouldn't have anything to do with your dinner guests that my brother saw you with on Friday, would it?"

Linc shrugged. "I had a great dinner." He didn't bother trying to deny it, knowing that Alejandro would tell his brother that he'd seen Linc with Tomi and Mitch at the restaurant.

"So I see." Pedro reached out and pushed the collar of Linc's shirt aside, exposing the bruise on his neck that was still visible from where Tomi had bitten him. "From the looks of things, dinner wasn't the only thing you had. So, which one was it, the woman or the man?" he asked, well aware of Linc's sexual orientation.

Linc sat back in his chair, a smile tugging at the corners of his mouth. Several seconds of silence passed before Pedro's eyes suddenly widened as if he finally realized the answer to his question. His head fell back, and he roared with laughter.

"*Tú híbrido!* You did both of them, didn't you? Oh, man, you are such a fucking dog!" There was no heat in Pedro's tone despite his words. He was still grinning when he said, "No wonder you looked so damn happy when I walked in here. I guess Miguel's no-show on Friday worked out all right after all. Otherwise, you might have missed out on your weekend entertainment."

Pedro shook his head, a look of mock disappointment on his face. "Shit, I'm in the wrong line of work. I should have gone into business with you when I had the chance, then I'd have access to all the hot customers too. Men aren't my thing, so I'd leave them to you, but if I met women even half as beautiful as the one Alejandro described with you on Friday, it'd be worth it." A smile suddenly spread across his face. "I don't suppose you need another driver, do you? I'm sure I can fit a few runs into my schedule."

"It's not like that," Linc objected. "Tomi and Mitch aren't like some of the customers that I've told you about." The need to defend them, to differentiate them from all the other easy fucks he'd met over the years, was great. "They're not here trying to get laid; they're here to get married."

Pedro's brow arched. "If they're here to get married, what are they doing fucking you?"

Before Linc could find a way to explain the seemingly unexplainable, to put into words the undeniable connection that existed between the three of them, Lorna walked into his office unannounced and interrupted their conversation.

"What is it, Lorna?"

"You forgot your messages, baby." She reached past Pedro to hand Linc several pink slips of paper. "Don't forget, you got a meeting across town this afternoon."

"Thanks." Linc scanned the messages. Lorna knew him well. He'd completely forgotten about the meeting. She could be a complete pain in the ass at times, but she kept him organized.

Lorna turned to leave, making certain to brush against Pedro in the process.

"Hola, Pedro." Her voice dropped seductively. "*Estás pareciendo bueno, como de costumbre.*"

Linc sighed, knowing what would come next. He should have known Lorna couldn't make it back to her desk without hitting on one of them.

In true Lorna fashion, she spent the next several minutes all but falling to the floor, spreading her legs, and offering herself to Pedro. His cousin didn't help the situation as he laughed at her provocative comments, seeming to enjoy, even encourage, her flirtatious behavior.

Finally, Linc couldn't take anymore. "I pay you to work, Lorna, not stand around trying to fuck my relatives," he snapped, a little more harshly than he'd intended.

She looked at him in surprise before turning on her heel and all but stomping from the room, muttering something in Spanish that sounded suspiciously like the word bastard.

"Relax, cousin." Pedro sounded amused. "Lorna's harmless."

"Then you hire her to work for you." Linc glared back at him. "You can have the pleasure of listening to her bullshit all day."

"I don't need the extra help." Pedro laughed, appearing completely unfazed by Linc's irritation. "Besides, I already told you, I'm still trying to get a job here."

"Yeah, right." Linc snorted. "You know damn well that Tracee would kick your ass—and mine—if you came to work here," Linc told him, referring to Pedro's longtime girlfriend.

The smile fell from Pedro's face. "You're probably right about that."

"Speaking of work," Linc began, "how's your work schedule this week?"

Pedro shrugged. "The usual. I'm booked solid with tours Friday through Sunday, but the rest of the week doesn't look too bad. Why?"

"I was thinking of taking Mitch and Tomi on a private boat tour around the island one day this week, and I wanted to know if you had any time available."

Pedro looked at him thoughtfully for a moment. "So I take it this thing between you and them isn't just a weekend fling, huh?" Linc didn't bother to respond. It was a rhetorical question, and they both knew it. "Actually," Pedro finally said, "I was planning to block off Thursday evening so that I could spend some time with Tracee on the boat. I'll check with her, but I'm sure she won't mind if you and your friends join us." He smiled again. "You know Tracee adores you. She'll do anything you ask."

"She should." Linc laughed. "If it weren't for me, she'd never have met you." He'd dated Tracee a few times before he introduced her to Pedro. That was two years ago, and they were still together.

Pedro's voice suddenly sobered. "This couple must be really special if you're calling in favors just to spend more time with them."

Linc held his gaze. "They are," he said simply.

Pedro nodded. "In that case, I can't wait to meet them."

Chapter Nine

The sounds of salsa music filled the air as Pedro's boat floated in the calm waters of the San Juan Bay. They were anchored a couple of miles away from the mainland, giving them an incredible view of the brightly lit San Juan shoreline.

Linc looked up as Tomi walked onto the deck wearing a bikini top and low-slung cutoff shorts, a smile curving her lips and her unruly curls gently blowing in the light wind. She had a seat next to him, and Mitch flanked his other side on the U-shaped, bench-style seat.

"You know," she began, "when you said you were going to take us on a boat ride, I had no idea you meant something like this." Her arm gestured around the boat.

"I can see your point." Linc looked around as well. Referring to it as a boat did seem like a bit of an understatement. The forty-foot catamaran easily held fifty people and included all the comforts of home.

It was more than just a boat for Pedro as well. It was how he earned a living. He'd invested all of his money—and some of Linc's as well—into purchasing this boat to start a chartered tours business. It turned out to be the best investment Pedro could have made. The boat had more than paid for itself within a few years.

"This is a great boat, man," Mitch said to Pedro, who walked onto the deck carrying a bottle of wine and several glasses.

"Thanks." Pedro set the glasses down on the built-in table. "It's my baby. My pride and joy." The look on his face confirmed his words.

"Hey, I thought that was me," Tracee joked as she joined them on deck carrying a tray of food in her hands.

Pedro took the tray from her and set it on the table. "Of course you are." His voice was soothing as he pulled her into his arms, whispering, "*Sabes te amo*," before giving her a kiss.

"That's more like it." A smile spread across her pretty face when Pedro finally let her up for air. Tracee pushed a colorful pillow to the side and had a seat on the bench across from them as Pedro poured the wine.

"You make a very nice couple," Tomi commented, accepting the glass Pedro held out to her. "How did you meet?"

"I stole her from Linc." Pedro winked at her.

Linc laughed hard. "I think that's stretching it a bit, but hey, whatever helps you sleep at night." He looked at Tomi. "Tracee and I dated for a while before she met Pedro," he explained.

"Speaking of couples," Tracee spoke up, "Pedro told me that the two of you were gorgeous, but I didn't expect for you both to be so perfect. I can see why Linc likes you so much. He has a weakness for beautiful women"—her gazed shifted to Mitch—"and men." To Linc, she said, "I definitely approve."

Linc groaned and shook his head. He could always count on Tracee to say exactly what was on her mind. Thankfully, Tomi and Mitch didn't seem to mind, judging from their soft laughter.

"That would explain why he dated you," Tomi told her. "You remind me of my last girlfriend. She was so full of energy and had a great personality." Tomi looked at her appreciatively. "Physically, she was nowhere near as beautiful as you."

"Thanks." Tracee smiled. "That's a huge compliment coming from someone who looks like you."

"No problem." Tomi shrugged. "Although, I'm only stating what's obvious."

"I agree," Mitch added. "When it comes to looks, Tracee, you have absolutely no reason to worry." Mitch looked at Pedro, who sat next to Tracee. "And you should consider yourself very lucky to have her."

Pedro put his arm around Tracee and placed a kiss to her temple. "Trust me, *mi amigo.* I do."

"So I hear that you're a professor," Tracee said to Tomi, who nodded.

"That's really cool. I did a couple of years at the University of Miami before I came back home. I thought about finishing up my degree here at the University of Puerto Rico, but I can't seem to find the time." She looked slightly sheepish. "Besides, I love what I do for a living."

Tomi smiled understandingly. "A college degree is great, but it can't replace doing something that you're passionate about. It sounds to me like you've already found your passion."

"What kind of work do you do?" Mitch asked.

Tracee practically beamed. "I'm a massage therapist. I work in a couple of spas at some of the larger hotels in San Juan."

"I love massages," Tomi said. "It's been way too long since I had one."

"Oh, I highly recommend them—and not just because I do them," Tracee added. "As far as I'm concerned, massages are one of the best forms of therapy in the world."

"I think you're right about that," Mitch told her. "I encourage all the people who I train to get regular massages. It's great for loosening sore muscles, especially after a hard workout."

"What kind do you specialize in?" Tomi asked.

"I do just about all of them, but my favorites are the Deep Tissue and the Trigger Point massages."

"If you ask me," Pedro chimed in, looking at Tracee, "nothing compares to your Tantric massages."

Linc had to agree with that. He was well familiar with Tracee's Tantric massages. He'd experienced them on several occasions—before and after she'd started dating Pedro—and he could attest to just how incredible they were. He felt his cock start to swell at the mere thought of one of those sessions with Tracee.

"Isn't that the sensual massage?" Tomi asked.

"Yes, but it's a lot more than that," Tracee told her. "If it's done right, a Tantric massage can be the most pleasurable nonsexual experience of your life."

"Wow." Tomi laughed. "When you put it that way, I'll definitely have to make sure to have one."

"If you'd like, I'll give you one before you leave," Tracee offered. "Trust me; it's like nothing you've ever felt before."

"What about right now?" Tomi asked and then hesitated. "That is, if you wouldn't mind."

"Would I mind the chance to touch you for the next thirty minutes? Are you kidding me?" Tracee's sultry laughter rang out. "I'd love to." She stood up and looked at Tomi. "We both have to be completely undressed. Are you okay with that?"

"I don't think that will be a problem." Tomi smiled, her voice sounding soft, sexy.

Tracee returned her smile. "Good. Let me grab some towels and oil, and I'll be right back."

As Tracee disappeared inside the boat, Linc took a moment to survey the surrounding waters, feeling satisfied that they were far enough away from other boats to have privacy. The lights of the nearest boat appeared to be several hundred yards away, making it next to impossible for the occupants to see the activities that were about to happen on their boat.

Tracee returned several minutes later, carrying a stack of towels and a bottle filled with liquid. Linc sat transfixed, outwardly trying to hide his arousal and excitement as Tomi and Tracee made quick work of stripping off their clothes. He looked at Pedro, then Mitch. From the looks on their faces, it was obvious that Linc wasn't the only one affected by the sight in front of them.

Physically, Tracee and Tomi were as different as they were beautiful. Tracee, the taller of the two, had full, naturally large breasts and pleasing curves with long black hair that hung to the middle of her back. Tomi stood a few inches shorter with her perfectly proportioned hourglass frame.

He'd been with both of them sexually, knew the pleasure they were capable of giving. As enjoyable as sex had been with Tracee, Linc would be the first to admit that no woman had ever made him feel like Tomi.

Tracee arranged a towel and pillows on the deck and positioned Tomi so that she lay on her back with a pillow under her hips, her legs spread apart, and her knees slightly bent. The built-in lights overhead provided Linc with a clear view of her exposed pussy, the folds already wet as she waited for the massage.

"Just relax," she encouraged Tomi. "Take slow, deep breaths." Tomi closed her eyes, and her chest began to rise and fall steadily as she did what Tracee instructed. "That's good," Tracee said softly as she began. "This particular massage is called the *Yoni* massage." Her hands moved slowly over Tomi's body as she spoke. "The word yoni means sacred space. It's a term used to describe the vagina." She opened the bottle of oil and poured some into the palm of her hand. The scent of lavender and vanilla filled the air. "The purpose of the Yoni massage is as much about loving and respecting the body as it is about pleasuring the body." She rubbed her hands together and began to massage the oil into Tomi's skin.

At some point, the music changed, becoming slower, softer, the volume too low for Linc to distinguish. It didn't matter, really. The only thing he could focus on was the way Tracee's hands moved over Tomi's body, starting at her calves and thighs, working her way over her hips and up her abdomen until she reached her breasts.

"Mmm, so pretty," Tracee murmured as she cupped Tomi's breasts in each hand. She bent and sucked one, then the other nipple into her mouth before gently kneading them, taking time to roll the wet berries between her thumb and forefinger.

Tomi moans grew louder, her excitement evident as her fingers clenched into fists each time Tracee stroked her nipples.

"*Jesús que coge a Cristo.*" Linc looked up at the sound of Pedro's whispered oath. His cousin made no effort to hide his arousal as he stared unblinkingly at Tomi and Tracee while rubbing his dick through his shorts.

Without even realizing it, Linc moved his hand between Mitch's thighs, feeling the heat of his erection through his jeans. Mitch groaned and reciprocated the move, covering Linc's hard cock and squeezing it gently.

The sounds of moans drew Linc's attention back to Tomi and Tracee. Tomi's eyes were open and locked on Tracee. They held each other's gazes as Tracee slowly poured oil on Tomi's pussy and set the bottle to the side before slowly massaging the oil into the lips. Tracee stroked Tomi's clit, rubbing the knob between her thumb and index finger for a few moments before she slid her middle finger inside. Tomi cried out, and her hips rose off the deck as her thighs began to shake.

Another finger soon joined the first one inside her pussy, even as a third eased into her anus. Tracee used her other hand to continue Tomi's massage, gently rubbing, kneading, and caressing over her stomach, her breasts, and her face.

Without breaking eye contact, Tracee leaned down and covered Tomi's lips with her own. They kissed until Tomi cried out, her body jerking as she came. They were both breathing heavily as Tracee lay next to Tomi and continued to stroke her body.

"So, was that normally how you do this massage, or did I just luck out?" Tomi asked.

Tracee chuckled breathlessly. "I think it's safe to say you got the special treatment."

"I was hoping you'd say that." Tomi's hand slid into Tracee's hair. "Now it's time for me to return the favor." She pulled Tracee's head down, kissing her hungrily. Her hands moved eagerly over Tracee's body, exploring her back, her ass, and her breasts. It was Tracee's turn to moan as Tomi pulled away from the kiss and dipped her head, taking one of Tracee's nipples into her mouth and swirling her tongue around the hardened tip.

"Sí, Tomi," she whispered. "*Que te sientes bien.*"

They became a tangled mass of arms, legs, and hands moving greedily over each other, their oily bodies sliding together, the light and dark hues of their contrasting skin tones glistening under the soft lights on the boat. They shifted positions, adjusting their bodies until Tomi lay on top of Tracee, their heads facing in opposite directions, their faces buried between each other's legs.

Linc watched them, feeling the pressure of Mitch's hand on his cock increase. The heat of Mitch's breath feathered across Linc's skin as his lips trailed up the column of his neck. Linc turned his head, meeting Mitch halfway, pushing his tongue inside Mitch's mouth, feeling desperate for a taste of him.

Suddenly, the act of touching Mitch through his jeans seemed far from adequate. Mitch seemed to share his sentiment, and they moved simultaneously, wasting no time unzipping and removing each other's clothes. He glanced briefly at his cousin and saw that Pedro had already shed his clothes. He sat on the bench with his dick sliding rapidly between his fingers, watching Tomi and Tracee as he pleasured himself.

Linc reached out and wrapped one hand around Mitch's cock and the other around his own, stroking them both, feeling the heavy weight of Mitch's dick in his hands, the heat of it intense. Their juices dripped down their shafts, adding to the unbelievable friction. He quickened his strokes, pumping hard until he felt Mitch tighten against him, and then liquid fire ran between his fingers.

"Fuck," Mitch whispered. It was just one word, but it was all he needed. As a chorus of women's voices rang out with cries and moans of pleasure, Linc felt the shudder start in the pit of his stomach and work its way out to his extremities until he finally trembled, jerking hard against his hand, calling Mitch's name as he came with a gasp.

Mitch's lips found his, his tongue darting out to map the crease of Linc's mouth, his teeth making tiny nips at Linc's upper lip. As they kissed, Linc's heart raced. His cock was still hard as stone and aching between his fingers, demanding more. In that moment, he looked up and saw Tomi crawling toward him. The look on her face told him she knew exactly what he needed.

* * *

Tomi's body still vibrated from the aftereffects of the two orgasms she'd already had. Yet as much as she enjoyed her experience with Tracee, it wasn't enough. She needed more, she needed...them. Her body craved her fiancé, who loved her more deeply than she ever imagined being loved, and their new lover, who pleasured her more completely than she'd ever experienced. During the last few days, the two of them had given her more joy, more happiness, than she thought possible.

She reached Linc first. Her mouth traveled up the calves of his legs and over his inner thighs, her tongue licked a line to his balls and up his shaft. Her lips closed over the crown and moved downward, taking him all the way to the back of her throat, holding him there, swallowing several times around his thickness before releasing him and repeating the entire movement over again.

"*Oh, Dios, sí. Se siente bien.*" Linc's head fell back, his throat worked as he whispered words of praise.

As she sucked Linc, Tomi wrapped a hand around Mitch's dick, working his shaft just how he liked it, taking him from half-erect to fully hard in seconds. She switched then, giving Mitch the same treatment that she'd given Linc, moaning at the familiar and welcome taste of him that mixed with the new but equally pleasing flavor of Linc.

Her body began to tremble; the need to have them fill more than just her mouth was great. Mitch seemed to sense her urgency, always so attuned to what she needed, when she needed it. He eased from between her lips and positioned himself behind her, pushing in deep as Tomi's mouth closed over Linc's cock again. The sounds of Tracee and Pedro's lovemaking provided the background music as they fucked her deep, turning the blaze inside her to an all-out inferno that raced through her, setting her body, her soul on fire.

As her latest orgasm flowed through her, she felt Mitch behind her, pumping hard, his fingers clenching convulsively on her hips. "Tomi...love you." His voice shook, his body shuddered, and he exploded, filling her with his heat.

Linc's fingers wrapped in her hair, holding her head steady, pumping in and out of her mouth, his frantic movements signaling how close he was to release.

"Dios, Tomi, gonna come." He tried to warn her, tried to pull her head away, but she wouldn't let him, quickening her pace instead, her mouth demanding he give her everything he had.

Linc didn't disappoint as a yell burst from his lips, and he filled her mouth with his cum. The taste of it was just like him, strong and spicy with sweet undertones. He leaned against the seat, panting. His dick slid from her mouth, and Tomi sat back on her legs. Mitch wrapped his arms around her. He lifted her face toward his, covered her lips with his, and kissed her hard, as if he were searching out Linc's flavor.

Their lips slowly parted, and Tomi felt herself rising as Linc lifted her from the deck and onto the bench next to him. Mitch sat on her other side, allowing her to snuggle between the two of them. She looked across the boat at Pedro and Tracee, who sat in a similar fashion, watching them with smiles on their faces.

"Watching the three of you together is the sexiest thing I've ever seen in my life," Tracee said.

"Thank you." Tomi's gaze settled on Tracee. "By the way, if you ask me, I'd say forget about going back to college." She smiled at the other woman. "Massage therapy is definitely your calling."

Chapter Ten

Linc pulled open the tinted glass doors and entered the lobby of his limousine company. Pedro stood at the reception desk talking with Lorna. They were speaking too softly for him to make out their words, but from the looks on their faces, it wasn't their usual, sexually charged exchange.

Their conversation abruptly stopped when they saw him, the expression on Lorna's face becoming guilty as she mumbled a greeting and quickly went in the direction of the restroom.

He looked at Pedro. "What's up?"

"You tell me." Pedro's brow arched, his gaze scrutinizing. "You're the one who's been MIA for the past week. I haven't seen or heard from you since we were out on my boat last Thursday. And Lorna tells me that you've been virtually nonexistent around here as well."

Goddammit. He should have known Lorna wouldn't be able to keep her big-ass mouth shut. No wonder she'd hightailed it out of here like her panties were on fire. If he didn't need her so badly, he'd pack up her desk and have her box waiting for her when she came out of her hiding place in the restroom.

To Pedro, he said, "Lorna needs to mind her own fucking business and focus on her job."

"It would seem she's been focusing on her job and yours as well lately."

"Tell me, *primo*." Linc stared at his cousin, feeling uncharacteristically irritated with him. "Did you come here for a reason, or are you conspiring with Lorna to fuck up my morning?"

That drew laughter from Pedro. "Come on, cousin, you know me better than that. Besides"—he smiled broadly—"if I wanted to ruin your day, I could think of a lot more creative ways to do it." He sobered some. "Seriously, we were just worried about you."

"Well, don't be," Linc snapped. Fuck. He'd been in such a good mood when he came to work this morning, still riding a high from the last several days he'd spent with Tomi and Mitch.

Linc glared at Pedro. "I'm fine. I've just been busy lately." He snatched his messages off Lorna's desk and headed for his private office with Pedro on his heels. He reached his office and had a seat behind his desk, completely ignoring Pedro's presence in the doorway.

"Would those things have anything to do with your two new friends?"

Linc sat back in his chair and stared at Pedro. "What's your point?" He ignored Pedro's question. Why bother responding to something they both knew the answer to?

"Listen, Linc." Pedro walked farther into his office and closed the door behind him before taking a seat in one of the chairs. "I like Tomi and Mitch a lot. They're both good people, and I can see why you're so attracted to them. But it doesn't change the fact that in just a little over a week, they're getting married, and they'll be gone shortly after that." A pained look flashed in his eyes. "Don't forget that I'm the one who found you after everything happened in New York. I don't ever want to see you hurt like that again."

Linc remembered those days in New York City more clearly than he'd like. He didn't admit it often, but he truly believed that Pedro had saved his sanity—if not his life—all those years ago when he'd rescued him from his own private hell. He looked at his cousin; the sincerity and concern were palpable on Pedro's face and in his voice. In an instant, Linc's irritation faded away.

"Look, it's nice to know you care, but you don't need to be worried." Linc tried to keep his voice light, his expression neutral, so that Pedro wouldn't see the truth he wasn't willing to admit to anyone behind his words. "It's like you said, Mitch and Tomi are good people, and I enjoy being with them, but I know this isn't going to last forever. And when they're gone, I'll move on to someone else like I always do. Really," he insisted, when Pedro still didn't look convinced. "It's no big deal, okay?"

Pedro studied him for another moment before he sighed and nodded. "Okay."

Linc smiled, trying to change the subject. "Now, are you ready to tell me the real reason why you're here in my office bothering me so early?"

"That's right." Pedro's mood lightened. "I wanted to make sure you were coming next Tuesday."

When Linc looked at him blankly, he said, "Don't tell me you forgot." Linc still didn't respond, and Pedro's expression turned incredulous. "You know, *La Noche de San Juan*, one of our family's favorite holidays that we celebrate *every year* with a big party and lots of food down at the beach."

"Of course I remembered." It was a blatant lie, and they both knew it, but Pedro seemed willing to overlook it.

"Good," Pedro said. "You can even bring Tomi and Mitch if you'd like."

"Thanks, man. I will."

Pedro stood, stretched. "Well, I gotta run. I'll see you next week." He walked toward the door. "Hey." He looked back at Linc. "Do me a favor and go easy on Lorna. I know she's a pain in the ass and she talks a lot of shit, but she really cares about you—and not just because she wants to fuck you, either." Pedro chuckled and walked out the door without waiting for Linc's response.

* * *

Linc stared at his computer, seeing nothing, his brain refusing to focus on anything other than the two people who had occupied his every waking thought since he met them nearly two weeks ago.

Pedro's observation about him was right. In the privacy of his office, Linc would admit that he had it bad for them. He felt himself sinking deeper and deeper into Mitch and Tomi, and he made no effort to do anything about it. Since he'd met them, Linc had spent nearly every day with them, every night wrapped in their arms. It had gotten to the point where he could barely sleep without them next to him.

The sound of female voices suddenly caught his attention. One he easily recognized as Lorna. It was the other voice, however, that made him nearly leap out of his seat and all but sprint down the hallway toward the lobby.

As he got closer, Linc could hear Lorna in full guard-dog mode, ready to attack anyone who tried to gain access to him without her consent. Typically, that included every woman who ever asked for him, unless she was seeking the company's services.

"*Tomi?*" She practically spat out the word. "What kind of name is Tomi for a woman?"

"Well, I—" He heard Tomi try to speak, but Lorna cut her off midsentence.

"There's no *Tomi* on Mr. Castillo's calendar." Linc reached the lobby in time to see Lorna standing less than a foot away from Tomi, her arms crossed in front of her body, her tone confrontational, the look on her face filled with disdain. "You know, Mr. Castillo is a very important man. He's too busy to waste his time talking to just anybody."

"Relax, Lorna." Linc felt a smile tugging at his lips in spite of Lorna's less-than-polite behavior. "She comes in peace."

Tomi turned at the sound of his voice, smiling brightly at him, relief evident on her face. "Hi." She spoke softly.

"Hi, yourself." He was grinning like an idiot, but Linc didn't care. Tomi had that effect on him. The mere act of being in her presence was more arousing than it had any right to be. It amazed him the way his body responded to her, as if he hadn't seen her in days instead of hours. At that very moment, he felt himself hardening at the memory of waking up this morning with those lips wrapped around his cock.

Out of the corner of his eye, Linc saw Lorna looking back and forth between them, her expression far from pleased. Linc ignored her.

"Come on." He grasped Tomi's arm and led her back down the hall toward his office. "We can talk in my office."

Linc barely closed his office door before he pulled Tomi into his arms. "Now I can greet you properly." He kissed her the way he'd been dying to since he saw her standing in the lobby. She moaned and molded herself to him, her body fitting perfectly against his. He backed up until he was resting on the edge of his desk with Tomi standing between his legs, her forehead resting against his.

"So, that was Lorna?" At Linc's nod, she said, "Wow, she's a lot nicer—and a hell of a lot less scary—over the phone."

Linc laughed and kissed the tip of her nose. "Don't worry about Lorna. She's a little protective of me, like a mama bear, but otherwise, she's harmless."

Tomi snorted, and her tone remained doubtful. "Be careful; some mama bears are known to eat their young."

Linc erupted in laughter. "So," he finally managed to say, "where's Mitch?"

"He went on one of those all-day tours."

"You didn't want to go with him?"

Tomi looked guilty. "I told him I wasn't feeling well."

Linc frowned; his hand immediately went to her face, brushing her hair away, and cupped her cheek. "Are you okay?"

"Oh, yeah." She smiled. "I'm fine." At Linc's confused look, she said, "I just told him that so I could have some time alone to look for a wedding gift for him. That's why I'm here." She looked slightly desperate. "I don't know where to go, and I don't have a lot of time left before the wedding to get a gift. I was hoping that you could tell me some nice places around here to find one."

"I can do better than that." He stood and picked up his keys off his desk. "I can show you myself." She tried to object, but he cut her off with a kiss. "I want to. Okay?" When she nodded, he smiled, grabbed her hand, and led her out the door. "Let's go before all the good stuff is gone."

* * *

Three hours and five stores later, they returned to Tomi's hotel. After rejecting every type of gift imaginable, they finally came across a local artist who drew an incredible picture of Tomi and Mitch based on a photo she carried around in her wallet. They had the picture mounted and framed before they left.

Linc was the first to admit that he was hot, hungry, and—most of all—horny. In the short time he'd known Mitch and Tomi, he'd grown accustomed to touching, kissing, and fucking them as he pleased—and it pleased him often. The last few hours had been complete torture, as he hadn't been able to do any of those things. Now his body screamed for release.

Tomi turned around slowly in the middle of the room, her expression thoughtful.

"What's wrong?" Linc gave in to the urge to touch her as his hands slid around her waist. He loved the way she automatically relaxed against him, as if her body knew it belonged next to his.

"I'm trying to figure out where to hide this until next week."

He looked around as well. His gaze landed on a floor safe that was the size of a small fridge. "What about that safe there?"

She shook her head. "No, that's where we put all our important things now. Mitch goes into it all the time."

Linc thought for a moment before an idea suddenly occurred to him. He released Tomi and moved over to the bed. Getting down on his knees, Linc lifted the spread.

"What are you doing?" Tomi asked.

"I'm looking for a safe. Many of the beds in the hotels here have built-in safes at the bottom that most people don't even know about." He moved his hand across the wood paneling until he felt a cool metal surface. "Found it."

"No, we—" Linc opened the safe before Tomi had a chance to finish speaking and stopped short.

Well...damn. Obviously, they knew all about this safe as well. Linc could only stare at the collection of toys inside the safe. One piece in particular held his attention.

"I was trying to tell you that we were using that safe too." He glanced at Tomi, who now crouched next to him.

"So...uh, you and Mitch...you use all of these, right?" His gaze remained fixated on the strap-on penis.

"Yep, and some"—her fingers brushed over the strap-on—"we use more than others." Obviously, she knew which toy fascinated him the most. "We don't have a third partner in our relationship anymore, but Mitch still enjoys being fucked. And I enjoy fucking him." She chuckled softly. "Now that we met you, I haven't had to use this once since we got here." She spoke right next to his ear. "Have you ever been fucked like this before?" Linc shook his head mutely. Her words went straight to his groin, turning his cock to stone. "Would you let me fuck you?"

Linc considered himself as adventurous as the next man—even more so when it came to sex. For some reason, this seemed wholly different.

"I know it doesn't compare to the real thing, but I promise, you'll like it." Apparently, Tomi sensed his hesitation. "Please," she whispered, "I just want to make you feel good, the same way you make me feel."

Who in the fuck was he kidding? Just the mere thought of Tomi strapping on that cock and fucking him with it had his dick trying to claw its way out of his pants

Linc didn't bother with a verbal response, allowing his actions to speak for him instead. He pulled Tomi close, moaning when she melted against him. He grabbed the strap-on out of the safe before he stood, bringing her with him as they collapsed onto the bed. Their clothes came off easily, and Linc sat back, watching as Tomi quickly fastened the strap-on to her body.

She sat back on her knees between his legs, the rubber phallus a slightly darker shade of brown than her skin. Tomi bent forward and kissed him before leaning over the edge of the bed and coming back with a small tube of lubricant in her hand. After squeezing some into her hand, Tomi inserted two lube-coated fingers inside him while her other hand wrapped around his cock, stroking him inside and out. Her fingers finally slid out, and she carefully pushed the dick inside him.

"*Fuck.*" Linc groaned as the cock slid all the way in and brushed against his prostate.

Tomi paused. "Is it okay?"

"Oh, yeah." He smiled. "It's definitely okay."

Tomi kissed the side of one bent knee, gripping him around his thighs, and pulled out halfway before pushing back in again. Her pace was slow and easy, her strokes steady and deep. She'd obviously had sex this way many times before, her experience with using a strap-on evident by the way she fucked Linc with it like a pro, angling her thrusts so that she nailed his prostate every time.

"*Cogida, bebé… Sí.*"

Linc reached behind him, gripped the headboard, and used it as leverage to meet her thrusts as his body spiraled toward release. "Oh, I'm ready, baby…gonna come."

One of Tomi's hands wrapped around his dick, working the shaft as she fucked him, increasing the pressure of her thrusts until he exploded and semen sprayed across his abdomen.

"Jesus…fuck!" he yelled out, his body shaking with spasms. He reached for Tomi as soon as she eased out of him, pulling her on top of him, kissing her hard, and grinding his body against hers. His dick was still as stiff as a board; his orgasm did nothing to decrease his erection.

Linc released Tomi just long enough to wrestle the strap-on from her body before he rolled over, placing her beneath him and pushing inside her wet heat, fucking her hard and deep.

"Linc...oh, baby, make me come."

"Uh-huh. Let it go...let me feel it." His pace increased, his strokes became frenzied. Adrenaline raced through him as he pumped furiously inside her. Tomi's pussy rippled around him, her screams rang in his ear as she came. He was right behind her, shooting hard enough to make his back arch as he came inside her.

Linc rested his head against her shoulder as they both struggled to catch their breath. Finally, he found enough strength to lift his head.

"That was...damn." He panted.

"I know." Satisfied cognac eyes stared back at him. "I told you that you'd like it."

"I think *like* might be a bit of an understatement." Linc chuckled. "What I felt was a hell of a lot better than that."

"Good." Her hands moved down his back and rested on his ass, where she gripped his cheeks and thrust herself against him, while clenching her vaginal walls around his softening erection. "Now you have an idea of how I feel when I'm with you."

Linc moaned as pleasure rippled though his cock. God, he couldn't seem to get enough of this woman. She and Mitch had become an addiction he couldn't resist.

His lips teased the line of her jaw, working his way toward her ear. "I think," he admitted, "I might be in trouble where you and Mitch are concerned." For the first time, Linc verbalized the feelings he'd developed for them.

Tomi remained silent for so long that he began to doubt the wisdom of his impromptu confession. Finally, she turned her head and looked into his eyes. "I think," she whispered soft and low against his lips, "that goes for us as well."

Neither of them spoke again, choosing silence over words, holding each other until Tomi's deep breathing signaled she'd fallen asleep. Sighing, he kissed her on the temple, carefully extracted himself from her embrace, and eased from the bed.

Linc took a quick shower, wanting to be clean before getting dressed again. When he came out of the bathroom, he found Tomi awake and watching him.

"I have to go." Regret laced his words. "I have to meet with some clients soon."

Tomi stretched out in the bed, watching him as he redressed. "I understand." Her beautiful brown face held a look of contentment. "We're still going to see you tonight, right?"

Linc leaned down, kissing her. "You couldn't keep me away." He straightened and finished dressing. As he prepared to leave, his eyes landed on the painting, still leaning against the dresser where they'd left it.

"We never found a place to hide your gift." Tomi looked in the direction of the painting. From the expression on her face, it was apparent that she'd forgotten all about it. Linc could relate. For the past hour, it hadn't been high on his priority list, either.

"If you'd like, I can take it home with me." Linc offered. "I'm sure I can find someplace to hide it there."

"Would you mind?" Relief filled Tomi's face. "I don't want to inconvenience you, but it would work out perfectly if you did that."

"You could never be an inconvenience to me." Linc grabbed one more kiss before walking over to the painting, picking it up, and heading to the door. He paused in the doorway and turned around.

"Damn, it's going to be a long afternoon waiting to see you and Mitch again." He closed the door without waiting for her response, afraid she'd say something that would make him turn back, strip off his clothes, and fuck her until Mitch returned from his tour. He'd never been in so deep so fast. Hell, if he were truthful with himself, he'd admit that he'd never been in so deep, period. And that's what scared him the most.

Chapter Eleven

The beach resembled one gigantic block party, with people covering nearly every visible part of the sand, most of them arriving early that morning to secure their spots for the all-day celebration. To an outside observer, it probably seemed like complete chaos, but for Linc, it represented home and heritage.

He looked around at the groups of families celebrating together, loving every minute of it, from the loud and sometimes raucous crowds to the overlapping sounds of ear-splitting music blaring from every direction and the intermingling smells of food filling the night air.

Their group was huge, at least sixty people, spread out on blankets and in chairs on the sand. It was like this every year. His family loved this holiday, loved that it gave them a reason to get together and catch up with family members they hadn't seen in a while.

Everyone he knew was there, including Pedro and Tracee, and Alejandro and his wife, Marissa. Even his wayward cousin and less than model employee, Miguel, was there, still acting skittish around him, as if he expected Linc to fire him at any moment. Linc took pity on him, stopping to speak to him and introduce him to Tomi and Mitch.

"This is my cousin Miguel," he told them. "He was your original driver when you arrived in Puerto Rico." They talked for a moment before Miguel moved on to join his friends.

"Truthfully," Tomi whispered to him as Miguel walked away, "I'm glad Miguel never showed up that day."

Linc smiled, fighting the urge to kiss her as he continued to take them around, introducing them to the rest of his family, wanting to make sure Mitch and Tomi knew they were welcomed there. They blended in as easily and comfortably as if they were born there instead of just visiting. In a matter of hours, they'd become a huge hit. His entire family took an immediate liking to them and included them as official members of the family.

"So, *mi muchacha hermosa*, what have you and your *hombre hermoso* seen on our island so far?" Linc's aunt, the family matriarch, asked Tomi.

She was the oldest living member of his family, but it was hard to tell by simply looking at her. Still healthy and active, her tanned skin minimally marred by wrinkles, her silver hair more of an asset than a hindrance, his aunt's physical appearance easily belied her eighty-seven years.

"I think a better question to ask them, *Tía*, is what they *haven't* seen yet," Linc joked to his aunt. "I'm sure it's a much shorter list."

Mitch laughed. "Linc is probably right about that."

"Well, let's see." Tomi paused. "So far, we've seen the *Jardín Botánico* at the University of Puerto Rico, the *Catedral de San Juan Bautista*, *El Morro*, the *Coamo* thermal springs, and the Bacardi rum tour"—she chuckled, holding up two fingers—"twice."

"Don't forget about *El Yunque* rain forest." Mitch's hands rested on Tomi's shoulders, his eyes meeting Linc's over her head. The heat in those blue eyes was evident even in the dark.

"And soon you get married." Linc's aunt smiled happily.

"Yes, in four days, on Saturday." Tomi's hands covered Linc's on her shoulders. Mitch leaned down and kissed her cheek. "And all of you are invited," Mitch added, his invitation drawing cheers and whistles from the group.

"Has the rest of your family arrived yet?" Marissa asked. Linc saw Tomi and Mitch exchange a look, their expressions a conflicting and uncomfortable mixture of emotions. He opened his mouth to intervene when Mitch spoke.

"No, it's just us," Mitch spoke quietly. "Our families won't be joining us."

There was a moment of surprised silence, and Linc watched the disapproving looks flicker across the faces of his family members, especially his aunt.

Finally, she reached out and grasped their hands, her smile bright. "In that case, we'll be your family," she declared, as others in their group nodded their heads in agreement. "And after your wedding, we'll have a big reception to celebrate. Come"—she stood, taking Tomi with her—"we should move to the water, so we can be ready at midnight."

"What happens at midnight?" Tomi asked.

"We get in the water," Marissa explained, standing as well. "It's an old tradition to walk into the water exactly at midnight on La Noche de San Juan. It's supposed to bring good luck."

Tomi and Marissa stripped down to their swimsuits along with several others in the group before they all headed toward the water. He and Mitch opted to stay behind and keep an eye on everyone's belongings.

"You have a great family," Mitch told him.

"Yes, I do." Linc watched Tomi and Marissa splashing around in the water with other members of his family. "I'm very lucky." He paused for a moment before glancing at Mitch. "Can I ask you something?"

Mitch looked at him. "Anything."

"What's the deal with your family? I mean, I've never been married before, but if I did, I know they would be there." Linc chuckled. "You saw how excited they were about your wedding." He sobered. "I just can't understand why your parents wouldn't want to share this special moment with you."

"My parents don't agree with my lifestyle." Bitterness tinged Mitch's voice.

Linc nodded. "I take it they have a problem with you being bisexual."

"Actually, they don't." Mitch released a humorless laugh. "They couldn't care less how many men and women I fuck, as long as Tomi isn't one of them." Mitch grew quiet, his gaze focused on the water. Linc remained silent, waiting for him to continue.

"Did you know that Tomi has two doctorate degrees?" Mitch suddenly asked. When Linc shook his head, he continued. "She doesn't like to talk about it, but the truth of the matter is that she's an extremely intelligent woman, smarter than my parents and I combined. She's more generous and loving than any person I've ever known, including my parents, but as far as they're concerned, she'll never be good enough for me because of the color of her skin."

Linc thought about the myriad of people he'd dated over the years of all races, colors, and genders. Considering the varied hues of the people in his own family, he knew that something as trivial and unimportant as skin color would never be an issue for any of his relatives.

To Mitch, he said, "Do Tomi's parents have the same issue?"

"No, their issue is strictly Tomi's lifestyle," Mitch told him. "Tomi comes from a deeply religious family. On top of that, her father is a career military man. For him, 'don't ask, don't tell' isn't just a military rule; it's a way of life. Tomi has openly dated men and women since she was a teenager, but her parents chose to pretend it wasn't happening. Their moral and military values just won't let them accept the idea that their baby isn't in the traditional heterosexual relationship with a man who only fucks her in the missionary position once a month."

Mitch shook his head. "I remember the one and only time they came to visit us in New York, when Alec still lived with us. It was easy to act as if they didn't know what type of relationship the three of us had together, but once they saw the bedroom with the one bed that we all slept in, they couldn't pretend that they didn't know anymore. They gave Tomi an ultimatum. They told her that she could either leave with them at that moment or stay with us and continue to"—Mitch made quotation marks with his hands—"live in sin." His eyes drifted back to the beachfront. "Luckily for me, she chose to stay."

Their conversation halted as Pedro approached. "Your lady is asking for you." He spoke to Mitch. "I think some of my male cousins may be taking more of a liking to her than she can handle."

"That's not surprising." Mitch laughed as he stood. "Tomi has that effect on people." Mitch made his way through the crowds of people toward Tomi. Linc's eyes remained glued to him every step of the way.

"Oh, *mi Dios*," Pedro murmured. "You got it bad, don't you?"

"Look," Linc began, knowing exactly what his cousin meant, "I already told you—"

"Yeah, I know." Pedro cut him off. "You just enjoy being with them." He sighed. "Take some advice from your primo and try not to get in too deep, okay?" He patted Linc on the shoulder and headed back toward the water.

Linc watched Pedro go, thinking his cousin's words of advice had come much too late.

Chapter Twelve

Linc smiled when Mitch answered the phone. His morning voice was deep and rough, the sound so sexy, it made Linc's dick hard.

"My clients had to reschedule their appointment, so I'm free for the morning," Linc told him, trying to focus on driving and not the image of Mitch spread out in his bed, which was where he'd left him and Tomi earlier that morning. "I thought I'd take you and Tomi out to celebrate your big day tomorrow."

"That sounds good, but you already missed Tomi. Tracee picked her up, and they went back to the hotel for an appointment at the Spa. Tracee hooked her up with a bunch of complimentary services, so she'll be there most of the day. I'm still available, if you're interested."

"Trust me, when it comes to you and Tomi, I'm always interested." Linc swore he heard Mitch groan.

"Let me get in a quick workout and after that, I'm all yours." His voice was more a growl than actual speech; the sound vibrated through Linc and made his cock throb.

His mouth went dry. "Uh, yeah…" He pictured Mitch, his body sweaty, his muscles straining as he worked out in Linc's exercise room, and suddenly any thought he had of leaving the house again to celebrate went right out the window. "That's fine. I think I could use a good workout myself."

"In that case, I'll wait for you." Mitch's voice dropped to a whisper. "I'll work you out as well as myself."

Jesus. Linc disconnected the call without responding. His foot slammed on the accelerator as he raced toward home.

* * *

Linc got home in record time, ran up the stairs three at a time, and removed his clothes as he went. He changed into a pair of shorts and a T-shirt before he grabbed the lube from the dresser and shoved it into the pocket of his shorts as he left the room. He went in search of Mitch.

He finally found Mitch in the exercise room, running on the treadmill. Actually, that wasn't quite accurate. Mitch's pace more resembled a sprint than a run. His flushed skin glistened with sweat, his hair looked plastered to his head, and his wet clothes clung to his body.

Mitch turned down the power when he saw Linc, slowing down until the treadmill finally stopped before grabbing a towel and wiping his face.

"Hey." He barely sounded winded, despite the evidence of his strenuous workout. "You made it."

"Uh-huh." There was no way in hell that he would miss the chance to be with this man.

"Good." Mitch moved toward him. "I was waiting for you." Obviously, he wasn't waiting for Linc in order to exercise—at least, not in the traditional sense.

He stopped directly in front of Linc, their bodies nearly touching, their lips barely an inch apart. "You ready for me to work you out?"

"Oh, yeah." Linc leaned forward, closing the slight gap between them. He covered Mitch's mouth with his, pouring as much heat and hunger as he could into the kiss.

Mitch pulled back first, slowly sinking to his knees, taking Linc's shorts and underwear with him. His mouth wrapped around Linc's cock, sucking hard, those lips an intoxicating mixture of soft and firm. Linc rocked into his mouth, feeling Mitch swallow around him before he began to suck harder, faster, his throat closing convulsively around the head.

As Linc pulled his T-shirt up and over his head, he felt a hand on his balls, a thick finger at his perineum, circling his hole before the tip pushed slightly inside. Linc glanced down and saw Mitch's hand pumping his own cock, his muffled groan buzzing around Linc's dick. God, just the thought of Mitch coming from sucking him off was enough to push Linc over the edge, and it took all of his focus not to give into the urge to blow in Mitch's mouth. No, he wanted to save that load for another part of Mitch's anatomy.

He eased Mitch off his cock, helped him to his feet, and gripped him by the back of the head, pressing their lips together and sweeping his tongue deep inside. As they kissed, his hands slid under Mitch's shirt, lifting it up, briefly forcing their mouths apart as he pulled it off and threw it to the side. Linc's lips covered his again, guiding Mitch backward until his legs pressed against the weight bench. He placed a hand in the center of Mitch's chest, encouraging him to lie down on the bench before removing his shorts.

After he finished undressing Mitch, Linc stepped away just long enough to grab his own shorts from the floor and remove the lube from the pocket before he tossed them to the side and returned to the bench where Mitch lay waiting for him. Linc straddled the bench facing him, placing Mitch's legs over his thighs. He took a moment to admire that body, from the sculpted pecs to the rippling planes of Mitch's tight abdomen. Damn, he was a fine specimen of a man.

Leaning down, Linc kissed a path from Mitch's throat, across his chest, and down his stomach, enjoying the way Mitch's skin quivered beneath his lips. When he reached Mitch's hard, thick cock, Linc took it into his mouth, working the shaft, refusing to stop until the tremors in Mitch's body signaled he was on the verge of losing control.

He sat back, pausing just long enough to open the lube and squeeze enough into his hand to prepare Mitch as well as himself. Linc dropped the lube to the floor before he gripped his cock and pushed in, moving closer and closer, until Mitch's ass rested against his thighs, his cock buried deep. Mitch's hands gripped the weight bar above his head, his legs wrapped around Linc, holding him tight. He started to move, slowly pulling out halfway before pushing in hard, his hips slapping against Mitch's ass. He increased his thrusts, his cock bumping against Mitch's prostate every time. Mitch's body rippled around his cock, squeezing and clenching.

When he looked down, the look in Mitch's gaze ate him alive. It said, *I belong to you, and I'm giving you everything I have and then some.*

"Come on," Linc spoke through clenched teeth, sweat pouring down his face. "Give it up for me."

Mitch nodded and shot, his body going tight around him. Linc held back long enough to watch Mitch's face, watch his features transform from need to pleasure to satisfaction, before he groaned, everything in him shaking, building in his thighs, spreading throughout his frame, overwhelming him. Then he was lost, pushing in one last time before he blew, drowning and yelling out Mitch's name like a fool.

For several seconds, neither of them moved, both caught in the moment, in each other. Slowly, he lowered himself, his gaze still holding Mitch's, unable to look away.

"Damn," Mitch whispered. "That was..." His words trailed off, his expression filled with awe.

"I know." It wasn't much of a response, but it was all Linc had. He eased out of Mitch and stood, pulling Mitch along with him.

"Man." Mitch stretched. "I'm going to feel you all day."

"Good." Linc growled against his lips, kissing him hard. "I want you and Tomi thinking about me all day, every day."

The look in Mitch's eyes made him pause. "We already do."

Linc nodded. It was the same way for him.

Christ, he was so fucking screwed.

* * *

Mitch closed the hotel room door, his gaze immediately searching for Tomi. He followed the sound of her voice to the patio, where she stood with her back to him, talking on the phone.

He leaned against the patio doorway, watching her for several minutes until she finally became aware of his presence. Smiling, she reached for him, pulling him against her when he grabbed her hand.

"Okay, we'll see you tomorrow." She disconnected the call and turned in his arms. "Hi." She leaned forward and kissed him. "That was Linc. He said he'd see us in the morning. Rosa has a special breakfast planned for us tomorrow."

He nodded as he placed kisses on Tomi's forehead, her nose, and her lips. "Did I tell you I love you today?"

Her smile grew even wider. "Yes, but you can feel free to tell me again as many times as you'd like."

"I love you more than you can ever imagine, more than I could ever express."

She reached up, and her warm, soft hand stroked his face. "I love you too. Tomorrow can't arrive soon enough for me."

"I know you do." Mitch cupped her face. "I know that your love for me is equally as strong and true as mine is for you. It's deeper than anything I've ever felt before, and I know that it will never change, never fade." He looked into her beautiful eyes and smiled. "The love we have for each other can handle anything, Tomi"—he took a deep breath— "including being in love with someone else."

Several emotions flashed across Tomi's face all at once. She closed her eyes for a moment and when she opened them again, they reflected the resignation she felt. "I didn't mean for it to happen." Her voice trembled, her eyes turned watery. "I—"

"Shh." Mitch stopped her, using a finger to wipe away a stray tear rolling down her cheek. "It's okay. Neither of us meant to fall for him, but it doesn't change the fact that we did." He pulled her close, and Tomi clung to him as if she never wanted to let him go.

"What are we going to do?" she whispered.

Mitch didn't respond immediately. Finally, he chuckled sadly. "Unfortunately, I'm fresh out of answers." His face grew serious again. "We'll talk to Linc, but not until after our wedding." He brushed her hair away from her face. "Marrying you is my one and only priority right now. It's more important to me than anything and anyone." Mitch leaned down and kissed her. "Everything else will work itself out." He tried to assure her, while silently praying that he was correct.

Chapter Thirteen

Linc stood at the edge of his aunt's large yard, watching the reception party in full swing. The wedding had been beautiful, but he hadn't expected anything less. It took place a couple of hours earlier in a secluded section outdoors on the grounds of Tomi and Mitch's hotel.

Tomi was stunning in a long, white, strapless dress made out of silk. The style was simple, but Tomi made it look incredible. Fresh orchids adorned her normally free-flowing tresses, which she'd pinned up for the occasion. Mitch was similarly clad in a long-sleeved shirt and loose-fitting slacks. The white silk material emphasized his newly tanned skin.

As promised, Linc's relatives showed up in full attendance, taking up every available seat. Mitch and Tomi made several last minute changes, electing Tracee as the maid of honor and Linc as the best man. Pedro had the honor of escorting Tomi down the aisle.

They looked picture perfect as they stood in the gazebo facing the setting sun and overlooking the Atlantic Ocean. The ceremony didn't last long—maybe twenty minutes at most. By the time it ended, all of the women—and a substantial portion of the men—were teary-eyed, including Linc.

When they exchanged vows, Linc remembered silently saying them as well, wishing with everything in him that he could put a voice to the love that he felt for them, just as they'd done with each other. As they kissed, Linc felt it clearly, as if he were kissing them as well. He smiled and clapped with everyone else when the officiator announced that Mitch and Tomi were husband and wife. Inside, he was dying, aching to be a permanent part of the bond they shared, but knowing it wasn't possible. The handshake he'd given Mitch and the chaste kiss he placed on Tomi's cheek didn't scratch the surface of the emotions that he felt for them.

As everyone followed Tomi and Mitch back into the hotel, he caught Pedro staring at him knowingly, his cousin's expression a mixture of disappointment and sympathy. Linc ignored him and headed to the waiting vehicles parked in front of the hotel.

He'd arranged for Tomi and Mitch to have a separate limo take them to his aunt's house. They'd asked him if he wanted to ride with them, but he'd declined, hiding his true feelings by joking that they should take advantage of their private time before they reached the reception and wouldn't have a moment alone for the next several hours.

The truth of the matter was that Linc couldn't handle being alone with them, too afraid that he'd ask them for things that he had no right to request.

He felt a hand on his shoulder just moments before he heard Pedro's voice. "How are you holding up?" Linc remained silent, certain that the answer to his cousin's question was already apparent. Hell, it was obvious that Pedro was right all along about his feelings. If Linc were being truthful with himself, he'd admit that he hadn't just fallen for Tomi and Mitch, he'd jumped in headfirst and heart wide-open.

"You know you have to end it between you and them, right?" Pedro said softly. "I know it's not what you want to hear, but you know it's true. And the longer you wait to do it, the worse it'll be for everyone when it finally happens."

He continued to watch Mitch and Tomi, looking more at home with his family than he did now. As far as he was concerned, they were exactly where they belonged, and if he had his way, this is where they would always be. Christ, why couldn't life ever be simple?

"I think"—he paused and cleared his voice—"I'm going to head out a little early. I need…" *Mitch and Tomi, but I can't have them the way I want, and it's killing me to know that they'll never be mine.* "…to get up early tomorrow."

It was a lie, and they both knew it, but Linc didn't care. He looked longingly at Mitch and Tomi once more, before he turned away and walked toward his car.

"I'm here for you, primo, if you need me." Pedro's voice followed him. He waved over his shoulder without turning around.

On the way to his car, Linc passed his employee, Mario, who he'd assigned as Tomi and Mitch's limousine driver for the day. "Take them wherever they want to go when they leave here." Mario nodded in understanding, and Linc got in his car and drove away.

The ride home was a blur, and before Linc knew it, he was outside his house. He'd told himself that he was going straight to bed, but he couldn't seem to shut down his brain, so he wandered around his house instead, thinking about Tomi and Mitch. It wasn't until his doorbell rang that he looked at the clock and realized that more than an hour had passed since he'd gotten home.

Linc opened the door and found them standing there, looking as gorgeous as ever.

"Hi," Tomi said softly. "You disappeared on us. You tired of our company already?"

He could live two lifetimes and that still wouldn't be possible. Linc forced a smile, looking from her to Mitch. "No, I just figured that you two wanted to be alone tonight."

"We do want to be alone." Mitch held his gaze. "With you."

Linc couldn't refuse them any more than he could refuse his next breath. He waved at Mario, who still waited by the limo at the curb, before he stepped to the side and let them in.

* * *

They undressed Tomi together, carefully removing her wedding dress and laying it to the side. Mitch was next, and they removed his clothes with equal care before placing them with Tomi's dress. When it was his turn, Mitch and Tomi took their time, slowly stripping off his clothes one piece at a time.

Tonight was different for so many reasons. They all seemed to feel it, yet neither of them appeared willing to acknowledge it. Their kisses became more gentle, their touches held more reverence, their bodies joined together with more passion, more emotion than ever before.

Somehow, Linc found himself in the middle with Tomi beneath him, her legs wrapped around his hips, and Mitch behind him with his hands on Linc's ass. Groaning, he sank his cock deep inside Tomi, and then he pressed back, aching to feel Mitch's dick inside him. As he slid smoothly in and out of Tomi's heat, she moaned for him, the sound filled with promises of things that there weren't even words for.

His slow, easy rhythm faltered when two of Mitch's lube-coated fingers pushed inside him, and then he started up again, riding the sensations in his cock and his ass. In one easy movement, Mitch's cock replaced his fingers, and he pushed in, spreading Linc wide, the sensation aching, burning, making him gasp and push deeper into Tomi.

He bit his lip, forcing back the words that threatened to overwhelm him, knowing that if he let it go, he'd say something he'd regret, something about how he desperately wanted and needed them, how far he'd fallen in love with them already. No, Linc couldn't do that. His body said too much already. He couldn't help it. Tomi knew just where to kiss; Mitch knew exactly where to touch him to send him flying.

Mitch's hand slid between them and found Tomi's clit, rubbing and teasing until she was screaming. Her walls tightened around Linc, causing his own muscles to clench around Mitch's cock as his bellow of pleasure filled the room.

Mitch's roar matched his, and Linc felt the heat from Mitch's pleasure shoot deep inside him. Linc jerked a few more times, rocking back and forth between them, trying to make it last as long as possible, knowing he'd probably never share this with them again. Finally, he went still, panting heavily, holding himself up so he didn't collapse on top of Tomi.

They settled in next to him, falling asleep long before he did. Linc lay there for hours with his cousin's words repeating in his head.

It killed him to admit it, but Pedro was right. However, that was little comfort when he had no idea what he was going to do without Mitch and Tomi in his life once he'd said good-bye to them forever.

Chapter Fourteen

Linc stood in his home office, staring out of his window, looking at nothing. His mind was spinning, his heart heavy with the decisions he'd made. He'd been up most of the night arguing with himself, trying to figure out the best way to end things with them. No matter how he tried to spin it, no matter how he wanted to position it, the outcome was always the same: heartache. Finally, just before dawn arrived, Linc settled on the quickest option of all; the one guaranteed to push Mitch and Tomi away without them making any effort to change his mind.

He stiffened, sensing more than hearing a presence behind him. When Mitch's strong arms wrapped around him, Linc mentally braced himself for what would come next.

"Hey." Mitch's warm breath caressed Linc's neck, his hand cupped Linc's cock. "Are you still joining Tomi and me for brunch?" His whispered words were right next to Linc's ear. "We, uh…there's something we need to tell you."

Tell him now, before he admits too much and you lose the courage to do what you know has to happen. "It's over." His voice sounded foreign to his ears.

"We still have time." Mitch massaged his balls, the sensation so intense it made Linc's eyes roll back. "Brunch doesn't—"

"Not brunch." Linc pushed his hand away and pulled out of Mitch's embrace, turning to face him. "Us."

Mitch went completely still, his eyes slightly narrowed. "I don't understand."

"Don't you?" Linc chuckled, his brow arched.

"No, I don't think I do." Mitch continued to stare at him unblinkingly, those blue eyes growing stormier with each passing second. "Why don't you explain it to me?"

"Come on, you can't be that naive." Linc's tone turned mocking. "Listen, the past few weeks have been a lot of fun, but it's over now. It's time to move on."

Mitch's throat worked. "I thought—"

"You thought what?" Linc interrupted him. "That this was a relationship?" He laughed contemptuously. "We were fucking!" Linc practically yelled. "Don't try to romanticize it, Mitch. It was good—hell, it was great—but that's all it ever was. It's all I ever wanted from you and Tomi. And if you thought differently, you obviously don't know me."

There was a sound in the doorway, and they looked in that direction. Tomi stood there with tears in her eyes, the look on her face so devastated, it made him want to weep. She turned and left the room as quietly as she'd appeared.

Mitch turned back to him, his eyes practically black, the muscles working in his jaw, his hands balled into fists. Linc prepared himself to be hit, knew he deserved at least that. Shit, he even welcomed it, hoping that the physical pain would distract him from the emotional agony he suffered.

"You finally said something that I actually agree with." Mitch's voice was unnaturally calm. "We obviously don't know you at all. We had no idea that the caring, decent man we thought we met three weeks ago was really a bitter, shitty bastard. Well, you don't have to worry. We can take a hint, and we have no interest in staying where we're not wanted."

He walked toward the door, pausing for a moment in the doorway before turning to look at Linc. "You got what you wanted from us, and now you're done. I get it. It's fucked up, it hurts, but it's okay. I'm not angry. In fact, I feel sorry for you. Eventually, Tomi and I will get over this, and in the end, we'll always have each other. You, on the other hand, will still be here, choosing to be miserable and alone for the rest of your pathetic life, just because you're too afraid of being hurt again to man up and admit your feelings."

Linc stood there long after Mitch was gone, frozen in place, unable to move, to think. Shit, he could barely draw a decent breath as he listened to his front door close as Mitch and Tomi walked out of his house and his life for good.

* * *

Three days. That's how long it'd been since he'd seen Tomi and Mitch. Linc spent most of that time sitting in his office, replaying that day when he'd destroyed the two most important people in his life. He stared out his window, wishing he had the power to roll back time, erase everything he'd said to Mitch and Tomi, and replace it with the truth of how much he loved them.

He couldn't even look at himself in the mirror. The way he'd treated them made him physically sick to his stomach.

God, what the fuck had he been smoking that made him think it was okay to hurt them so badly? The looks on their faces would haunt him until the end of time.

Linc rubbed a hand over his face, as if doing that would somehow erase the memory. Jesus, he was even worse than their previous lover, Alec. He knew the pain they'd suffered after that breakup, yet he still deliberately went out of his way to devastate them.

He'd convinced himself that he'd caused this chaos in order to save everyone unnecessary heartache by ending the relationship before they became too attached to each other. He could admit now that was complete bullshit. Mitch's words cut him like a knife, but he was right. Linc had been too afraid to share his feelings with them, too scared to hear how they felt about him. He shook his head. What made sense at that time seemed so ridiculous now.

Well, he was officially done running from his feelings. Linc picked up his cell phone from his desk, determined to reverse some of the damage he'd done.

He dialed the number to their hotel room from memory, listening to it ring, silently praying that they would give him a chance to tell them how he truly felt.

"Hola?"

Linc paused when the accented voice answered the phone. "*Lo siento.*" He apologized, certain he'd dialed incorrectly. "*Llamé el número incorrecto.*" Linc hung up and tried again. When the same voice answered the phone, he knew something was wrong.

He hung up without responding, immediately calling the main hotel number. "I'm trying to reach the Elliotts in suite twelve twenty-three." The operator placed him on hold for several long moments before returning. "I'm sorry, sir. The Elliott party has already checked out."

Linc sat in stunned silence. He was too late. They were already gone.

Chapter Fifteen

Mitch walked into the bedroom where Tomi sat at a small desk in the corner, looking at the computer screen. He came up behind her and wrapped his arms around her.

"Hi, beautiful." His lips grazed along her neck. She stood and stepped into his embrace, leaning up to give him a kiss.

"How was your day?" he asked her.

"Much better, now that you're home." Mitch smiled at that. Tomi always knew what to say to make him feel like he was the most important person in her world.

"I got an e-mail from Tracee today," she said quietly.

Mitch paused. "Oh, yeah?" He kept his voice casual. "How is she doing?" One of the good things that they'd brought home with them from Puerto Rico was a new friendship between Tomi and Tracee. They exchanged e-mails with each other several times a week.

"She's good. She's trying to take a few days off to come and visit before my classes start in a few weeks."

She smiled, but her eyes remained slightly sad. He knew that look. He'd seen it a lot lately. It had been a month since they had last seen Linc, and despite everything he'd said, everything he'd done, she still missed him. Hell, they both did. And that really pissed Mitch off.

Every time he looked into Tomi's face, every time he saw the tears that she tried to hide from him, it made him so fucking furious that he wanted to hop on a plane to Puerto Rico, march back to Linc's house, and bust him right in the face. It wouldn't solve a damn thing. Mitch knew that, but it sure as hell would make him feel better.

It wouldn't be so bad if they both didn't still love the bastard so damn much, and time definitely had not done a thing to lessen the way they felt about him. If anything, it made it worse.

In the short time they'd known Linc, they'd developed feelings for him that were deeper than they even realized. It wasn't until they returned home and tried to get back to normal that they truly understood what an impact Linc had had on them and their life. It made their relationship with Alec seem insignificant in comparison.

Mitch held Tomi a little tighter, remembering how much she suffered when Alec left. At that time, he'd sworn to Tomi, as well as himself, that he would never allow her to go through that again, never watch sadness and sorrow eat away at her and nearly tear them both apart. And he was willing to do whatever it took to keep that promise.

"What are you doing tomorrow?" His tongue traced along her ear.

She moaned. "Nothing. Why?"

"Well, it's Friday, which means I don't have any clients scheduled, and I thought we could spend the entire day in bed, alone, with no distractions, doing horizontal workouts."

He sucked on her earlobe. "How does that sound?" Mitch whispered.

"Mmm." Tomi shivered slightly. "That sounds perfect."

Mitch began to undress her, his hands moving over her familiar curves, exposing smooth brown skin for his touching, tasting, and teasing pleasure.

"Speaking of which," Tomi began, "you might want to recharge your cell phone. I tried to reach you several times today, but your calls kept going straight to voice mail."

Mitch chuckled. Damn, she knew him so well. "I know. My battery died early this morning."

"Here"—she unclipped it from his belt—"I'll plug it in for you so it can charge." Mitch stopped her before she could walk away.

"Don't worry about it." He took the phone from her and placed it on the desk, pulling her into his arms again and unfastening the front closure of her bra to expose her breasts. "In fact, we should turn off all the phones." He bent and sucked a nipple between his lips before he picked her up and carried her toward the bed. "The only voice I want to hear for the next twenty-four hours is yours screaming my name."

* * *

"*Madre de Dios.*" Pedro's voice barely registered with Linc. He was only distantly aware of his cousin speaking softly to someone else before he began moving around the room. Finally, the smell of coffee filled his nose.

"Here." Linc felt the cup press against his mouth. "Drink this." His eyes felt fused together, and he struggled to open them. Pedro's blurry image appeared in front of him, and

Linc absently took the coffee from his hand and swallowed several huge gulps, ignoring the burn of the strong, hot liquid as it flowed down his throat.

Sighing, Pedro sat across from him on the leather couch in his office, silently watching him as he drank, refilling his cup once he finished. Linc had no idea how long he'd been there. The bright sun shining through his windows confirmed that it was morning, and from the look of his rumpled clothes and the empty bottle of rum on his desk, he'd obviously slept there—again.

It'd become the norm for him lately. Drink until he couldn't remember his former lovers, couldn't feel his pain, and then pass out in his chair.

After he'd had his third cup of coffee, Linc felt the fog finally lift. Pedro seemed to notice it as well.

"How are you feeling?" he asked quietly.

Linc snorted, rubbing his eyes as his hangover kicked into full gear. "How do I look?" In spite of all the coffee he'd drunk, his throat was dry, his voice raw.

Pedro nodded. "I see your point." He set the nearly empty coffeepot on a nearby table before standing and walking over to Linc's desk and holding out his hand. Inside were two aspirin, which Linc gratefully accepted, washing them down with the remaining coffee in his cup.

"How did you find out?" Linc asked as Pedro had a seat in the chair in front of his desk. He didn't bother to explain what he meant. He was certain that Pedro would understand.

"Lorna called and said that she hadn't seen you in a few days. I didn't worry about it too much. I figured you probably needed some time because of...well...you know. Then, Rosa called today when she found you in here." He paused. "You ready to talk now?"

Linc didn't respond. There was nothing for him to say that wasn't already glaringly apparent. He hadn't left his house in days, he only ate when he absolutely had to, and he couldn't sleep unless he was unconscious. He didn't need a mirror to know that he looked a mess and probably smelled even worse. It was safe to say he was completely falling apart.

"Well," Pedro began after a long silence, "since you don't want to start, I will." He shook his head and stared up at the ceiling for a moment before he looked at Linc again. "I can't even believe I'm about to say this, but I was wrong about your relationship with Tomi and Mitch."

Pedro spoke the words very softly, and for a moment, Linc wasn't sure he'd heard him correctly.

"You heard what I said." Pedro smiled slightly, responding to Linc as if he'd read his mind before his expression turned serious again. "I knew you loved them, but I had no idea just how much until now. I never would have believed it if I hadn't seen it with my own eyes, but you are in worse shape now than you were when Paul and Ava died."

Linc could not argue that. Everything Pedro said was true, and the pain of it all was killing him slowly from the inside out.

He looked into Pedro's eyes. "I fucked up," he finally said. "Paul and Ava died before I had the chance to tell them how I felt. Not that it would have changed anything between us, because I didn't love them, not like this, anyway." Linc took a deep breath; his throat was tight with emotion.

"This time, it was different. I had the chance to tell Mitch and Tomi how I felt, and I chose to push them away instead..." Linc's words trailed off, and he closed his eyes, the throbbing in his head and his heart becoming too much to bear.

"So, what's stopping you from doing it now?" Pedro asked quietly.

Linc laughed sadly. "Aside from the fact that they live thousands of miles away? Even if they lived right next door, they probably hate me so much, they'd just as easily kill me as look at me—which I really couldn't blame them for, considering how I treated them."

"Well," Pedro began, "I can't tell you what to do, but I will tell you this. I've known you all your life, and I gotta be honest with you and say that I don't recognize the person I see in front of me. The Lincoln I know is a man that I have admired and looked up to my entire life. He isn't just my cousin; he's my best friend, and the strongest person I know. I've seen him at his best and his worst, and I know that it's not in his nature to just give up and stop trying, especially when he wants something—or someone. The Linc that I know is better than this." His hand gestured in Linc's direction. "*You* are better than this."

He stood, pushing in his chair and picking up the empty coffee cup and the coffeepot on his way out the door.

Just before he left the room, Pedro turned and said, "More than anything, Linc, I want you to be happy. If being with Mitch and Tomi makes you that way, then you should do whatever it takes to make that happen. It's the least you deserve."

Linc sat in silence after Pedro left, his mind going a million miles a minute. Finally, he reached for his phone and made a call. A few minutes later, he raced upstairs to his bedroom to shower and pack an overnight bag before he headed to the airport. He had a flight to catch.

Chapter Sixteen

Linc awakened in an unfamiliar bed, and it took him a moment to remember where he was. *New York City*. It felt like forever and no time at all since he'd been in this city. He remembered rushing to the airport, trying to catch the last-minute flight he'd booked here, arriving at the airport barely thirty minutes before his flight took off. Linc had had just enough time to find his seat and make a quick phone call to Pedro to tell him where he was and to thank him for rescuing him once again.

His flight from Puerto Rico had arrived at LaGuardia at nearly eleven o'clock last night. Once he finally made it to his hotel and checked into his room, it was well after midnight—too late to contact Mitch and Tomi. Besides, he'd been far too exhausted and nervous to do anything more than crash for the rest of the night.

Although the heavy curtains blocked the windows, Linc knew it was morning, and time for him to do what he came here for. He picked up his cell phone from the table by the bed and dialed Mitch's cell number from memory. Linc didn't know exactly where they lived, so calling them was the only option he had.

The phone rang once before Mitch's recorded voice message began. Damn, just the sound of the man's voice made Linc's heart race. At first, he wasn't sure if he felt happy or disappointed when Mitch didn't answer, and he considered hanging up without leaving a message and waiting until later to call him again. Linc was still weighing his options when he heard a beeping sound, and before he knew it, he started talking.

"Hi, this…it's Linc. Um…" He paused, suddenly so nervous, he could barely form a complete sentence. "Listen, I, uh…I'm here…in New York. I flew in for the day, and I was hoping to see you and Tomi before I leave in the morning. I know I'm the last person you ever thought you would hear from again. I wouldn't blame you if you deleted this message as soon as you heard my voice, but I hope that you won't do that without listening to what I have to say first. I know that this won't automatically fix things between us, and I know that I could say I'm sorry a million times, and it still wouldn't be enough to reverse the damage I've caused. I just…I hope that you and Tomi can find it in your hearts to forgive me. But"—Linc swallowed hard—"if you both still decide that you never want to see me again, I'll understand."

He blew out a breath. "Man." He chuckled uncomfortably. "This is a lot harder than I thought it would be." Linc leaned against the headboard and closed his eyes. When he opened his mouth again, he spoke straight from the heart.

"There's not a single minute that goes by since you and Tomi left that I don't think about the two of you. I remember every moment down to the smallest detail of the time we spent together. More than anything, I remember that day when I hurt you and Tomi, when I said things to you that make me feel disgusted with myself. You have no idea how much I wish I could take back what I said that day, to take back the hurt and anger and pain that I caused you and Tomi." His throat tightened, his voice thickened with emotion as he tried to hold it together long enough to say what needed to be said.

"You were right about me, Mitch. I lied to you, to Tomi, and to myself. I was too afraid to tell you the truth, too afraid to let you know how much I loved you both—how much I still love you—or to allow myself to even dare to hope that you and Tomi could ever love me in return."

A computerized voice interrupted Linc, warning him that he only had thirty seconds left to finish his message.

"God, I miss you both…so much," he whispered hoarsely. "I am not the same without you; my life is not the same without you and Tomi in it. Everything I do, everything I see, reminds me of you, and I'd give anything, do anything, to be with you both again, to be a part of your relationship again." He sighed heavily before he continued.

"There's one last thing I want to tell you before I hang up. You were wrong about one thing, Mitch. I didn't just use you and Tomi and then walk away. The two of you have owned me since the moment I saw you. In those weeks we spent together, you became a part of me, and losing you feels like I've lost a part of myself. Regardless of whether we ever see each other again, you and Tomi deserve to know that you mean so much more to me than just a convenient piece of ass. You have a right to know that I love you and want forever with you, even if that isn't possible."

Linc quickly left his hotel information and his cell phone number, whispering, "I love you," just before he heard a *beep* signaling the end of his message. He disconnected his call and laid the phone on the bed before he got up and headed for the bathroom. No use in sitting here, driving himself crazy while he waited.

As Linc stepped into the shower, the same thought repeated in his mind, like a mantra: *God, please let them call.*

* * *

He spent his day reacquainting himself with the city he'd called home for years, the place he'd sworn never to set foot in again. Linc's first stop was just a few doors down from his hotel at the Roxy Deli on Broadway, his favorite breakfast spot.

He grabbed a sandwich and coffee to go before he continued his walk down memory lane. Linc passed the CitySpire building on West Fifty-sixth Street, where he once lived with Ava and Paul, the Bamboo 52 bar, on Fifty-second Street, where he used to meet his lovers and friends for dinner and drinks, until he finally reached the place where his life changed forever.

Linc stood at the site of Ground Zero, so overwhelmed with memories that he couldn't speak. Somehow, he found the courage to go inside the memorial museum, searching through the victims until he located Paul and Ava's names.

He lost track of time, unsure of how long he stood there, reliving that day several years ago, alternating between outbursts of laughter and uncontrollable tears as he remembered both the good and bad times he had had with his lovers before they died. By the time he finally left, his heart felt a little lighter, his conscience a little clearer, now that he'd finally gotten the chance to say good-bye.

His last stop was his parents' home in Brooklyn. Linc showed up unannounced, knowing that if he'd given them advance warning, his mother would have spent the entire day cooking. As it was, her regular meal was far more than enough to feed the three of them, and Linc enjoyed his first dinner in their home in more than a decade.

As they ate, Linc updated them on the rest of the family in Puerto Rico. Although he talked to them regularly on the phone, Linc had not seen his parents in over a year. His father's health wasn't as good as it used to be, forcing them to cancel their yearly trip to Puerto Rico. Linc wanted them to move to the island permanently; he'd even told them they could live with him. He definitely had more than enough space. So far, he had not been able to convince them to do it. As he once used to, his parents loved the big city life and weren't ready to give it up just yet.

"So, how long are you in town, *hijo?*" his mother asked.

"Not long. I'm just here for the day. I flew in to see a couple of friends."

His father looked at him thoughtfully. "They must be some very special friends, if they got you to fly all the way here just to see them."

"Yes, *Papá*," he said quietly. "They are."

His father nodded, as if Linc's answer explained everything.

An hour later, Linc said good-bye to his parents and prepared to leave. At the door, his mother asked, "Are you happy, Lincoln?"

Linc paused. Her question caught him off guard. "I'm trying to be, *Mamá*," he finally said. "Hopefully, I will be by the time I leave in the morning."

"Good." She smiled, and kissed his cheek. "You deserve to be happy."

It was the second time in as many days he'd heard that. Linc desperately wanted to believe it was true.

He rode the train from Brooklyn and by the time he reached Manhattan, it was already after ten o'clock. As he walked to his hotel, Linc refused to think about Mitch and Tomi or the fact that he had not heard from them yet. When he reached his room and found no messages from them, he ignored the disappointment he felt. And when he woke up Saturday morning and realized that they still had not responded, he headed to the airport alone, finally admitting to himself just how devastated he truly was.

Chapter Seventeen

Tomi rolled over and reached for Mitch, finding only empty space next to her instead. Her eyes blinked open, and she stretched, smiling when she felt the tenderness in her body, knowing it was the result of the lovemaking marathon she'd indulged in during the previous day.

Her smile broadened. God, just thinking about the things he'd done to her yesterday made her wet all over again. No one ever loved her body, her mind, her very soul, the way this man did. Well, she could think of one man who came surprisingly close, who could make her body throb, her heart race in ways she never thought possible with anyone other than Mitch.

Tomi refused to go there. Thoughts of Linc already invaded her mind on a regular basis. Voluntarily thinking about him only made things worse.

Her thoughts turned to Mitch again, always trying to make sure she was okay, always willing to do whatever it took to make sure she stayed that way. She knew he worried about her, especially since they'd come home from Puerto Rico. The feeling was mutual for her as well. This thing with Linc had been hard—harder than either of them would ever have imagined. Some days, it felt as if the pain and longing would never go away. There was nothing worse than wanting, needing someone so bad, and not being able to have them.

Thankfully, they had each other, and no matter how much she would like to have Linc in their life, Tomi had no regrets that it was just Mitch and her. Even in her wildest dreams, she could not have imagined a better, stronger, more caring man to spend her life with than Mitch. He was, by far, the best thing that had ever happened to her.

She climbed out of bed and went in search of the source of her current state of wedded bliss. Finally, she found him in the living room, sitting on the couch, staring at his cell phone.

The look on his face stopped Tomi in her tracks. "What is it?" She finally convinced her feet to move and went to Mitch, sitting next to him on the couch. "What's wrong, baby?"

He opened his mouth as if he wanted to say something, but no words came out. Finally, he held the phone out to her. Tomi looked at him questioningly as she took the phone from his hand.

"Press number one." Tomi did as he instructed and put the phone to her ear, listening to the familiar voice on the other end. For the next several minutes, she sat with her mouth open, barely able to believe what she was hearing. When the message ended, she played it again, needing to make certain that she wasn't imagining this, trying to be sure that she hadn't misunderstood when Linc said he was there for them, dying to know that she wasn't just dreaming that Linc said he loved Mitch. Loved her.

After replaying the message twice more, Tomi finally disconnected the call and looked at Mitch. "I...I..."

"I know." Mitch took the phone out of her hand and set it on the table. "That was my reaction as well."

"I just can't believe he came all the way here to New York to see us." This city held so many memories for Linc, and most of them were bad. Tomi knew that. She'd discussed it several times with Linc. The fact that he would disregard the promise he made to himself about never returning here in order to see them again was more shocking, more humbling, than she could express.

Mitch's hand slid around her shoulders, and she automatically leaned her head against his shoulder. "I guess the real question is whether this changes anything between him and us."

Tomi thought about telling him that it didn't change anything between them, she had everything in her life that made her happy. She thought about saying many other things, but they all would have been lies, and they both knew it. She opted for the truth instead.

"When we first went to Puerto Rico, I thought we'd never need a third person in our lives again. Then we met Linc, and suddenly I found it hard to imagine our life without him in it. Don't get me wrong, the way he treated us in the end was incredibly shitty, and how I felt afterward was even worse, but I stopped being angry with him a long time ago. I won't pretend that I don't wish every single day that things had turned out differently with him and us."

Tomi stared into his eyes, praying that she wasn't hurting him with her admission, but refusing to be anything but honest about how she felt.

"God knows I love you, Mitch, more than I can even begin to articulate, but it doesn't change the fact that since we came home, I feel...incomplete, like something's—"

"Missing." Mitch finished her sentence for her. There was no judgment or anger in his voice. He pulled her tighter against him. "I know what you mean. I think we both know that something is Linc. Although he acted like a complete dick the last time we saw him, and despite the fact that I'm still more than a little pissed off at him, I won't deny that I love him as much today as I did last month." He cupped her face with both hands. "I suspect you do as well."

Tomi nodded. "I do."

"Then, there's only one thing left to do." He picked up his cell phone and replayed the message, writing down the number Linc left.

Tomi watched anxiously as he called the hotel, silently hoping that Linc was still there. From Mitch's conversation, though, that clearly was not the case.

"He's already gone, isn't he?" she asked when Mitch disconnected the call. When he nodded, she said, "What about his cell phone? Maybe he hasn't left the city yet." She waited while he dialed that number as well.

Mitch sighed. "His voice mail is full. I can't leave him a message." He looked as disappointed as she felt.

"Fuck." He shook his head. "He came all the way here to see us, and we missed him." He looked at Tomi, his eyes filled with guilt. "I should have recharged my phone like you told me to do. Now he probably thinks that we don't want to be with him because we didn't respond."

"Hey." She touched his face. "It's not your fault. We had no idea that we would ever hear from Linc again, much less have him travel here to talk to us."

Tomi laid her head against Mitch's chest. "Now what?" Mitch remained silent. Obviously, he didn't have an answer for that one, either.

"It's not supposed to end this way." Tomi hadn't meant to say that out loud, but it didn't make it any less true.

Mitch kissed the top of her head. "I know," he whispered.

Tomi remained quiet as one thought kept flashing through her mind, growing stronger, more persistent, until it suddenly seemed like a real possibility instead of a mere fantasy.

"I can teach anywhere," she blurted out, putting a voice to her thoughts. "When I visited the University of Puerto Rico, they had positions available for instructors with credentials like mine."

She looked at Mitch, watching him closely, trying to gauge his reaction to her words. After a moment, he slowly nodded.

"I can move my personal training business anywhere as well. People still need to work out no matter where they live. I'm sure I could always work at one of the health clubs or the hotels until I get some new clients lined up."

She stared at him. "Are we seriously considering this? Are we really willing to completely change our lives around and give up everything that we have here?" Tomi could not believe they were even having this conversation. Just this morning, she'd thought she'd never see Linc again, and now they were sitting here, talking about moving to another part of the world in order to be with him. It should have seemed crazy, yet the only thing Tomi felt was the excitement and anticipation of being with Linc again.

Mitch returned her stare. The look on his face was determined, his eyes certain. "For the chance to have Linc in our life permanently, yeah, I'm positive."

"Good." She grinned. "So am I." She leaned up, and Mitch met her halfway; his mouth covered hers, his kiss was hot and slow. "I love you, Mr. Elliott."

"I love you right back, Mrs. Elliott." He nipped her bottom lip, her chin. His tongue slid along the inside of her ear. "Come on," he whispered before he stood up, took her hand, and pulled her up from the couch.

"Where are we going?" She followed behind him as he led her to the bedroom.

Mitch glanced back at her with a smile on his face. "We're going to see if there are any flights leaving this morning to Puerto Rico that we can catch."

* * *

Linc sat in his office chair with his eyes closed. He'd been home for several hours, and he hadn't managed to get any further than his favorite place of solace, feeling so physically and emotionally drained that all he could do was sit there and lick his wounds.

The truth of the matter was that he'd completely blown his chance to be with Mitch and Tomi. There was no use in pretending otherwise, and it hurt like a son of a bitch to admit.

He leaned forward and rested his elbows on his desk and his head in his hands. He had no one to blame but himself. After acting like a pussy for the past month, he'd finally grown a pair of balls and decided to tell them the truth about how he really felt, and then he was hurt when they didn't feel the same way.

What did he expect them to do? He'd accused Mitch of being naive, yet he was the one being unrealistic. Did he really think they would just welcome him back into their lives after he treated them like shit and practically kicked them out of his house just a few weeks ago? Linc snorted in disgust. He shouldn't be surprised that they didn't want to have anything to do with him. If he were Mitch and Tomi, he wouldn't, either. God, he was so fucking stupid.

"Christ."

"No, it's just me." Linc glanced up at the sound of Pedro's voice. He stood just inside the doorway looking at Linc.

"How did you get in?"

"Rosa." Of course. Linc should have known she'd call Pedro to tell him that Linc was home. She worried over him as much as his family did.

"So, I take it things didn't go too well." Pedro leaned against his desk.

"What was your first clue?" Linc asked dryly.

Pedro laughed. "Well, I see you haven't lost your sense of humor. That's a good sign." He sobered. "What happened, Linc?"

Linc rubbed his hands over his face. "It's over. They don't want to be with me." He stood up from his desk and

stared out the window, unable to stand seeing the pity he was certain would be on his cousin's face.

"Did you see them? Is that what they told you?"

Linc sighed. "No, I didn't see them, and no, they didn't tell me that. Their silence spoke loud and clear for them."

"Well, I wouldn't be too sure about that if I were you."

Frowning, Linc turned around. "What the hell are you talk—" Anything he'd planned to say died in throat.

"Look who I found outside." Mitch and Tomi stood mere feet from him.

"I'll just leave the three of you alone." Pedro walked toward the door. "It's good seeing you both again." To Tomi, he said, "I'll let Tracee know that you're here. I know she'll want to stop by and see you." He paused and smiled. "I'll make certain that she visits later, like tomorrow, or maybe the day after that. I'm sure you all have a lot of…catching up to do."

Pedro left without waiting for their response, not that anyone in the room seemed very interested in giving him one. Their focus remained on each other instead. One moment, they were standing still and the next, they were moving toward each other as though they were thinking the exact same thing. They reached out for him, pulled him into an embrace, and Linc held on tight, refusing to let go.

He leaned down, kissing Tomi with all the love he had inside him, before doing the same thing to Mitch, pouring his apology, his regret into the kiss, before their lips separated.

"Please tell me I'm not dreaming. Tell me my jet lag hasn't made me so exhausted that I'm starting to hallucinate."

"It's no hallucination." Mitch's lips found his again. "We're real, we're here, and we love you." Those blue eyes held his with such intensity, it made his heart ache.

Linc's eyes closed, and he groaned as he pulled them close. "You don't know how badly I've wanted to hear you say that." He swallowed past the lump in his throat as he blinked back tears. "God, I love you too, both of you...so much."

He held Tomi around the waist, lifting her just enough so that she could join in their kiss. Their tongues stroked inside each other's mouths, their moans rang out as they whispered words of love and forgiveness to each other.

They made their way to the couch and sat down, with Tomi between them on their laps, kissing and touching each other as eagerly and urgently as if they were doing it for the first time.

"There's so much I want to say to you."

"Shh." Mitch silenced him with another hungry kiss. "Later...need you."

"Yeah." Mitch was right. Whatever he had to say could wait. Right now, he needed both of them in the worst way. Impatient hands pulled, snatched, and even tore clothes off, throwing them in various places throughout the room. Desire made everyone far too anxious to go slow and be careful.

Once their clothes disappeared, Linc shifted on the couch, pulling Tomi on top of him, spreading her legs as wide as possible and pushing his hard dick inside her. Linc moaned when their bare skin touched, their bodies connected together. He lost count of how many times he'd dreamed of having this with them again, so afraid that it would never become a reality.

He felt Mitch's weight, solid and welcome, when he covered Tomi's back, as he carefully entered her from behind. Linc felt Mitch's cock slowly sliding into her anus, rubbing against his shaft as he went deeper. He watched Tomi's face the entire time as it changed from a slight discomfort to a look of pure bliss in a matter of seconds.

There was nothing slow or gentle about their lovemaking. This was about urgency and possession, the need to lay claim and take ownership. When Linc finished with them, there would be no doubt in either of their minds that they belonged to him, just as much as he belonged to them.

He fucked Tomi hard, thrusting deep until she was screaming his name, telling him that she loved him as she came, her wet pussy clenching around his cock.

Linc pulled his still-hard dick out of her, desperate to be inside Mitch as badly as he'd needed Tomi. Mitch seemed to understand as well, and he followed Linc's lead, easing out of Tomi and lying back on the couch, offering himself to Linc.

Linc didn't waste time, pressing into Mitch's hole, fucking him wildly, angling his thrusts so that he hit Mitch's prostate every time. It didn't take long before they were both yelling, and Linc's seed spilled deep inside as Mitch's cum sprayed over his stomach.

They collapsed together in a wet, sticky heap. Linc felt Tomi behind him, moving up his body, placing warm, soft kisses along his spine until her warm body rested on his back. Linc lost track of how long they lay that way, seeming perfectly content to let the sound of their breathing be the only noise in the room. It didn't bother Linc one bit. As far as he was concerned, they could stay that way forever, and he'd never complain.

"We didn't know that you came to see us." Tomi's soft voice broke the silence. "We didn't get your message until after you were gone."

"It's okay." Linc reached behind him and caressed one rounded globe of her ass. "You're here now, and that's all that matters."

Mitch looked up at him and smiled. "I can't believe you came all the way to New York for us."

"It's no big deal." He shrugged and looked away, attempting to downplay Mitch's words. "Besides, you did the same thing for me."

"No." Mitch shook his head. "It's not the same thing." He disagreed. Mitch's hand cupped his face, practically forcing Linc to meet his eyes. "We don't feel the same way about Puerto Rico that you do about New York. Yet in spite of how you felt, you came anyway, and that makes it a very big deal to us."

Linc nodded, unwilling to trust his voice to speak without breaking. He traced Mitch's lips with his finger. "I'd do anything for the two of you," he managed to whisper before kissing Mitch softly. He felt Tomi move and then her lips joined theirs. Jesus, this felt so perfect, so right. He couldn't lose this, lose them, not now, not ever again.

"I don't want you to go."

"Don't worry." Mitch kissed him hard, his tongue pushing deep into his mouth, his hand reaching between them to stroke Linc's semierection. "We're not going anywhere."

Linc paused. "No, I mean, I don't want you to go back...to New York. I want you to stay here in Puerto Rico with me." He shifted until he sat on the couch between them.

He looked from Tomi to Mitch. "I know it's a lot to expect, and I probably have no right to ask it of you, but I...I just love you both. I need you so fucking much, and I don't think I could stand living without you."

"Well, that's good to know." Tomi had tears in her eyes. "We're not willing to live without you, either."

Linc pulled her close, so overwhelmed by her words that he couldn't speak. "Thank you." He kissed her. "Love you."

"Like I said, we're not going anywhere." Mitch gripped him by the neck, pulling Linc's face toward his for a kiss, his hand stroking Linc's now fully erect shaft. "Although"—he smiled suddenly—"you might get tired of having two unemployed lovers living off of you, at least until we can find jobs."

"Take your time." Linc moaned. "You can live off me as long as you need to. Everything that I have is yours."

Tomi kissed up the column of his neck. "Everything?" she whispered in his ear. "What about this?" Her hand joined Mitch's on his cock.

"Oh, yeah." Linc's eyes rolled back.

One of Mitch's thick fingers traced the crease of his ass. "This too?"

He started to pant. "Uh-huh."

"And this?" Tomi's hand covered his heart. "Is this all ours too?"

Linc opened his eyes and looked into their faces. He picked up Mitch's hand and placed it on top of Tomi's. "Especially that." He looked from one to the other. "Every beat, every breath, will always belong to you for as long as you'll have me."

"How does forever sound?" Mitch asked. "Because that's how long we need you in our lives." Their mouths met in the middle for a slow, breathtaking kiss.

Tomi pulled back first. "Want you." Her voice was soft, needy.

"You still hungry?" Linc's teeth pulled at her bottom lip.

"For the two of you?" Tomi looked from him to Mitch, those warm brown eyes smoldering. "Always." She stood and grabbed their hands, leading them from the room.

Always with Tomi, forever with Mitch. Linc smiled. That worked just fine for him.

~ * ~

Kori Roberts

Kori Roberts writes erotic tales of love, lust and passion—stories filled with strong, adventurous, and exciting characters who love hot, kinky, no-holds-barred sex.

Kori's novels reflect her belief that beauty comes in all forms, shapes, and sizes; love crosses all colors, races, and genders, and happiness can be found in the most obvious and the least expected places.

Whether you're seeking contemporary, fantasy, paranormal or suspense novels with single partners, multiple partners, same-sex partners, or all of the above, you'll find what pleasures you within the pages of Kori's books.

Visit Kori on the Web at http://www.kori-roberts.com, or send an email to her at kori@kori-roberts.com.

REDESIGNING ADELE

Talya Bosco

Dedication

Pat and Kelly: As always, I owe you everything.

Laura and Jess: Thanks for reminding me what I already knew.

Chapter One

"Goddamn it! Who the hell thought it was a good idea to keep my shit on the top shelf?" Adele snapped to herself as she climbed up one more shelf. Since she was vertically challenged, anything above five and a half feet was difficult for her to reach. And of course, some idiot had taken the step stool out of the stockroom, probably to decorate for the stupid holidays.

So here she was, five feet three and two hundred pounds in her stocking feet, climbing shelves to get pads of paper that her assistant, Gabby, hadn't gotten her before leaving for lunch. Although to be honest, Adele hadn't told her she needed them right away. It wasn't like it was the stuff she used every day.

And the damn paper wasn't what was really annoying her. If she hadn't had that damn dream last night again, she'd be fine. But no, her subconscious couldn't go more than one night without playing her fantasy over and over again. Her secret fantasy where Max and Leo fuck her until she passes out. She'd been having the same dream, or some variation of it, for over a year now. Too bad it wasn't real, 'cause it always left her hot and bothered, tense and ready to snap.

And her damn batteries had picked this morning to die on her.

Leo and Max alone were enough to get her fantasies going. When you mixed the two of them together, she was a goner. If Leo was sexy, then Max was sex on a stick. The man had the body of someone who had spent most of his life performing physical labor, which he had. She hadn't seen better bodies on models.

His black shoulder-length hair, deep, chocolate brown eyes, and Latino features were enough to grab the attention of any woman in a room, as well as many of the men. By the time they got through examining his face and moved on to his body, most of them were in love without ever having said a word to him. And he seemed oblivious to it all.

And Leo. Despite the fact he was basically an office jock, he was just as impressive. He had short brown hair cut in a professional, dignified style, which always made Adele giggle when she thought about it. She wanted to run her hands through the short tresses and feel the ends tickle her skin. He spent almost as much time on work sites as Max did and never failed to lend a strong back when it was needed. Spending time with them was always a treat. In more ways than one.

"What are you doing?" The soft baritone ran down her spine, waking up parts of her body that had no business being awake in the middle of a workday. It didn't matter that Leo was her best friend, and unattainable to boot. He made her body tingle and her blood boil whenever he was near. She shivered in response and started to fall backward. Quickly, she grabbed the shelf in front of her and held still.

Last night's dream came back full force, instantly soaking her undies as her pussy clenched in desire. Next time she was buying a multipack of batteries. Damn it.

"What does it look like I'm doing, Sherlock? Gabby left for lunch without getting me the damn paper I need, so I have to get it myself."

"Didn't it occur to you to ask for some help?"

Of course it had, but it was lunchtime, and the office had emptied quickly. People had things to do this close to the holidays and didn't make a habit of hanging around.

Instead of answering him, she turned away and looked up. Leave it to her to work in the only building in town that had ten-foot ceilings, and shelves that went almost to the top. Hell, even if she had asked the six-foot Leo for help, he'd have had to climb, too.

The warm hand on her calf made her jump and almost lose her balance again.

"Leo! Stop that, you scared me!" She held on for dear life, not looking down at him, afraid her face showed how much she enjoyed his touch.

"You never wear skirts to work, Adele. Why today?" His hand stroked her calf. Heat shot from his hand straight to her pussy. Her leg quivered under his touch.

She took a deep breath, hoping her voice didn't reveal how shaky she was feeling. "The meeting with Gunderson. He prefers women to look like women."

Leo growled and she smiled, looking down at him quickly.

"You think I like it any better?" she asked. "I'm the one that had to spend all morning with the sexist bastard. But he's brought a lot of business to the company, and I can suck up to the man for a couple hours once every few months. He lets me decorate his buildings the way I want to with little to no interference."

"You know Max and I don't expect you to put up with that kind of harassment."

Adele almost choked on Leo's statement. His hand had tightened on her calf when she mentioned Gunderson, and here he was accusing the old man of sexual harassment. If she hadn't been four feet from the ground she would have doubled over in laughter.

But it wasn't sexual harassment. Leo was a touchy man. Just because he'd never touched her like this before didn't mean anything. He'd stroked her arm countless times before; this was no different.

She looked up again, trying to ignore the feel of his hand against her skin. *He doesn't mean anything by it, Adele. Calm down. It's the dream. You're just all wound up from waking up in the middle of it. It means nothing.*

"I love your legs, Adele. I don't know if I've ever told you that. They are so muscular and toned."

Adele stifled a groan. Her legs were the only thing toned about her. She knew she should wear dresses and heels more often, show off her good points, but it always seemed to be too much of a bother to do so. Sure, low-cut blouses got the looks, but as soon as the guys moved past the cleavage and started seeing the rest of her rounded figure, they lost all interest. But that still didn't answer why he was touching her like this.

"Leo, let go. You're distracting me."

"Hmmm," was the only response she got from him as his hand moved up her leg, under the hem of her skirt to the back of her knee, stroking her slowly.

Oh God. She closed her eyes. Did he know what he was doing to her? Her body was alive with sensation, tingles starting where his hand lay on her leg. If he moved his hand any higher, she'd come just from the excitement of having him touch her. She'd dreamed for years of having him look at her as more than a co-worker, more than a friend.

But that was all they would ever be. He was in a committed relationship with Max and had been for seven years. Even though he was bi, there was no way she would try to interfere with their relationship. She loved the both of them too much to ever try to get between them. And that was part of the problem. She loved them. Both. And still none of that explained why he was now caressing above her knee.

"Are we still on for tonight?"

"What?" Leo's sudden change of subject and removal of his hand from her lower thigh threw her like a splash of cold water.

"The dinner party? You promised you'd come early and make your chocolate orgasm. Max has been looking forward to it."

Orgasm. It was the only word she heard. Oh God, wouldn't she like to go to their place tonight and have an orgasm. Or ten. Hell, she'd almost had one with just the stroke of his hand on her leg, and he hadn't even realized it. *Get a grip, girl. It was nothing. He asked you a question.*

Taking a deep breath, she tried to concentrate on what he had just asked. The dinner party. Max and Leo had invited some friends over to help them celebrate the near completion of the house. The ground floor was done, as well as the master bedroom suite and a guest room and bath on the second floor, and the two of them had decided to celebrate with a get-together. Max had said something about wanting to christen the new kitchen.

Adele had forgotten all about it. Well, to be honest, she had tried to forget all about it. She had already decided she wasn't going but hadn't gotten the nerve up to tell the two of them. Leo was bad enough, but she didn't have the strength to tell Max to his face that she wouldn't be there.

"Well?"

Adele shook her head. "What? Yeah, of course. Sorry, distracted."

"Come down from there and let me get the damn paper, woman. You're gonna fall and break your neck."

"No, I'm fine. I've got them." Adele reached up and grabbed the pads of paper off the top shelf, before handing them down to Leo's waiting hand. She started to climb down and then stopped. Leo was still watching her. He had a strange look on his face, his eyes trained on her body.

"What?" she asked, nervous again.

"What, what?"

He smiled and her heart thumped rapidly. Oh God, she had it bad. Going to their place tonight definitely wasn't a good idea. Thank God she'd turned him down.

No, you didn't, you idiot. You just told him you'd be there.

Shit, she had. Damn, well she'd have to take it back. Find some excuse. As soon as she got him to stop staring at her like that.

"You're looking at me funny, Leo."

"I am not looking at you funny. I just don't remember the last time you wore a dress this short."

"It's not short!"

"Just come down before you give me a heart attack." She started to climb back down. "And don't do that again."

"Yes, oh, lord and master," she muttered under her breath as she put her shoes back on. But the look in his eyes told her that he heard it anyway.

* * *

Leo watched the little spitfire walk out of the stockroom with a sway to her hips he didn't often see. He sucked in his breath sharply. If heels got her hips moving that sharply, then he was going to do his damnedest to make sure she wore them more often.

Heels and skirts. Preferably short skirts. Maybe a mandatory change in dress code was in order.

Easy boy, calm down. Get your hormones in check. You're still at work. There's nothing you can do now.

Leo gritted his teeth as he swallowed a growl. He and Max had waited long enough. Tonight was the night they would stake their claim on little Miss Adele Waters. She belonged with them, whether she knew it or not.

The conversation he and Max had earlier in the week replayed in his head.

"*Are we sure we want to do this?*" *Max asked, lying naked on the bed, hard body glistening with sweat from their earlier bout of lovemaking.*

Max was a large man, six-four and well over two hundred pounds of muscle. Built like a Greek god, he made Leo salivate regularly.

He'd been a construction worker all through college, and then a crew boss, learning the business from the ground up before finally getting his degree in architecture. Even now, he could be found putting his back to work on job sites as often as his brain. He asked no one to do anything he wasn't willing to do himself.

His wide, muscular chest was Leo's favorite body part. Well, almost. Leo stroked it as he responded, "Aren't you?"

"You know I love you, Leo, right?

"Of course."

"If we go ahead with this, it will affect our relationship. There's no way to prevent that. And I know that, but I'm ready. We need her, Leo. I feel it deep within my soul. I'm happy with you, but we need her to be truly complete."

Leo nodded. "I know. I feel it, too. This past week has been hell not seeing her or talking to her other than during working hours. We need her with us. I love you, Max, but she is part of this. Of us."

"But is this the right time?"

"It's now or never, Max. We're losing her."

"Then I say we do what we intended and seduce the little witch out of her pants, love her senseless, and never let her leave us again."

Max nodded and met Leo's lips in a kiss that seared Leo to his soul. He would never get tired of his lover's kisses. He felt warm and comforted, content in their decision, and drifted off in Max's arms.

Leo smiled as he thought of the plans they had made this morning. Adele had managed to avoid him earlier today for breakfast, but this little incident in the stockroom had gone better than he could have hoped. He hadn't expected to find her there, but the surprise had been a pleasant one.

Tonight was going to be the most important night of their lives. She would either accept what they had to offer or likely leave their lives forever.

They knew she thought of herself as a "fag hag." The fat chick with the gay best friends, but they didn't think of her like that. They saw the inner beauty that shone every time she looked at one of them. She made both of them feel special and treasured.

Max had described it once with the words, "She makes me feel worth something, almost like a superman whenever I do anything for her. As though even the smallest thing I do is a gift for her."

She brightened up any room she walked into with her energy and positive attitude. If they could bottle her zest for life, they'd put companies that manufactured antidepressants out of business.

Neither of them had been conscious of it as it happened; they'd just included her in more of their activities, invited her over more, enjoyed being with her.

It had taken Max going away on a business trip last year right before Christmas to make them realize what it was.

When he'd come home he'd told Leo how he felt. That he'd missed Adele as much as he'd missed Leo. That his feelings for her had changed. It should have caused a rift between the two men, but it hadn't. After just a short time of thinking about it, Leo had realized he felt the same way. But neither of them knew how to change the status quo.

Until last week. When she'd stormed out of the house in such a hurry it left them confused and worried. Then all week Adele had avoided her and Leo's usual breakfast before work. Oh, she always had an excuse, calling his voice mail when she knew he wasn't at his desk or didn't get service on his cell. But the fact was that things had changed.

That was when they'd concocted their plan for tonight. Tonight was a testing of the waters. Starting with today. Leo was supposed to flirt with her and infringe on her personal space as much as possible. If she had acted normally, like nothing was bothering her, then they would talk about forgetting tonight. But he hadn't had the chance. He had forgotten about the meeting this morning, and she hadn't been in her office any time he'd been by.

Seeing her in the stockroom had been too much of an opportunity to pass up. Hell, even if they hadn't wanted to test her reactions, he couldn't have passed the chance up. Her smooth skin had begged to be caressed. He didn't know what had stopped him from doing anything further, but he thanked God something had. Because if he'd had his way, she would have been screaming out in orgasm within a few more minutes.

But it didn't matter. She'd tried to hide it, but she'd been as affected by his touch as touching her had affected him. He readjusted himself as he thought of it again. No more waiting. No more pussyfooting around.

Tonight was the night they started their assault on their woman.

Chapter Two

"Breathe, girl. Just breathe."

Adele sat in her car alone, talking to herself. She'd started when she left her place twenty minutes ago and hadn't stopped. She'd visited Leo and Max hundreds of times before and never had this reaction. So why today?

It was Leo's fault. If he hadn't cornered her in the stockroom today at work, she wouldn't be dithering like a fool instead of heading inside where it was nice and warm.

What the hell had gotten into the man's head? How could he not know how he affected her?

Probably because she'd hidden it pretty damn well over the years. It hadn't been that strong at first; she'd just thought him an attractive man. The knowledge that he was gay and in a committed relationship had always been there, and she'd been fine with it. Even after finding out they were actually bi, she was okay with it. Hell, when they'd first met, she'd been dating another guy, though that hadn't lasted. But then things had started to change.

She didn't know when or how, but her feelings for both Leo and Max had begun to grow. She found herself wanting to spend more time with them and enjoying the time more than with any of her other friends. The feelings she had for them were no longer those of a best friend, they were those of a hopeful lover.

It had gotten worse over the last year, though. The guys had bought an old house and had been spending a lot of time renovating it. She'd been helping them almost every weekend and sometimes during the week after work. They'd spent so much time together, it was almost like she lived with them.

Despite the stereotype, the decorating gene had skipped both Max and Leo. That was her contribution to much of the house, suggestions on decor as well as some minor physical labor. Maybe that gene only came with being gay, not bi? Adele never really thought of them as bi, since they'd been together for the last seven years and never even looked at a woman. At least not in the five years that she'd known them.

She knew what they thought was sexy in a woman. It was normally the down-home Sandra Bullock type, and she didn't run anywhere near that league. Although Max had commented more than once that Marissa Jaret Winokur was kind of cute when they'd watched her on TV last year. She wasn't shaped much differently from Marissa. Was it too much to hope for that Max might find her attractive?

Adele shook her head. *Stop it. You've been letting your thoughts get away with you ever since Leo touched you today. You're being stupid and you know it. It's that stupid dream you've been having. And waking up in the middle of it today had your body all primed for something more.*

Both of them have touched you before and never meant anything by it, and you've been perfectly fine. Get your hormones in check, and get through the night. By the time you see them again, you should be over this horniness and things will get back to normal. Just cut down on the time spent with them and it'll be fine.

Maybe that's why it had gotten so intense. Seeing them all the time, relaxed, at home with each other. Watching them, half naked as they painted the living room, sweat dripping down their chests. Feeling their bodies rub up against her as they bumped her for one reason or another. Seeing their love for each other in everything they did. It made her want to be a part of that love. In a way she never could be.

It had finally gotten too much for her last weekend, and she'd practically run out of the house, yelling something about a forgotten appointment. In reality, she'd gone home and cried herself to sleep. Happy for her best friends, but feeling beyond sorry for herself.

She'd been having the same dream now all week. It was what helped her decide to loosen the ties she had to them. She was in love with the both of them and would never do anything to hurt them. If they knew how she felt, then it would affect how they treated her. She valued their friendship too much to be the recipient of their pity. It was better to leave now.

So then why was she sitting here on a Friday night, looking at their front door like it was a pastry box full of yummy things to eat? A box she couldn't open?

Because Leo had shocked the shit out of her today. Because she'd agreed to it without thinking, only eager to get him out of the stockroom and away from her body. So she could panic in secret.

Adele sighed. Time to get a move on, or they would wonder what the hell was taking her so long. She opened the door and got ready to face her men, less eager to see them than she'd ever been before.

* * *

Leo looked out the curtain one last time and saw the light in Adele's car come on as she opened the door. Thank God. If she hadn't gotten moving within the next two minutes, he had planned to go out after her.

He knew she'd reacted to his presence today, but after telling Max about it, now he was afraid he'd scared her away. Adele could be very touchy at times, they both knew that, but they were beyond taking things slow. This week had proved that to both of them.

Her reaction had brought a smile to his face and a feeling of contentment to his heart. Their little Adele wasn't getting tired of them, she was just as affected by them—or at least by him—as they were by her. Tonight was their chance to find out how affected, and if she was interested in both of them.

They'd detected a change in the relationship, and something had to give. There was no going back, only forward.

This afternoon Leo had barely been able to stop himself from taking her in the middle of the stockroom. The sight of her legs, defined sharply as she reached for the top shelf, had turned his mind to mush and his cock to steel. He hadn't even been aware when he'd reached out to touch her. It had been instinctive; he'd needed to touch her.

It hadn't been his fault. He loved her legs. He hadn't been feeding her a line today in the stockroom; they were beautiful. She'd done a lot of biking since she was young, and they were toned and muscular, capable of wrapping around a man's waist and pulling him into her tightly as her pussy milked his cock for all it was worth.

Adele opened the door slowly, not like her usual barging in with a smile. It was so unlike her, Leo felt his heart trip in worry.

"Adele, are you okay?"

She turned and looked up at him, and his heart kicked into overdrive. Her bright green eyes and vibrant smile filled him with a desire that even Max couldn't quench. God, the woman was hot. Leo couldn't understand how she didn't know how sexy she was. Plus-sized, yes, but well proportioned and beautiful. Her green eyes sparkled when she was angry or happy and grew lake-sized when she was sad. Long brown hair framed her face perfectly. Her full, pouty mouth just begged to be kissed, or for a cock to be placed between her lips. Her breasts were made for loving and tasting. A man could get lost in cleavage like that, and never want to find his way out.

His half-erect cock perked up at the vision in his mind's eye. *Not now, buddy. Later. I promise.*

"Of course I am, silly. What makes you ask?" She handed him the garment bag that obviously had her outfit for later tonight. He couldn't help but hope it was a short dress with high heels.

Her blue V-neck shirt showed more cleavage than usual, and he was sure she hadn't looked at herself in the mirror too closely before coming or she never would have worn it. That or her old, tight jeans that begged to be peeled off. He couldn't wait to see that soft white skin in all its glory. He was sure she would be exquisite in the nude. Hell, she was exquisite in or out of her clothes. Whether in a skirt like earlier or jeans like now, her beauty couldn't be hidden.

He shook his head, realizing he had to answer her. "Nothing. Sorry."

"Hey, sexy. We've been waiting for you." Max leered at her from his position in the hallway.

She laughed and reached up to pull him down for her usual kiss on the cheek. He turned at the last minute and met her lips with his. Leo's cock stirred at the sight of the two of them in a lip-lock at the same time a twinge of jealousy curled in his belly.

Adele broke the kiss quickly with a murmured "sorry," before pushing past him toward the kitchen.

Leo raised an eyebrow at his lover.

Max shrugged. "I couldn't help myself. You got to touch her this morning. Tit for tat."

Leo pushed down the feeling that rose at Max's words. If he couldn't deal with the two of them kissing, he wouldn't be able to handle the rest of what they had planned tonight. They'd planned this too long for him to get cold feet now.

"You think she suspects?" Max asked, his mouth quirked in amusement.

"No, but she's definitely confused."

"Good, all the better for us."

"So what do the two of you have planned for tonight?" Adele's voice called to them from the kitchen. Leo laid the bag over the stair banister and followed Max back into the kitchen to see what their woman was up to.

Adele had made herself at home, as usual, and opened a can of Diet Coke. Leo frowned. He knew she didn't like the stuff, but she refused to drink anything else other than an occasional glass of wine or mixed drink.

She'd propped her delectable ass on one of the bar stools at the kitchen counter and looked at them out of the corner of her eye. The newest edition of a decorating magazine lay open in front of her. They ordered them for her to look through. She thought they were decorating impaired, but she had yet to see the turret room they'd made up for her in the attic. It was their attempt at providing her with her own space if she agreed to move in with them.

"That, my sweet"—Leo leaned close, imposing on her personal space—"is for us to know and you to find out. Now get your cute little ass out of the chair and get to cooking. Your job is the dessert."

Adele grumbled and did as she was told, walking to open the large stainless steel refrigerator. Leo watching her ass in her tight jeans, nearly forgetting he had things to do as well. A nudge from Max had him moving again.

* * *

Adele took her soda and magazine and sat on the comfortable couch in the refurbished family room. The boys had done a lot to the house, including opening up the kitchen to the family room, creating a great room that was perfect for entertaining. She could just see a large party with everyone from work and their friends from other areas mingling and mixing in the large living spaces. They had definitely put their expertise to good use in the house. Tonight would be a success just by nature of the space alone.

They'd told her the house had at one time been a bordello and then fallen into disrepair as owner after owner had failed to perform even the most minor of upkeep. When they'd bought the place, it was close to being condemned, despite the fact it was on an up-and-coming street in a popular neighborhood. No one was willing to go through the expense or time necessary to make it what it could be.

Leo and Max had changed that. Being architects and in the construction business, they'd managed to gut most of the place and create a home for the twenty-first century with all the charm of the nineteenth.

The first room they'd done was the kitchen. Max had designed a large dream space for any cook. The stainless steel gas range had four burners, a grill, and two industrial-size ovens, perfect for a large get-together or someone who loved cooking. Granite countertops and tile floor sandwiched the cherry oak cabinets, creating a kitchen that Adele would kill for.

The attached family room had wood floors and comfortable furniture that welcomed her whenever she sat down. The large television and entertainment area could be viewed from almost any seat in the room, but the couch was the best viewpoint. She always made sure to sit front and center, and if the guys had to fit around her, so be it. It was one of her little pleasures in life. By the end of a night of movie watching she usually would find herself with her head in one of their laps, her feet in the other's.

She remembered the day they went furniture shopping. They'd made her try out everything with them, reminding her that if she wasn't comfortable, she'd make them pay the price. And they were right; she wasn't a quiet person, especially when she was unhappy.

Unless it came to them. But losing their friendship wasn't a price she was willing to pay. She knew someday she'd get over this infatuation; she had no choice, she had to. They never had to know about the dreams and fantasies she'd had about them over the past year.

"Okay, time's up, gorgeous."

Adele looked at her watch. "Shit! I didn't realize it was so late. Dammit, I still need to take a quick shower."

"No problem, we've both taken ours. You don't have to worry about losing water pressure."

Adele looked up and nearly dropped her soda. Max stood there in all his gorgeous glory, and her pussy grew wet. He was dressed in black slacks and a white silk shirt that set his dark skin off to perfection. His brown eyes were full of cheer and contentment, obviously happy about the upcoming night. Her heart thumped as the thought, *I love you*, ran through her head. But that was the only place she would ever speak those words. In her head.

"Oh, great. Okay. Um, thanks." Adele backed out of the room and headed to the guest room she used when she needed a place to shower. Leo had said he'd put her clothes in there.

She managed to get to the room and close the door without running into Leo on her way up. Leaning against the door, she breathed a sigh of relief. Oh God, what was she doing here? She wasn't sure she would be able to handle this tonight.

"Get a grip, girl. It's a dinner party. The rest of the guests will be here any minute. You aren't gonna be alone with them for much longer. After a couple hours you can make your excuses and leave. They'll be none the wiser."

If she didn't start acting her normal self, they'd begin to wonder what was up, and that was the last thing she needed, them prodding and prying at her trying to figure out what was wrong. She never could resist them, and pretty soon she'd be crying her tale of woe and want to them.

Talk about a blow to any friendship. "Hey guys, I know we're just friends and everything, but you know, for the last year or so I have had the hots for you. Both of you. All I can think of is you both fucking my brains out."

Wouldn't that be a nice pre-Thanksgiving surprise. Shit, she'd totally forgotten. Thanksgiving was Thursday. The guys had closed the office for the week, figuring it was a good time to get some of their own stuff done. Other than a skeleton crew, the entire company had the week off, and that included her. The three of them had plans to work on Leo's home office and one of the extra rooms upstairs.

There was no way she could spend an entire week with them if she couldn't spend one night acting like everything was normal. She'd have to figure out some sort of excuse, something that wouldn't hurt their feelings.

A quick glance at her watch had her getting into gear. She only had to survive a couple hours, and could worry about next week later.

Decision made, Adele walked over to the hanging garment bag and pulled down the zipper. Inside was her outfit for the night. One she now regretted choosing.

She'd bought it last week when she'd been out shopping with her friend Lisa. Lisa had convinced her to try it on, despite the fact Adele was sure it wouldn't look right. Adele should have known better, Lisa was never wrong about clothes. It was perfect for her.

The deep emerald green dress was sleeveless, the bust held up only by inch-wide straps over either shoulder. The silk dipped in a deep V in both the front and back, preventing her from wearing a bra, but the empire waist and cupping material made one superfluous.

She picked it up, the material sliding against her hands with a soft slithering sound, making her feel sexy just at thinking of putting it on. The matching wrap was the same color and Lisa had insisted the entire outfit made Adele's eyes look brighter and larger. That thought alone was enough to make Adele buy it, as she always considered her eyes her best feature.

A handkerchief hem varied in height from above her knee to halfway down her calves, giving the skirt a sense of movement and freedom. Paired with the four-inch matching stilettos Lisa had made her buy, as well as some of her grandmother's art nouveau jewelry, Adele felt almost ready to face the world.

At the very least two very sexy men and their dinner guests.

Chapter Three

Max turned at the sound of Adele coming down the stairs and froze. Oh God, was she beautiful. His cock tightened at the sight of her strong calves highlighted by her heels. Shit! Those heels. They had to be at least four inches high and screamed "Fuck me!" better than anything he'd seen in a long time.

The material flowed around her body, giving him teasing glimpses of her legs and hips as it caressed her skin. What he wouldn't give to be that piece of silk right now.

"No one's here yet?"

Max swallowed and pasted a smile on his face. "No. You know Michael and the rest of the crew. Fashionably late every time."

Dinner was supposed to be at eight, with cocktails starting at seven. It was already quarter past, and as he had told Adele, no one had shown up yet. They'd pretty much expected it, though, so neither he nor Leo were worried about it. In fact, they thought they'd take this extra time to put their plan in action.

"What do you guys need me to do?"

"Leo was hoping you'd help him in the kitchen while I finish the dining room and bar."

She smiled in agreement as she turned down the hallway to the kitchen. Max swallowed hard, again. Leo was right, she did sway that ass of hers more when she was in heels. He wondered if she did it purposely or it was just a result of the shoes.

She screamed sex and screamed it unconsciously. She didn't even know her power. When they'd gone out dancing or to a bar he'd seen men stare after her, wanting to ask her to dance, or perhaps more, but he and Leo had always kept them at bay. It was unfair of them, he knew, but they weren't going to risk losing her before they caught her.

Whatever it was, he had to press against his hard-on to remind it to calm down. Now wasn't the time. Later.

Unlike Leo, he had no doubt that she loved the two of them. That she wanted them both sexually. He did, however, wonder how she would handle the thought of both of them at once. It wasn't a common arrangement, and she had grown up in a strict Catholic household. Something like this was beyond her normal expectations.

They had friends who were in nontraditional relationships, from gay and lesbian couples to swingers, and even another triad, but it was one thing to accept it in your friends and another to accept it in yourself.

He and Leo knew they should take it slow tonight, but they were beyond patience. They wanted to get moving on their hopes for a relationship with her. There would be a lot of issues for her to overcome though.

In her family, she had always been the one to give in. Whenever there was an issue that her father took offense with, or she did something he didn't like, he made no secret of the fact. And she would bow to whatever pressure he exerted.

In fact, being friends with the two of them was probably the only thing that she had openly defied her father about. She'd refused to drop their friendship, though, going so far as to limit contact with her family when he and Leo weren't invited.

Hell, if being friends with them was hard, he could only imagine how hard living with them would make her life. Her father wasn't the only one in the family that did his best to make her life miserable. Her sister was already a judgmental woman, never missing a chance to berate Adele for anything, whether it be her job, her clothes, or her weight. Adele's weight and friendship with the two of them seemed to be Beverly's biggest targets.

Neither of them could count the days that she'd come to them crying over something her sister or father had said to her. Over the last year or so, she'd been separating herself from her family more and more, turning to him and Leo for support. If Max had his way, she would cut her relatives out of her life forever, but it wasn't his call. All he could do was be there to help whenever and however needed.

* * *

Adele stopped short at the kitchen entrance when she saw Leo standing at the counter setting up the hors d'oeuvres. Like Max, he wore slacks, only his were charcoal gray and hugged his ass perfectly, falling gently after the curve of his cheeks to his shoes. His dark blue shirt stretched across his back, and the rippling of his muscles as he moved caused her pussy to moisten as she thought of how those muscles would move under her hands.

She bit back a groan at the images that ran through her mind She needed to get her head on straight and stop obsessing over things she couldn't have.

"Max said you needed my help?"

Leo turned and smiled at her, and her heart thumped in tune with the pulse in her crotch. This time she did groan.

"Baby. Yeah, could you do me a favor and set up the olive tapenade and bruschetta?" He gestured with his head to the pile of ingredients, homemade and store-bought, that sat on the counter beside the fridge. Adele headed over to start arranging the food.

She hadn't been at it for longer than a minute before she felt someone at her back. An arm reached around her, brushing against her breast, to grab at a small square bowl in front of her. Leo's body pressed up against her back for an instant and then was gone.

"Sorry, darlin', need this."

Adele nodded, not saying anything, not trusting her voice, and kept working. A few minutes later he was back.

"Sorry, need to get something out of the top cabinet." This time he crowded her a bit closer before opening the cabinet in front of her. He leaned over and reached for something above her head, pressing his body against her ass. It took every thing in her not to push back and rub against his crotch.

"Why don't you just let me move out of your way?" Adele grabbed hold of the countertop and sucked in her stomach, pulling herself into the granite as close as she could. If she didn't, she knew she'd do the opposite.

"No, no, that's okay." He pressed against her just a bit more before moving away again.

Adele stood there a moment longer. "Breathe, girl, breathe," she told herself under her breath. Her body tingled where he had brushed against her. "Breathe," she repeated.

"Did you say something?"

"No, not at all." Adele shook her head. "Okay, all done, where do you want this stuff?"

"Why don't you put them both on the coffee table with the crostini?"

Adele nodded, biting her lip and proceeded to do as he asked. *Just a couple hours, Adele, just a couple hours.*

* * *

Hours later, Adele downed what had to be her tenth glass of wine, wondering why she was still there. Okay, so she wasn't in any condition to drive home, but she could call a taxi. Hell, she should have left at least an hour ago. But she was nothing if not a glutton for punishment and spending more time with Leo and Max definitely fit that description.

Staying here was pure stupidity. It was time to go home.

A rattling startled Adele and she jumped, nearly spilling the little bit of alcohol left in her glass. She looked over and saw her new iPhone vibrating against an empty glass.

Confused, she thought for a moment and then remembered bringing it downstairs to show someone who had asked about it. A quick glance at the display revealed it was her cousin Sarah calling. What did she want?

Adele looked around. What would it hurt? No one was in the room and probably wouldn't be looking for her; it wasn't like she was the hostess or anything. So she plopped on the couch sloppily and picked up the phone.

"Adele? Are you there?"

"No, this is not Adele. You have reached her answering machine." Adele hiccupped, sending her into a fit of giggles before she could continue.

"Oh, stop that. What the hell are you doing? You sound like you're drunk."

Adele looked at the glass still in her hand and sucked down the last few sips. "You know, Sarah, I think I very well may be."

"Where are you? Are you safe? Do you need me to come get you?"

"I'm with the guys."

Sarah's sigh was audible. "Good, then you'll be okay. They'll take care of you."

"Take care of me? Take care of me! Oh, yeah, sure the little shits will take care of me. That's all they've been doing all night. Taking care of fat little Adele."

"What the hell are you talking about?"

"Them. The guys. The bastards." Adele realized she was raising her voice and tried to lower it. "They won't leave me alone."

"Adele, honey, I don't understand."

"Well neither do I, dammit. Them. They keep touching me. Rubbing up against me, pushing me against counters, brushing my boobs. I'm so fucking wet it's not even funny. Every time I turn around they're there. They won't leave me alone. Hell, Max practically growled at one of his cousins when he took my hand."

"Touching you? Explain."

Adele ignored her cousin's demand. "And kissing! Max kissed me and made my toes curl, dammit! The bastard put his tongue down my throat."

The "woohoo" was impossible to miss, even through the phone. "Well, dammit, girl, that's what you want, isn't it?"

"No. Yes. Oh, shit, Sarah. I want it. But not like this. I don't know what the hell they're doing. It's not like they want me."

"How do you know that? Have you asked them?"

"No, I haven't asked them. They're my friends. You don't ask them that."

"Well, sweetie, what else can it be?"

Adele recognized the tones of someone trying to calm a drunk person. Hell, she'd used it often enough on Sarah herself. "I don't know. Maybe they had a fight before I got here and are using me as a shield."

"Well, are they acting strange?"

"I just told you they were!"

Sarah sighed. "I mean with each other."

"I don't know, I haven't noticed."

"Do you want me to come get you?"

Did she? Hadn't she just been thinking that she should go home?

"No. That's okay. I need to stay and help them clean up. I'll get a taxi or have Max's brother drive me home. I'll be okay."

"If you're sure…"

"Yeah. I'm sure."

"Okay, then. But don't forget about tomorrow night."

Adele tried to figure out what Sarah was talking about. "Tomorrow night?"

"Yeah, our double date."

"Sarah, you know I hate blind dates. I never ag—"

"Adele, you have to come. I already told them you'd be there."

Adele debated arguing with her cousin, but she knew she'd never win in her condition. Hell, she never won even when she wasn't drunk. "Fine, but don't expect me to be all happy about it."

Sarah laughed. "Please, even when you're bitchy, you're nicer than me on my best days. I'll call you later tomorrow when I have the details."

Adele grunted her agreement and disconnected the phone. She stood up and walked around the room, muttering loudly. "Damn cousins. Damn men. Who do they think they are, playing with me like that?"

They *had* been crowding her, and she knew she wasn't the only one to notice.

"So Adele, when are you going to leave our two hosts alone and let them live in peace? Aren't you tired of hanging around waiting for crumbs of attention?"

The snaky voice ran down her spine, bringing a chill with it.

Adele turned to face Krista, Max's soon-to-be sister-in-law. Or at least that's how Krista made it sound. Adele had been watching her and Michael tonight and she wasn't so sure.

Krista walked into the small library, swinging a bottle of wine from her hand as she gloated at Adele.

Emboldened by the wine she had drunk, Adele answered her instead of ignoring her like she normally would. "They are living in peace, Krista. And unlike some of us, I don't throw myself at anything with a cock."

Krista had grown up with Max and his twin brother, Michael. She had lived next door to them from the time she was nine. According to Leo, she'd always had a crush on Max and tried whatever she could to get him interested in her. Max had even found her naked in his bed in his dorm room at college.

After being rejected by Max, she'd left town for New York. She'd returned a year ago, and upon finding out Max was in a committed relationship, she'd apparently decided to settle for Michael.

Krista tsked at her and shook her head. "I am surprised at you, Adele, that you haven't given up yet. The boys will never turn to you, no matter how desperate they are or how drunk you get."

"What is your problem, Krista? I thought you were in love with Michael? Why are you obsessing over a man you can't have?"

"Oh, please. If I wanted Max, he'd be mine."

"That's not what I heard. Why don't you just give up? Max may be bi, but that doesn't mean he'll fuck anything that comes along."

Krista slammed the wine bottle down on the table, the only visible sign of her anger. "You're right, he won't and neither will Leo. If they would, then they would have fucked you by now. They have better taste than that, though, and if they ever did pick up a woman to join them for a bit of fun, it would be a real woman. Not a fat marshmallow like you."

Adele cringed inwardly before straightening her back. No matter how drunk she was, Adele was not going to let this shrew see how much she could hurt her. "You know, Krista, I will never see what such a good man like Michael sees in a backstabbing, lying slut like you."

"I'm good in bed, honey."

"Not that good." The cold, hard voice came from the doorway. They both turned to see Michael standing in the entryway, a look of disgust on his face. How long had he been standing there? "It's time to say good-bye to everyone, Krista. You won't be seeing them again."

The look on Krista's face should have turned Michael to stone, but he ignored it and turned to Adele. "I'm sorry, Adele. She promised to be on her best behavior, but I should have known better. I won't be bringing her back here again."

"But, sweetie…" Krista walked up to Michael and stroked his face, but he moved his head and grabbed her hand to pull it away.

"Don't 'sweetie' me. I told you before I was tired of your attitude. This time you've gone too far. Get your coat."

Krista turned and glared at Adele before walking out of the small room in a huff.

"Ignore whatever she said, Adele. She's a sour bitch."

Tipsy though she might have been, Adele could still hear the pain in Michael's voice. "Why do you put up with her then, Michael? You deserve so much better."

His smile was crooked as he answered her softly. "I know, but I thought I loved her." With that, he nodded and walked out of the room.

Adele watched after him with sadness in her heart. The man deserved so much better. Maybe someday.

After grabbing the half-empty bottle that Krista had put on the table, Adele filled her glass. No use letting it go to waste. The boys never bought cheap wine, and she drank so rarely, she might as well enjoy it.

* * *

"She's in here!" Max stood in the doorway watching the woman he loved more than anyone but Leo sleeping on the couch. "We should have looked here first, but after what Michael told us, I figured she'd head upstairs."

"Well, our little lady is nothing if not contrary, isn't she?" Leo walked over to Adele and stroked a small curl off her face. She was absolutely beautiful.

"You can say that again."

"Did she really call Krista a backstabbing slut?"

Max smiled. "Yeah, she did. Our little kitty is growing claws."

"Maybe we should get her drunk more often."

Max reached down to cradle her and lifted her in his arms to take her upstairs.

She murmured sleepily and then curled tight into his arms.

"Where you taking her?"

"To bed. I'll be down to help with the party mess in a few minutes."

"No, I mean which bed."

Max stared down at her for a long moment before answering. "Ours. We've waited long enough, and I want her to know she'll always have us to protect her."

Leo nodded. "Good. She needs to know she's been alone long enough. Never again."

Max smiled grimly and headed up the stairs. She felt right in his arms. Like she belonged there. He hugged her tighter against his body as he turned at the top of the stairs toward the master bedroom.

"Marshmallow."

Max glanced down at the woman in his arms. "Sh, sweetheart. It's time for bed."

"Marshmallow. That's what I am. Big, fat marshmallow."

"Sh, you aren't a marshmallow. You're perfect." He reached out to pull the blanket back before placing her on the bed. Her arms snaked around his neck before he could move back.

"You have to say that. You're my dream man. You both always say that in my dreams. But I know you don't want me. You're happy." A frown ran across her face. "Dumb, fat bitch."

Pain sliced through his heart at her words. She was right; he was happy with Leo, but they knew they could be happier with her in their lives.

"Oh, honey. We love you. We both want you more than you can ever know."

Adele drunkenly shook her head. "No, don't need me."

Max sighed. He didn't know what to say. He could only hope she wouldn't remember this when she woke up.

Instead, he bent down to take her lips with his. This time, she responded, opening her mouth and letting him in with a sigh.

He tasted her. Wine, chocolate, and a taste that was all her own. It ran through his body and ended in his hardening cock. Her moans of pleasure made it twitch erratically.

Reluctantly, he pulled away. Now definitely wasn't the time. But she wasn't getting away from them. In the morning was soon enough. No one was leaving before they had a chance to say to her what they should have said a long time ago.

He took off her shoes before covering her up. He had no doubts she'd sleep soundly until the morning.

By the time he got downstairs, Leo had already started cleaning up. The dishwasher was almost full and the leftovers were waiting to be put in appropriate containers.

"How's she doing?"

"Out like a light. But not until after she talked about being a marshmallow and fat bitch."

"Goddamn it!" Leo slammed the plate he was holding down on the granite countertop. Max heard a snap as the porcelain cracked in two and prosciutto and melon clusters went rolling across the counter. "What did that bitch say to her?"

Leo had never liked Krista, but she had grown up with Max, so he put up with her. Max always remembered her as the young girl with ponytails and skinned knees. But she had changed over the years, become poisonous. He could only hope Michael would see that before it was too late.

"Michael said that's what Krista called her. A fat marshmallow. He was gonna say something then, but that's when Adele called her a backstabbing bitch. He took that as his cue to interrupt rather than have a catfight on his hands. And we both know Krista is capable of taking it that far."

"I'm sorry, Max. I know she's your brother's girlfriend, but that woman is not welcome in this house anymore. No matter what."

Max nodded his head as he walked over to wrap Leo in his arms. "Agreed."

Leo sighed and relaxed into Max's arms. "Maybe tonight was a dumb idea. But we were getting to her, Max. I know we were. She was nervous at first, but I know she was turned on."

"Maybe it was the wine."

Leo laughed sadly. "Who knows, maybe it was." Leo looked away for a moment before turning back. "Are we fooling ourselves? Should we just let this go?"

Max thought about what Adele had said upstairs about her dream man and he knew they were on the right track. He was more confident than he'd ever been. "No. She's ours, dammit, and nothing is gonna keep her from us."

Leo nodded his head and brought his lips close for a kiss.

Max would never get tired of the taste of his lover. No matter what Leo had been doing prior to a kiss, Max always tasted his sweetness and gentleness backed with a strength of character that he could feel deep within his own heart.

"I want you, Max. Here, now."

"You first." Max smiled as he reached toward one of the drawers in the kitchen. Although there were other things that could be used in the kitchen as lube, they both preferred something made for that purpose. So, being the adventurous types they were, they always had some handy in unexpected places.

Leo smiled and shook his head. Before Max could say a word, Leo was on his knees in front of him and opening his pants. The thought of Adele lying upstairs in their bed had his cock pulsating even more. Of her maybe walking in on them, perhaps even joining them. Max groaned.

"She's out like a light, lover boy. You put her in bed. But I know you're burning for her just like I am. Consider this a prequel to what we shall have soon."

Leo continued setting Max free and once his cock was out of his pants, Leo took him in hand and slowly made love to him.

Leo's lips wrapped around him and tugged gently, forcing Max to grab hold of the countertop behind him and close his eyes. Leo's groan of satisfaction sent shivers down his spine as he fought against the need to thrust himself into his lover's mouth.

When Leo tugged harder with his lips and hand, Max looked down at him to see the love shining in his eyes. His cock popped free as Leo leaned back.

"Come on, Max. I know you want it. You need it just like me. Fuck my mouth hard, the way you like it. Take what I want to give."

Tears formed at the corner of Max's eyes as their gazes met in perfect harmony. Leo always knew what he wanted, what he needed. And he never refused. Max reached down and knotted his hands in Leo's lighter-colored locks and caressed his scalp as he began to thrust as Leo ordered.

Leo grabbed his ass and pulled him tighter into his mouth, opening wide as Max shoved in and pulled out, faster and faster, his lover teasing him with his tongue and teeth, sucking harder at each thrust.

Love and desire overwhelmed him at the look on Leo's face as he took him in his mouth. An acceptance that was unbelievable in its totality. Everything he was, he was because of his love for this man. And the growing love for the woman upstairs. They would have it all.

Max burned with need, all sense of control gone as he pumped between Leo's lips. He felt the beginning of his orgasm tingle at the bottom of his spine, tremors shooting straight to his cock as he imagined pumping into Adele like this. Hard. Fucking her for all she was worth. The picture of Leo fucking her pussy as he fucked her mouth filled his mind, and it was too much. He lost all control and exploded into Leo's mouth.

Leo took everything Max gave him and cleaned him with his tongue before standing up to kiss him on the lips.

"Better?" Leo asked as he pulled Max into his arms.

"How the hell do you do that to me?"

Leo leaned back and grinned. "It's exactly what you do to me, lover. We take care of each other. And now we have one more person to take care of."

Max nodded and adjusted his pants before helping Leo clean up. After they had put the leftovers away, they headed upstairs to their bedroom.

"What are we going to do with her?" Max asked softly, eager not to wake the woman sleeping in their bed. She'd thrown the blankets back, and the dress was curled up around her upper thighs, revealing a long stretch of leg.

"Well, she needs out of that dress for one thing."

"She'll kill us when she wakes up, Leo. You know she will."

Leo shook his head as he reached for Adele. "Well, she can't sleep in it. It's gotta be uncomfortable."

Max watched as Leo pulled Adele to him and unzipped the back of the dress before laying her back down on the bed. "We can't let her sleep in the nude. She doesn't do that when she's alone, and if she wakes up in bed with us naked, with no memory, her freaking out will be the least of our worries."

Leo sighed. "I guess you're right. Why don't you go get one of those pajama sets we were gonna give her for Christmas?" Max nodded and turned to walk out the door, only to be called back by Leo.

"And make it one of the skimpy ones. Not that warm, fuzzy set that covers everything."

Max smiled as he headed out of the room. He may be worried about Adele's reaction in the morning, but he wasn't stupid. If she was gonna be in bed with them, he wanted to be able to feel her, not her clothes.

Chapter Four

Adele woke slowly, groaning with the pain in her head, afraid to open her eyes and face the light. Good Lord, how much had she drunk last night? The last thing she remembered was Krista calling her a marshmallow.

Thank God the night was over. Her plan to avoid the two men started right now. She rolled over, content in her decision, and thinking a few more hours of sleep sounded good. Her movement was stopped, though before she made it more than a couple of inches.

What the hell?

Her eyes popped open, to find a chest. A nice, tanned, well-formed male chest. She gulped.

What happened last night?

Closing her eyes again, she took a deep breath and thought. *Okay, Adele, get a grip. There weren't that many guys at the party you could have gone to bed with, just roll over and climb out the other side. Deal with it as soon as you figure out who it is.*

Slowly, Adele rolled the other way, pretending to be asleep in case her strange man wasn't, only be to be caught on the other side.

Once again, her eyes popped open. She couldn't move. She was lying on her side, in bed, between—

"Good morning, sweetheart." Max's voice sent shivers dancing up and down her spine. She dragged her eyes up to meet his chocolate ones, which were full of mischief.

Suddenly her throat was dry and she found herself unable to say a word. Her mouth opened, but no sound came out.

A hand she hadn't been aware of a moment before tightened on her waist. "Mornin', darlin'. How are you feeling today?"

Oh God, oh God, OH GOD! She was lying in bed with Max and Leo, and at least Max had no shirt on. When Leo pulled her tighter against his body, she realized he didn't either. Hell, if she felt his warm, smooth chest against her back, then neither did she!

Quickly she looked down and saw she was wearing a baby-doll nightgown. She'd never seen it before, but it seemed to fit her perfectly. Except for the fact that it dipped down to show way too much cleavage.

Oh good Lord, what had she done?

"Um, well..."

"Mmm, do you know how gorgeous you are in the morning?" Max gently stroked her face, cupping it in his palm. It took all she had not to moan and lean into it. Instead, she took refuge in trying to find the facts.

"What happened?"

A deep chuckle came from behind her, waking parts of her body that had no right to be awake despite where she now found herself.

"Don't you remember?" Leo buried his head in her hair, teasing her ear with his nose.

What happened, what happened? What was the last thing she remembered? Krista had been a bitch, as usual, and then Michael had come and taken her home. After that, nothing. Well, nothing except a dream where she had started to make out with Max, but then those were normal dreams. Her gaze flew to Max's face. It had been a dream, hadn't it? She hadn't told him he was her dream man, had she?

No, impossible.

Then what the hell was she doing half naked in bed with two equally half-naked men? *Oh God, please let them be only half naked.*

"What am I doing in here?" Why wasn't she in the guest room she was usually given? What the hell was she doing in their bed? Because a quick glance around, at least what she could see, assured her she was most definitely in their bedroom.

Max answered sleepily. "Well, until about three minutes ago you were sleeping like a baby."

"Little baby snores and everything."

Adele felt her skin flush at Leo's teasing comment. "I did not snore!"

"You sure about that, darlin'?"

She had much worse things to worry about than snoring. *Get on topic, woman!*

Her voice shook. "What am I doing in your bed?" Oh God, please don't let her find out she'd crawled into it. That made her no better than Krista. What were they going to think of her after this?

No, she wouldn't have done that. No matter how drunk she was. At least she hoped she wouldn't have. No. Definitely not.

But then why was she here? How did she get here? Why were they acting like something had happened last night? And like they were happy something had happened?

This made no sense. Adele stopped and forced herself to think. It was pretty damn difficult given the fact she was where she'd wanted to be for as long as she could remember: smack dab in the middle of a Leo and Max sandwich. Did it matter how she got there or what she was doing there?

Hell, yes, it did. This didn't add up. She knew damn well no matter how drunk she'd gotten she'd never do something this stupid. She'd made a decision a long time ago not to let her life go down the path others she knew had chosen. Even drunk as she'd been, she would have still been in control of her actions enough not to climb into their bed.

And if she didn't have the control, she knew they would have taken her back to her bed and not said a thing. They knew her mother had had a problem with alcohol, and how much Adele feared following in her footsteps.

That was it. Maybe she had climbed into their bed, and this was their way of showing her how stupid she'd been. Nothing else would make her freak out like finding out she'd done something like this. Or maybe they'd put her in their bed just to confuse her. Just to show her how stupid she could have been.

Adele's brain ran through the conflicting and contradictory thoughts. None of them made sense. The guys would never purposely hurt her. So the only scenario that worked was they were trying to teach her a lesson.

They were setting her up.

Suddenly, she was on much surer footing. "And don't either of you dare lie to me and tell me I climbed in here. I may have been drunk, but I sure as hell wasn't that drunk. Now let me out."

"Now, darlin', don't be goin' all huffy on us."

That was it. Despite being sandwiched rather tightly, and nicely, between the two of them, she managed to wriggle herself free and out of the bed. "This isn't funny. I don't know how I got here, and I don't care. I'm gonna go change and then go downstairs. When you two are ready to stop behaving like immature fools, you come talk to me. *After* you get dressed!"

She just managed to keep herself from stomping her foot as she turned from the room and headed to her own.

Damn them! She had no idea what the hell had gotten into their heads, but this wasn't funny! Who the hell did they think they were, doing something like this to her?

Adele searched for her clothes and yanked her pants on, then took off the baby-doll nightgown and pulled on her shirt. As she dressed, more memories of last night came back to her.

The bastards had been flirting and teasing her all night. They'd been acting strange, and this morning was the icing on the cake. She didn't know what the hell was going on in their heads, and she didn't want to know. But she'd had enough.

Screw talking. She needed to get home and alone. She needed to be as far away from them as possible.

* * *

"What just happened?"

Max smiled. He'd seen Adele's face go from confused and scared to pissed off. He could pinpoint the exact second. And Leo accusing her of getting huffy just made her get to the boiling point that much faster.

"She's on to us."

"What do you mean she's on to us?"

"She knows nothing happened last night and thinks we were stringing her along."

"Well, what reason would we have for that?"

Max shook his head at the man he loved. "I don't know, what reason could we possibly have for trying to make her think she'd spent the night in bed with us, as more than just friends?"

"Oh fuck!" Leo flopped back on the bed. "She really thinks we're playing with her?"

"It's the only reason I can think of for her reaction."

"How the hell can't she know how we feel about her?"

"Have you told her?"

"Of course not! She'd bolt."

"Exactly. And I haven't told her either. So, although our little Adele is a talented young lady, mind reading is not her forte. We should have known she'd react like this."

"Well, dammit, why didn't you say something last night?"

Max raised an eyebrow. "I believe I did. Right before you took her dress off."

"Well, she couldn't have slept in that contraption. She would have hurt something. Not to mention ripped it."

"And the fact you got to see her practically naked had nothing to do with it?"

Leo's lips twitched. "I tried to keep my eyes averted."

Max snorted. "Yeah, I saw the reaction to your eyes being averted. Hell, I benefited from your reaction in the shower, now didn't I?"

"So what do we do now?"

Max eyed the door as though he could still see her storming out. "We do as she asked. Get dressed, go downstairs, and try to get this all sorted out. We fucked up. It's up to us to fix it."

"What do you mean 'date'?" Leo practically yelled over the phone.

Adele cringed. She knew she should have looked before she'd answered the phone. She'd managed to avoid the guys all day, between shopping with Sarah and getting ready for her date. She'd gone straight to Sarah's after leaving their house this morning and hadn't gotten back until about twenty minutes ago. Both her cell phone and house phone had at least five messages from each of the guys.

Why she'd picked up the phone now, she didn't know. Instead, she stood there wrapped in a towel while she listened to Leo yell at her as she brushed her hair dry.

"A date—as in go out, meet someone, and have a few drinks."

"Who is this guy?"

Adele cringed, again, debating whether to tell him the truth. But if she didn't and he found out later, she'd never hear the end of it.

"Sarah fixed it up."

"Sarah? Sarah! As in your cousin Sarah? The one who got herself arrested after attacking her last boyfriend? Sarah, the one who flew all the way to Acapulco to meet a man she'd only talked to on the Internet for two weeks and got stood up?"

"It's a double date."

Adele could hear the frustration coming over the silent phone line. In her mind's eye, she could see Leo firming his lips as he tried to keep himself from yelling. His next question came out as though through gritted teeth. "Does she even know the guy she is supposed to meet?"

"Do you really think she's that stupid?"

"Do you want me to answer that?"

"Jesus, Leo, get over it. I'm a big girl. I can take care of myself."

"Where are you going?"

"I don't know yet."

"You're going to meet a man you don't know at a place you don't know, and you have the balls to tell me you know what you're doing."

"Well, it's not like I plan on going home with the guy."

"So you say, but he may have other plans. Nope, sorry, you aren't going."

"Excuse me?"

"I said you aren't going."

"Dammit, Leo, last time I checked, you were *not* my husband. Or my boyfriend or anyone else that has a claim on what I do. Now get over it. I'm going out, and that's final. And for the record, if I want to go home with an entire hockey team, it's none of your damn business!" Adele slammed down the phone and glared at it, wishing she had the power to melt it with a glance. It and the damn man on the other end of it.

Who the hell did he think he was, acting like that? Their stunt this morning was bad enough, now he was trying to tell her whether she could go on a date or not? No sirree, not gonna happen.

The phone started ringing again, and she ignored it. She didn't need their shit. She was almost certain it was Max this time, calling in a calmer manner, reminding her how much of a hothead southern-born Leo could be, which was funny, given Max's Latin temperament. She didn't care. They weren't her keepers.

And if she couldn't have the ones she wanted, she'd find someone else. Adele looked at the outfit she had laid out on the bed for her night out. Jeans and her favorite sweater.

Screw that.

She reached into the back of her closet and moved some clothes around until she found what she was looking for. Perfect. Too bad they wouldn't be seeing her wearing it. Maybe she'd have Sarah take a picture.

It took less than fifteen minutes for Adele to get dressed and do her hair. She'd realized as she was dressing that it was likely one, if not both of them, would show up on her doorstep before she left.

Luckily, even going as fast as they possibly could, they'd never get to her place in less than twenty minutes, and her phone hadn't stopped ringing until five minutes ago. A quick glance at the caller ID readout assured her they'd been calling from home. She had another ten minutes for makeup, fifteen if she was really lucky.

She checked herself in the mirror before she started her makeup. A little bit over-the-top, but that was okay. It would make her feel good.

Her long hair was up with curls coming down in a casual, messy style that framed her face without making it look too round. The same necklace she'd worn last night hung down her neck, pointing straight to her breasts. Not that they needed any more attention called to them.

The dress was bustier fashion, made so someone her size could wear it without a bra. Her breasts lay on the shelf made by the bustier, practically spilling out of the material. Stiff, boned leather cupped her waist, drawing it in to give the impression of an hourglass figure, before widening over her hips to meet a shiny satin skirt that was too short for any kind of respectable activity. The bright red color alone would call attention to her, even if it hadn't been an advertisement for what she wanted tonight.

She had planned to wear it to the guys' Halloween party this year but had chickened out. She'd decided she was better off going as a well-covered angel, rather than the slutty devil she'd intended to be. Well, tonight she was taking that devil by the horns and would see what it brought her.

The tops of the thigh highs she wore were just hidden by the material, but the wrong—or right—move would make the black lace at the top visible to all who cared to look.

Her heels were the highest fuck-me heels she owned. They had been bought on a dare a couple of years ago and worn only once. Although, given the way they made her legs look, she was surprised. She should wear them more often. Her legs looked muscular and well defined, just like Leo had claimed in the stockroom.

Makeup done, if a bit heavier than normal, she was ready for a night on the town. And dammit, if her date didn't want to get laid tonight, she'd find someone who did.

* * *

The two men watched her walk to her car, coat over her arm. It was cool out, but they knew she hated to drive with the long wool coat on. It wasn't until she walked under the parking lot lights that either of them said a word.

"Oh my God, what the hell is that she's wearing?" Leo gaped out the window.

Max growled. "Or not wearing. Where the fuck did she get that?"

"I don't know, but I wanna know why we've never gotten to see her in it."

Max felt his cock rise at the sight of Adele climbing into her little two-door sedan. As she sat, the hem of her dress rode up and he saw the edge of her thigh highs glitter in the lamplight.

Thigh highs? How the hell did they miss her wearing those? She was a pantyhose kind of girl.

"I'd be willing to bet our little lady is going to do her best to get lucky tonight."

"To hell with that noise." Leo reached for the door handle. "I'm gonna grab her and put her ass back in that house. If she wants to wear those clothes, she can wear them for us. Before we rip them off her."

Max locked the door before Leo could open it. "No, Leo. That's not the way, and you know it."

"Well, subtle didn't work either, did it, Mr. Know-It-All?"

Max ignored his partner's sarcasm. He knew Leo was as frustrated as he was. "No, subtle didn't work, and neither will force. So tonight we take the bull by the horns and go for it. No more dancing around the subject. No more teasing. Tonight she learns what it means to be in our sights."

Leo turned his body completely to face his lover, a smile twitching at the corner of his lips. "Okay, Romeo, tell me what we're going to do."

Chapter Five

Adele sat down with a sigh. If she'd known wearing so few clothes would get even *her* this much attention, she would have tried it earlier. Although she wasn't sure she wanted all the kind of attention she'd been getting.

"Damn, girl, you are popular tonight."

Adele sipped her Diet Coke and smiled at her cousin. Neither of their dates had shown up, but they'd decided to hell with them; their goal was to have a good time tonight. Adele hadn't sat down for more than a couple minutes at a time. She didn't know if it was the short skirt or the low-cut top, but she felt like the pretty girl at the prom tonight.

In fact, she'd almost forgotten the insufferable men she was in love with. The little shits that tried to teach her a lesson about drinking too much.

How dare they? It wasn't like she drank that much normally. Hell, it was probably the first time in five years she'd gotten really smashed. And those bastards had to call her on it.

It made no sense, but she didn't know why else they would have done it. Her mother had done some stupid things under the influence of alcohol, and Adele had made them promise a long time ago to keep her in check.

Screw it. She took another sip of her soda. Now wasn't the time to worry about them. Now she just needed to concentrate on having fun.

"May I have this dance?"

Dammit. "How the hell did you find me?" She wasn't polite about it.

"Our secret." Max smiled and held out his hand. Adele debated turning away and ignoring him, but he wasn't the one who had pissed her off this evening. When she turned to say something to Sarah, she saw Leo already leaning over her cousin's shoulder, chatting her up as he pulled over a chair from a neighboring table to sit in. Max was the lesser of two evils. At least at this moment he was.

She let Max tug her to the dance floor, following reluctantly. As soon as he had her in the middle of the floor, he pulled her to him and started to dance.

Adele loved to dance; she always had. As part of their wellness program for the company, the guys had arranged ballroom dance classes last summer. They consisted of twelve weeks of classes for any employee and their significant other. It had been a big hit, and most of the crew still mentioned it as a fun and unexpected perk.

She, of course, hadn't wanted to go, as she didn't have a partner, but they'd insisted she do so. They'd needed someone to partner with and weren't about to put another female employee in a potentially uncomfortable situation. So she'd gone, and she'd been in heaven one night a week for twelve weeks. So many of the ballroom dances were so sexy and erotic, it was hard not to feel something more for your partner. In her case, it had been impossible. She'd already been in love with them.

They started to move and Adele lost herself in the beat of the music. It was perfect for a rumba.

"So, where's your date?" Max asked. His thoughts obviously ran the same way as he began the steps they'd learned in class.

"He's not here."

"I can see that. Where is he?"

Adele moved out, debating lying to him, but figured why bother. It wasn't like this was a pity dance, she'd been getting invites all night. When they came back together, she answered him. "He didn't show."

"That must be disappointing."

"Not really, I'm still having fun."

"Really?"

She glared at him. "Yes, really. I don't need a man to have fun, Max. And anyway, I've barely had a chance to sit down. I've been asked to dance more often tonight than I can ever remember."

"It's that damn outfit." He practically growled the response.

She smiled. "Yes, it is. Why? Don't you like it?" She twirled out, moving her hips to the beat.

He pulled her against him, hard. Their hips moved together this time, in perfect sync. Either Max had taken to carrying a gun in his pocket, or the man was excited. What had he and Leo been doing before they came in? Or was there someone here who had turned him on? Glancing quickly around, she wondered who it was.

She had to remind herself sometimes that they were bi, not dead. A good-looking guy, or girl, was just as capable of turning them on as for any other married couple. It was who they went home to that mattered.

"I didn't say that."

"So you like it, then."

"It's a bit revealing."

A half turn had her back to his front and she placed her backside against him. "You think?" she asked innocently before wiggling her ass against him. She crouched to the ground and then wiggled back up. What good was a sexy man if she couldn't irritate him as much as he irritated her?

He turned her, fast. "You know it is."

"Oh well, maybe I decided I deserved some fun." She swung her hips from side to side and arched back slightly. She'd be damned if she didn't enjoy every bit of this dance.

"You have fun with me and Leo."

Smiling, she shook her head as she moved in close enough to whisper, "Oh, but that's a different kind of fun. I'm gonna get laid tonight if it kills me."

Max opened his mouth to respond, but the music ended on an upward burst of volume, so she didn't hear him. Blowing him a kiss, she left him on the dance floor without looking back.

Adele barely got ten feet from him before a tall cowboy tilted his hat and asked her for the next dance. Glancing back at Max, she grinned and agreed readily.

The cowboy led her into a simple two-step as a popular song began.

"How well do you know that man you were just dancing with, ma'am?"

Adele looked up, startled. "We're friends. Close friends. Why? Are you the morals police?" Adele knew she hadn't done anything wrong, but there were some people who would be offended by some of her moves with Max. Not that she really cared what this stranger thought, but it seemed a strange beginning to a conversation.

"Do you trust him?"

Adele's brow furrowed. "Excuse me…"

"Tex."

Of course. "Tex, but what business is it of yours?"

"Well, ma'am, he and his buddy have been eyeing you from the other side of the bar for the last forty minutes before they joined you, and they didn't look happy."

Adele's head whipped in their direction and she saw the glare that was on both their faces.

"Kind of how they're looking now."

"They're friends. They were just worried because I was supposed to be on a blind date tonight." They'd been watching her for nearly an hour and she'd never seen them? Where the hell had they been hiding?

"Ma'am, you may think of them as just friends, but I'll tell you this, they definitely think of you as more."

"And how would you know this?"

Tex smiled. "Well, I could tell you I'm a cop and make my living reading people, which I am and do. And I could tell you that the only time I see men look at women like that is when they have something the men want, which is true.

"But to be completely honest, I heard them back at the bar planning how to get you home and at their mercy."

"Excuse me?"

"Their words, sugar. They talked about how you weren't gonna get away this time."

Adele blushed. What must this man think of her, that two men would plot to have her at their mercy. Then she realized what he had said. The boys wanted her. They were trying to figure a way to have her. That made no sense. Shit, nothing about this crazy weekend had made sense, why should it start now?

"Now, I'm not one to pass judgment if that's what you want. It's a free country and all that. But if it's not what you want, all you have to do is say the word, and I'll make sure those boys don't bother you again."

"But you don't even know me."

"My mama would kill me if I ever walked away from a woman in trouble."

Adele stared over his shoulder blindly for a long moment without responding. "No, they don't mean me harm. I've known them for years. They would never do anything to hurt me." She shook her head. "And anyway, how do I know you aren't putting me on? This doesn't make any sense; they've never made a move or anything like that. They're just friends."

"Well, your friends want to take it to the next level. So it looks like the ball's in your court."

A shiver of anticipation ran up her spine. It was what she'd dreamed about for what seemed like forever. But now that it was a possibility, could she really do it?

Tex smiled mischievously. "If it makes a difference, my sister is in a triad relationship up north, and she says she's never been happier."

Adele raised an eyebrow. Tex shrugged his shoulders. "Hey, just cause I'm a country bumpkin doesn't mean I don't know things."

The music was winding down, and they were in sight of her table when he pulled her close. He reached into his pocket and took out a business card.

"This is my card. I'm giving it to you for three reasons. One, if you need help, you can call me; two, if you don't need me, give it to that hot little redhead sitting with you; and three"—he folded it lengthwise and slipped it down between her breasts, grinning evilly as he glanced quickly at the table—"a little bit of jealousy might get those chickenshits off their asses and get them to claim their woman."

With a kiss on her cheek and a wink, he walked back onto the dance floor and was lost in the crowd.

Adele stood there, bemused, unsure of what just happened.

"Who was that?" Leo's voice snapped her out of her trancelike state as he pulled her around to face him.

Adele opened her mouth to snap at him to let go of her and remind him it was none of his business. Then Tex's words flitted back through her mind. If they did want her, then this sudden possessiveness was jealousy, pure and simple. Their behavior last night, as well as over the past few months could be explained away by the fact they were testing her. Trying to see what she wanted without actually coming out and asking her.

She didn't know if she should feel touched or be angry. How the hell they could be stupid enough to not know that she wanted them was beyond her. But then, she hadn't known they wanted her, either.

So she guessed that made them all a bunch of fools, didn't it?

"Adele. Who was that?" Leo released her without being asked. He was obviously trying to keep his cool as he ran his hand through his hair.

"Huh? Oh, just a guy. I don't know."

"Then why the hell did he put his hand down your dress?" Max came up on her other side and demanded an answer. He, on the other hand, wasn't doing anything to temper his mood.

Screw it. They wanted to make a scene; she'd help them. Only it wasn't going to be the kind of scene they were expecting. "Maybe he saw something he liked."

"And you let him do it?"

Adele's eyes narrowed. Armed with knowledge she didn't have ten minutes before, she opted to address his jealousy rather than his anger. "Well, Max, I told you my plans for the night. He just moved to the top of the list."

"Like hell."

"Well, unless you have someone else in mind for the job"—she looked him up and down, perusing his beautiful body suggestively—"he might very well be the one."

Before she could complete her turn away from the men, she was pulled back and forced to face Max yet again. She opened her mouth to yell at him this time, but it was immediately covered by his.

She'd been kissed by Max before. Soft, gentle kisses like you would give a friend or relative. Nothing like this. This was harsh, demanding, and burned her to her core.

She tasted desire, lust, and need in the way his mouth raked across hers in a kiss designed to stake a claim once and for all.

"You belong to us, Adele Waters. It's time you get that through your head." Adele was so surprised by Max's actions, she barely noticed when he grabbed her coat and wrapped it around her body before forcing her out of the bar. Leo followed close behind.

Adele had recovered her sanity enough by the time they got outside to think about fighting Max, but she realized it would be counterproductive. She'd egged him on, given what Tex had told her. If she'd gotten a slightly stronger reaction than she'd intended, it was no more than she deserved.

Instead, she tried to be reasonable. "Max, would you please let go of me?"

"No."

"Max."

"Not now, Adele. You're coming home with us. We'll wait until Leo gets home and then the three of us have to talk."

"But—"

"I'd do what he says, Adele." Leo spoke for the first time since Max had kissed her. "When we get home is time enough for explanations. Just do what he asks."

Adele once again debated arguing what they were doing to her. Manhandling her wasn't the way to her heart, but she couldn't find it within her to be truly mad at them. Instead, she was mad at herself. She knew Max was easy to get riled up, and she'd deliberately baited him, hoping for a reaction. So much for thinking he would be calmer than Leo earlier tonight.

So she let him put her into her own car with little more than a nod to Leo. He was right; now wasn't the time for arguments. Better to wait until they got back to the boys' place and Max had a chance to calm down.

* * *

Fuck, fuck, fuck! Max berated himself. This was not the way he'd planned it. Goddamn his temper.

Max willed himself not to look at the woman in the passenger seat, sure he'd see her cowering away from him. And that was the last thing he wanted: Adele scared of him.

Dammit! Wasn't he the one who was telling Leo earlier that they needed to be calm, take it easy? And now look at him. He'd dragged her out of the damn bar like a fucking Neanderthal. He was surprised no one had stopped them on the way out.

What must she think of him now? He'd lost all chance of getting her to trust him and the love he had for her. Hell, after that performance he wasn't sure he'd trust himself ever again.

Leo had to be infuriated with him right now, and he was fully justified if he was. Max had fucked up, pure and simple. He'd lost them the only thing they wanted other than each other.

Max closed his eyes in agony. If Leo still wanted Adele, and she'd have him, Max would bow out. It would destroy him, but he wasn't going to deny Leo anything. He loved him, and if he needed Adele, so be it.

He opened his mouth to say something, anything. To apologize for what he'd done at the bar, but the words stuck behind the lump in his throat. How the hell could he apologize for treating her like that? Better to just keep his mouth shut and let her cool down. Knowing Adele, she was infuriated right now, as well as scared. Back at the house, Leo would be a good buffer. Maybe he'd be able to salvage something of their friendship.

Chapter Six

When they pulled up to the house, Adele watched Max get out of the car and meet Leo as he pulled up behind them. He had followed them in Max's car while Max had driven hers.

Her door opened, and Leo held out his hand to her. It wasn't like she really needed the help to get out, but she took it and let him lead her to the house. There was no sign of Max.

Probably kicking himself in the ass, she thought. Max never liked to lose his temper, and he was probably as surprised at his behavior as she was.

"So, are we going to talk or not?" Adele tossed her coat on the living room couch before plopping her body down beside it. She knew that the guys preferred the family room in the back of the house, but she was damned if she was going to make any of this more comfortable for them.

First they made her night miserable last night, teasing and harassing her. Then they let her wake up in bed with them, sandwiched between them like a piece of meat. And finish it off with tonight, plotting a way to get her home and have their way with her? Not to mention the fact Max had been an asshole.

"Why don't we wait until Max gets inside?"

"Of course, we don't want to do anything without Max, do we? And of course, he didn't want to do any talking without you. So let's just sit here and wait for Max to calm down from his little hissy fit at the bar, and we'll talk like three normal adults."

Adele told herself to calm down, but all of a sudden she had started to get annoyed. Who did they think they were, treating her like this? Who cared what they wanted? She had a mind, too, dammit, and she was perfectly capable of making her own decisions.

"You know what, Leo, I think I'm gonna head home. I'm not in the mood to play games with the two of you tonight."

"It's not a game, Adele." Max's voice came from the front door. It was harsh and ragged, as though he was ripping every word out of his throat.

"Then what is it? What the hell is going on with the two of you?" She knew what Tex had told her, but she needed to hear it from them. Needed to hear the truth of it, not to mention the why of it. "You guys have been acting strangely for weeks, and this weekend is the final straw."

She turned to Leo. "*You* corner me in the supply room and feel me up." She turned back to Max. "And then when I get here last night, *you* lay a kiss on me that threw me for a loop. Then all freaking night you both spend your time rubbing up against me, touching me, stroking my ass, my hips, any part of my body you could touch.

"Not to even mention where the hell I woke up. And I know damn good and well that I did not climb into your bed of my own free will. So, if it's not a game, then what the hell is it?"

"We wanted to talk to you calmly about this, convince you it was the right thing, but everything got out of hand." Leo reached across for her hands, holding on to them tightly. "Last night we planned to broach the subject, but thanks to the bitch Krista, those plans flew out the window.

"And then you had to go and have a date tonight."

"I'm a single woman. I have a right to go on a date, you know."

Leo nodded. "We know. That's why it pissed us off so much. Because if we'd had our way, you wouldn't be a single woman. You wouldn't be on the lookout for Mr. Right."

"Or Mr. Right Now," Max added sullenly from the doorway.

Adele bit back a smile. By the time she'd gotten to the bar, she'd cooled down from her argument with Leo and had changed her mind, she hadn't really had any intention of going home with anyone tonight, despite what she'd told Max, but they didn't need to know that.

Suddenly, the anger that was so high seconds ago just disappeared. It was as though it flowed out of her body easily, leaving her empty and needing.

She loved Max and Leo and would give anything to be with them. The fact they wanted her, too, should be something that was accepted joyfully and celebrated. Not something yelled in the middle of an argument.

She realized they were scared too. It didn't matter that they had each other. If they wanted her, then they had every right to be as worried about it as she did.

Her voice softened as her gaze flew between the two of them. "Does this have anything to do with what Tex told me he overheard?"

"Who the hell is Tex?" Max still hadn't let go of his temper from earlier, obviously.

Adele looked up at him. "The man you objected to me dancing with. The man that slipped me his business card because he's a cop and was worried that the two men at my table had been spending the better part of an hour talking about me and plotting ways to get me home and, I believe his exact words were, 'at their mercy.'"

Max swore. Leo flushed.

"It's not the way it sounds, Adele." Leo tried to reassure her.

"It's not? You don't want me in bed with the two of you?"

"No! Yes!"

Max walked toward her, not saying a word until he stopped less than six inches from her and pulled her to her feet. "Yes. We want you in bed with us. We want to fuck your brains out and ruin you for all other men. We want you to join us as part of our relationship. Be the part you were always meant to be."

"Are you looking for a one-night thing?"

Leo stood up. "Fuck no. We want you forever."

"What the hell took you so long?"

It took a moment for her words to register. She could see indecision and confusion in their faces.

"Do you want to make love to me?" she asked them softly.

"With every breath I take," Max whispered the words.

"More than anything." Leo nodded.

"Then please, make love to me. Both of you. Here, now. Make me yours."

Max was quicker on the uptake than Leo, because he pulled her tight against him and slammed his mouth against hers. The kiss was hard and voracious, much as it had been at the bar, but more intense. She opened her lips on a sigh of contentment and he thrust his tongue into her mouth.

She tasted the beer he had been drinking at the bar as he caressed her tongue with his. The kiss had started out quick, but it seemed Max wasn't about to rush it as he stroked and caressed her mouth, tasting her as she tasted him. He wrapped his hands around her head, fingers weaving in her hair as he held her against him, making love to her mouth. Fireworks burst in her brain, all thought gone as she just let herself go and *felt*.

Low groans reached her ears, but they came from behind her. Suddenly she felt heat from behind as Leo came up and sandwiched her between them. Oh God.

This time she moaned when Leo grabbed her hips and pressed up against her. She felt his cock at the small of her back, hard and long, and she knew now, all for her.

Slowly, Max eased away from the kiss and stared into her eyes for what seemed like an eternity.

"I love you, Adele Waters. With all of my heart."

Emotions and feelings she was hard-pressed to name flooded her heart and soul. Love for him, for both of them, ran through her body like a river of fire as tingles ran up and down her spine. Her stomach fluttered as his words penetrated deep within her being, and she found herself unable to respond intelligently.

Before she could think of what to say, how to tell him she felt the same way, Leo turned her to face him and whispered, "My turn." He took her mouth with his.

Whoever said a kiss was just a kiss had never been kissed by two different men they were in love with. Leo's was gentle where Max's had been firm, but they were different in more than just that. Leo tasted smoother, softer, but caressed her heart just as deeply with just that kiss.

When he pulled away from her, he, too, looked her in the eyes as he gave her the promise. "I will love you till the day I die."

Tears pricked Adele's eyes. This couldn't be happening; this wasn't real. It was her dream come true, and she didn't know how to handle it. She opened her mouth to say something, what, she didn't know, but Leo placed his fingers over her lips and shushed her.

"Don't say anything now. Just tell us if this is what you want. Truly want. If you want to be with both of us, together. Here and now."

"Yes." It came out a whisper, a mere breath of sound, but they both heard it. Leo smiled gently, and Max scooped her up in his arms and walked to the stairs.

"Put me down, Max. I want to walk."

"No way in hell, woman. I'm not letting you out of my arms until I get you naked in bed and completely satisfied."

Warmth cooled in her belly and shot straight to her core at his words. It sounded perfectly fine to her.

He brought her to the master bedroom, the same room she'd woken up in this morning, only this time, she truly felt like she belonged, like she was wanted here.

When he walked through the door, she looked around, this time with a totally different viewpoint than she'd had in the past. She'd helped the guys pick out the decor, knowing the earthen tones were relaxing and suited them perfectly, but tonight she had a different perception of it.

Tonight she saw the softness of the bed she would soon share, the comfort of the coverlet that Leo was pulling back. She smelled the mingling of their scents in the air and was enveloped in the warmth of their private retreat. She felt like she was home.

He placed her on the bed and stood back to stare at her a moment. Max on one side of the bed, Leo on the other. They stood there, looking at her, and she began to get nervous. Were they having second thoughts?

"Do you know how long we've dreamed of having you here in this bed with us? Looking disheveled and as though you'd been kissed soundly? As though you'd been made love to and were replete from pleasure?"

Leo's words sent her body trembling in anticipation. She tried to swallow over the lump in her throat as she watched the two of them strip off their shirts to stand there, bare chests staring her in the face.

Max sat down beside her and turned her head to him. "Leo and I have plotted, planned, schemed, and devised what we would do to you once we got you here."

Her pussy dripped with desire, spasming as pictures ran through her head. Things she'd only dreamed about. Things she'd only read about.

"I've never…"

Max smiled. "Been with two men. We know. But we also know you've read a lot about it." She felt heat rush to her face at the thought of the erotic romance books they both knew she read. His smile turned into a grin that suddenly had her very worried. And very excited.

Leo sat down on her other side. "Just relax and enjoy." He turned his head and looked at Max. The two of them kissed above her. Adele had always found the love they had for each other incredibly sexy. Every time they touched each other she would feel a tingle of desire and need. And now it was multiplied tenfold. When they parted, she finally understood the love that shone in their eyes encompassed her as well. They wanted her, loved her, just the same as she did them. Adele closed her eyes, unable to face the evidence that had been staring her in the face for so long. Evidence she'd been a fool to miss.

She felt hands at her feet, and her shoes were gone. Hands massaged her soles, soothing away the pain of dancing with the high heels and sending shocks of pleasure through her body. The hands gently worked their way up her legs, erasing her tensions of the day and building more intimate ones. Tingles spread out from their touch, to her toes and up to the crown of her head, bringing her body alive to every sensation they had to offer her.

Adele bit her lip to keep herself from moaning again when the hands reached the top of her thigh highs. A whimper escaped her throat, though, at the hint of a caress when the nylons were rolled down her legs.

"We thought about taking you with your heels and hose on. But this time is for all of us. A slow lovemaking session that you will remember always. We'll save that as a treat for later."

Adele's breath caught in her throat at Leo's words.

"Will you help me take this off of you, sweetheart?" Leo tugged at her dress. She nodded quickly and sat up to allow him access to the zipper. Sooner than she realized, she lay there in only her panties, both men once again staring at her. Instinctively, she moved to cover herself with her arms, but a crooked brow from Max stopped her almost immediately. When he shook his head once, she lowered her arms and laid them at her side.

"You are beautiful, Adele. Perfect in every way."

When Adele opened her mouth to protest, Leo placed his fingers against her lips.

"To us, you are perfect. We don't care what society says, you know that, darlin'. You are perfect to us, and perfect for us."

Warmth spread through her body at his words as once again he kissed her gently, hands sliding up and down, gradually allowing her to relax into the moment.

One of his hands was replaced by one of Max's, and she tensed for a moment before forcing herself to relax. These were her men. Max and Leo, and she'd dreamed of this forever. She wanted them.

They seemed to sense her uncertainty, moving their hands no farther than her arms, calming her like a nervous filly.

Each bent down to kiss her softly, stroking her hair as they murmured words of love and encouragement. Gradually she lost herself in their touch, in their words, wanting more of what they had to give.

She arched herself into their arms, moaning as she begged for more.

Leo caressed the top of her chest with the back of his hand, her body slowly getting used to his touch. Max followed her arm down to her hand, massaging and stroking all the way before he linked fingers with hers.

Max's lips never left hers as Leo kissed her neck, her shoulder, working his way down to her chest. His hand cupped her breast, squeezing it, stroking it, as his mouth headed to her nipple.

Max's hand shifted to her stomach and drew lazy circles on her torso. Sharp sparks of electricity and need shot through her body at their touches, setting her skin on fire. She felt ready to detonate; each stroke, each touch, one more sensation for her mind to follow and lose itself in.

Hands were everywhere, caressing her, stroking her. Her entire top half was alive with sensations as electric impulses shot from her skin to their hands, her body alive with their touch.

Adele moaned more than once as they continued their slow torture of her.

Leo finally reached her nipple, stretching his tongue out to lick it quickly. Adele gasped at the cool, wet stroke, her nipple perking up to attention. She saw Leo's small smile before he took the bud into his mouth.

Lips, tongue, teeth, they all tortured her breast as he tasted her. Zings of pleasure started at her nipple, shot straight to her core, and then back out the top of her head.

Max had moved and now caressed and nibbled on her legs. He lay between them, moving up toward where she wanted his touch more than she wanted her next breath. His hands grasped the sides of her panties and slowly he pulled them down her legs. He stroked the outside of her thighs, moving his hands to the inside of them and she moved into his touch, urging him on without words.

A soft chuckle met her ears as he pushed her legs farther apart.

"I've waited too long, my love. You're not going to rush me." His words blew across her mons, a whisper of breath that popped up goose bumps along her body.

Adele was soaked. She had been since she'd learned what the men wanted, and every second with them just left her wetter, dripping with need.

She couldn't see Max, could only feel him as he stroked her pussy with one finger and she felt liquid run down the crack of her ass as he found her outer folds.

She moaned at his touch, wanting—needing—more.

Leo bit at her nipple, and suddenly her attention was back on him as he lifted his head up and grinned at her. "We're both here, darlin'. Don't be forgetting about me."

As if she could. He reached across her torso and took her other nipple in his mouth as he continued to tease and pinch at the first one, moist and erect from his previous attentions.

Max was obviously not to be undone, as he blew his breath across her core and used two fingers to part her outer lips before teasing her inner ones with another finger. He stroked her up and down and back up. "I've wanted to taste this pussy for so long, I know it will be as sweet as the rest of you."

Adele tensed, caught between sensations: Leo sucking and caressing her breasts, Max breathing on her pussy. Adele arched her body into Leo's mouth at the same time she jerked away from the coolness of Max's breath. But when Leo sucked hard, shots of pleasant pain shot through her breast, and she shoved her pussy toward Max, begging him silently for more.

Instead of tasting her as promised, he slid his finger inside her, pushing against her walls.

Adele had been without a man for too long, and even frequent sessions with her toys hadn't prepared her for this. She was tight, and his finger filled her as her body sucked at it hungrily. She thrashed her head and next thing she knew his tongue had found her clit and was playing with it, teasing her as he flicked and pressed against it.

Leo left her breast and kissed her hungrily, swallowing her gasps of pleasure as Max made love to her with his hands and tongue. A second and then a third finger joined his first as he pumped at her, sucking at her, nibbling at her. Her orgasm wasn't far off; she felt it building. The tension grew, heaviness overcoming her body while every muscle tightened sharply. Adele struggled for breath, short, quick gasps all that would come as her body quickly released, tightened, and released again, ripping screams from her throat. Leo swallowed her sounds, holding her tight while her body shook and thrashed in response to her release as the world as she knew it blasted apart in ecstasy.

Adele was aware of Leo stroking her back, murmuring sounds into her ear as her body calmed down, going limp.

She felt Max work his way up her body, kissing her gently until he lay by her side. "She okay?"

"Oh, yeah. But I think it's been a while for her."

Adele thought about protesting their talking about her as though she weren't even there, but chose not to. Instead she concentrated on getting her breathing and pulse to return to normal.

Max snickered. "She's ready for you, lover. But first, how about I give you a taste of her juices."

Max and Leo reached for each other once again, lips meeting in a kiss that even Adele felt the heat from. Max held his lover against him as he let Leo taste the juices that were still on his lips and tongue.

"Oh, that truly is ambrosia," Leo whispered when Max finally let him go. They both looked down at her, and her heart jumped into her throat, his corny wording sending warmth through her body.

"We know you haven't been with anyone for a while, darlin'. And although we both want you tonight, we want to take this slow. If it's okay with you, I want to make love to you first."

Adele whimpered. She wanted both of them tonight. Now. And she told them so.

"Sh." This time it was Max who laid fingers across her lips. "Maybe later, after we're sure you can handle it, but for now, let Leo love you."

Her gaze met Max's. Love and satisfaction shone through his eyes. That and excitement. He was excited at the thought of Leo fucking her as he watched, and she didn't need the pulse in her previously sated pussy to remind her that she was, too.

She nodded her head. They both quickly stripped the rest of their clothes off. Max lay down beside her again while Leo repositioned himself between her legs. Max kissed her gently when he lay back down beside her, and she allowed herself to be lost in his touch. The sound of a wrapper being ripped open pulled her attention, but before she could remind him she was on the Pill, Leo was positioned at her lower lips, ready to push inside.

Max rolled onto his side, letting Adele see Leo as he readied himself. Max's gaze danced back and forth between his two lovers, anticipation and excitement obvious on his face.

Leo leaned back and reached out to caress Adele's pussy, and it pulsed at his light touch.

"Adele, sweetheart, I know you said you wanted this, but I need to ask one more time. Are you really sure?"

Adele felt tears at the corner of her eyes once more. The love and need that came through in Leo's voice melted her heart as she felt a burst of love for him so powerful she almost couldn't find her voice. But now wasn't the time for just a nod. She might not be able to tell him how she felt at this moment, but she would at least try. She reached out and grasped Max's hand, squeezing it, including him in her assurances.

"I've wanted the two of you for so long, it's the first thing I think of when I wake up in the morning, and the last thought before I fall asleep at night. I burn for you both, and the thought of being with the two of you without this has been tearing me apart for too long. I need you, Leo. You and Max. I need you like I need oxygen.

"Please, make love to me."

Leo closed his eyes at her words, and a smile spread across his face. When he finally opened them again, he watched her, slowly pushing into her.

Adele was no virgin. She'd had sex before. Each of her lovers had been a bit different, but essentially the same. Not even her ex-fiancé had been able to make her feel this way. When Leo entered her, he filled her completely, in a way she never knew she could be filled.

He was a perfect fit, scraping against her inner walls as he pushed through into her body. But that wasn't it. His gaze never left hers. It penetrated deep within her heart as surely as his cock penetrated her body. Max's hand tightening around hers let her know that he, too, was experiencing this moment of pure joy, pure belonging, as the three of them became one.

Once he was fully seated, Leo bent down to kiss her and then kiss Max before laughing. "It's heaven, Max. Pure heaven."

Max growled and Leo laughed as he slowly began to make love to Adele. In and out he moved, waking her body to sensations she hadn't known she was capable of feeling. Each push and pull built an excitement in her body that scared her in its intensity, the tension growing tenfold with each stroke.

Max kissed and nibbled on her body, urging her with those small murmurs he seemed so fond of, never letting his hands leave her body, finding new and interesting ways to tweak her excitement to a fever pitch.

She reached for him, wrapping her hand around his cock and squeezing. When his gaze met hers, she whispered, "I want you too."

"But, Adele."

"No, dammit, I want you too! Now. In my mouth."

Max looked at Leo, who hadn't stopped moving. He was smiling. "The lady is the boss, partner. If she wants it, you have to give it to her."

Max quickly positioned himself, placing a couple of pillows under Adele's head as she turned and told him where she wanted him.

Leo stopped moving, and instantly Adele felt bereft and turned her eyes to him.

"Get positioned, darlin', and then we will both make love to you and take you as far as you want to go."

Adele smiled and turned to see Max where she'd asked. He was kneeling at her head, his penis within easy reach of her hands and mouth. Moving her hips to remind Leo to get going, she reached for the thick, pulsing cock in front of her and brought her lips to the tip.

She darted her tongue out to taste him first and was rewarded with his gasp as she connected. She smiled and once again stuck her tongue out, only this time to truly get a taste, to lick the entire head as she savored his manly essence.

Heat warmed her hand as she grasped his smooth shaft. She moved her hand up and down as she licked and suckled, until finally she placed her lips around the head and took him fully within her mouth.

All three of them groaned as Max wrapped his hand in her long hair and Leo began to move once again.

Adele sucked and nibbled, Leo pumped and fucked, and Max moaned and flexed as the three of them pleased each other in the most intimate of ways.

Max tensed in Adele's mouth, and she felt his cock start to twitch.

"Adele, honey." Max pulled out of Adele's mouth, tugging gently on her head. "Honey, you need to stop. I'm gonna come."

Adele narrowed her eyes. She didn't want to stop. The thought of him shooting his cum down her throat filled her with a joy she could never have explained. "I want you to come in my mouth, Max." He started to shake his head, and she tugged at the cock still in her hand. "Yes, dammit. This is my fantasy, my dream. I want you in my mouth. I want to swallow you, to taste you. Please, Max."

He stroked the side of her cheek with his thumb, caressing her, and nodded. She quickly engulfed him in her mouth, her action matched by Leo as he thrust hard into her pussy. She groaned around Max's cock, and he groaned right after her. "Oh God, Adele. Yes."

Again the cock in her mouth twitched, and Max tightened his hand in her hair. She, too, was close to her own orgasm, each thrust of Leo's hips bringing her closer to the edge.

Max leaned over, reaching with his other hand and cupping her mons before sliding a finger between her lower lips. His gaze still locked on her, he flicked at her clit, once, twice, and a third time.

She groaned around him, sucking harder. Max pushed into her mouth, crying out her name. It was too much for her. Max in her mouth, his fingers on her clit. Leo in her pussy, stroking her harder, faster. Her skin prickled as though the embers from a sparkler danced across her, heightening her senses. Every second stretched to minutes, her body tightening in response before she finally exploded into a million pieces as her orgasm shot through her hard.

As she convulsed, Max groaned and he, too, came, giving her what she'd wanted all along. She swallowed his juices quickly, eager to taste her lover.

Leo moaned and he thrust into her again. "Max, Adele. Oh God, that was hot." His voice came in gasps between each thrust until, with one final push, he shouted his release as his cock pulsed within her walls.

It seemed minutes later, although more than likely had been mere seconds, when they all three lay on the bed, her cuddled between the two of them, warm and comforted, feeling as though she belonged.

She felt like they should talk about what had happened, share what they had experienced, what their expectations were for the future, but she found no energy to speak. She was perfectly content to lie there in their arms and drift off to sleep.

* * *

"Sh, you'll wake her."

"Good, maybe we can get her to join in."

The chuckle pulled her further out of her sleep, but she waited with her eyes closed to listen to what they were going to do. Grunts and groans met her ears and shivers of excitement shot through her body. She had no choice. She had to open her eyes to see what was happening.

Leo and Max were at the foot of the bed, Leo standing, Max kneeling on the floor with Leo's cock in his mouth. They were standing perpendicular to the bed, so she could see everything they were doing. With a sense of glee, she watched them please each other through her partially closed eyes.

Their love was evident in the way Leo gazed down, cupping Max's head in his hands as Max pleasured him.

"Oh God, Max. I love when you do that for me. Yes, harder. Suck me harder."

Max responded to his request, moving his head faster as he brought his longtime lover pleasure. Adele hadn't gotten a real good look at Leo's cock earlier, given the positions they had been in, but now she saw it in all its glory. It wasn't as thick as Max's, but it was long and beautiful. She could see the veins in it throbbing as Max went down on him, moving him in and out of his mouth. It glistened with Max's saliva, making her want to take it into her own mouth just as Leo was doing.

Adele's hand crept to her pussy as she watched them. She was so turned on she found herself breathing heavily, pulse speeding along. Who would have ever thought voyeurism would turn her on so much? She never knew.

Leo's gaze locked on hers, and she realized he knew she was awake as a smile spread over his face. He pumped into Max's mouth while his gaze never left her body.

Emboldened, she rolled over on her back to spread her legs and started playing with herself. One hand on a breast, the other flicking at her clit. The two of them were so hot she knew she was going to come quickly. She teased herself as she watched them continue their loving.

The novelty of watching the two of them together, making love, drove her excitement higher, her body growing rigid as her orgasm neared. Small ripples ran through her muscles as her hand moved faster over her pussy, the other pulling and pinching at her nipple. Her orgasm slammed into her with all the subtlety of a freight train, sending her thrusting against her own hands with a cry. Her shout of pleasure was drowned out by Leo's as he came in Max's mouth.

"Oh, darlin', that was beautiful."

Adele looked up and realized that Leo was still looking at her, talking to her as he stroked Max's hair before he got down on his knees and kissed Max deeply. "Thank you, lover. That was wonderful."

"She saw, didn't she?"

Adele heard Max's whisper, and she blushed.

"Oh yeah, and I would say she definitely approved of it."

Leo raised his gaze and looked at her. Her hand was still between her legs, and she pulled back, shy all of a sudden. The smile that he gave her heated her body all over again.

His eyes narrowed, and he crawled up over the bed toward her. With a tiny squeal, she tried to scoot back, but he grabbed her ankle and wouldn't let her go anywhere. He planted himself between her legs.

"Mmm, I didn't get a taste of this earlier." He inhaled the scent of her mound deeply. "Max got it all. I think it's my turn."

"But aren't you tired?" Her voice squeaked as he slowly opened her lips.

"From being pleasured by Max? Hell no, I can go for hours yet." And with that, he buried his face between her legs and proceeded to show her how much energy he really did have left.

Adele had never considered herself a very sexual woman before. Sex had never been anything spectacular. It was a way to scratch an itch, pleasurable, but nothing to write home about.

But she'd never had lovers like Max and Leo. She hadn't known what she had been missing.

Leo licked at her, drinking her juices, which were spread across lips and thighs. His tongue and moans of appreciation had her fast approaching yet another orgasm. For a man who hadn't eaten pussy in over seven years, he sure as hell hadn't forgotten anything.

He tasted her, his fingers slowly sliding into her, massaging her, stretching her, as he pumped at her slowly first, then harder and faster.

"His tongue is absolute magic, isn't it?" Max asked at her side.

She'd forgotten about him for a minute as her body responded to Leo.

"I love when he pleases me with his mouth. Feel the way it moves against your skin. He uses his tongue like another cock, strong and stiff, but soft and gentle when he wants it to be." As Max talked to her, he slowly stroked her torso with one hand, the other running through Leo's hair again.

He bent down and whispered in Leo's ear loud enough for Adele to hear. "Tongue fuck her, Leo. Make her scream for you, lover."

Adele had been on the edge of an orgasm, eager to reach the pinnacle, but when Leo switched motions, he left her hanging.

"Goddamn it, Leo, no!"

Max's chuckle infuriated her as much as Leo's soft smile and shake of his head.

"You little shit, you know how close I was. Why'd you stop?" She gritted her teeth, screaming in frustration when he moved. Her body screamed out for release; it had been so close.

Before she could protest further, he adjusted himself, doing as Max ordered. He slid his wet fingers out of her pussy and replaced them with his tongue. He speared her with it quickly as he pulled her lips apart, getting into her as close and hard as he could.

She watched down the line of her body, watched him as he ate at her, munching on her as though he were starving. Tingles started anew, her toes curling into the sheets as her body responded.

One of his hands, wet from her juices, crept around to her anus and pressed against it gently. She'd never had anal intercourse before, never even had anyone touch her there before. She'd always been afraid. But who better than someone that practiced it regularly to introduce her to those pleasures?

His eyes swept her face, as though asking for permission before he went further. Adele nodded quickly, and he slid his wet finger in to the first knuckle. At first there was only pressure, and then a satisfying sense of being filled. Not completely, but in a way she'd never experienced before. She wiggled her hips, urging him on. Both mouth and hand.

Slowly, the finger eased in a bit more. She threw her head back, closing her eyes as she felt the sensations run through her body.

Her eyes popped open when she felt warm hands on her knees, pushing her legs wide. Max smiled from where he straddled Leo's back, forcing her legs apart and up toward her chest, leaving her wide open for Leo's attention

The angle of her waist changed, and Leo's tongue and finger went into her deeper and harder. A second finger joined his first in her ass, and he pushed into her as he fucked her with his mouth. His second hand was busy flicking at her clit, sliding the hood back as he played with her.

The sight of the two of them between her legs and the reactions they wrenched from her body were too much as she felt herself reach a crest again. Her nerve endings fired all at once, pinpricks exploding on her skin as she went flying over and screamed her release.

Still Leo didn't stop; he kept at her, sucking, eating, pumping. Bringing her over again and again. Fireworks went off in her brain, bringing conscious thought to a halt as all she could do was ride the wave of ecstasy that engulfed her body. Her head thrashed and her body rocked, bringing Leo closer and tighter against her body, driving her further over the edge until finally she screamed for him to stop.

"No more, please, Leo!"

With one more long lick, he pulled out of her and kissed her mons gently. An exhausted sigh was all the reaction she could muster.

Her breathing was ragged, hiccuping as the two of them massaged her legs that still shook from her orgasms. Oh, good Lord. Who'd have ever thought it would be this wonderful?

"I want you, Adele. Please." Max's voice penetrated her postorgasmic haze.

Adele looked down, thinking they'd just had her for what seemed like hours, although if she were to be fair, it was Leo that got the actual having. Well, sort of.

Max sat back, watching her closely. His cock stood at attention, ready for action. She'd forgotten he'd pleased Leo before Leo'd pleasured her. He had to be aching.

Leo reached for Max and stroked him softly. "If you aren't up to it, Adele, I don't mind taking Max's cock." He tightened his grip, and Adele saw Max's eyes close as he shuddered and moaned. Did Max want Leo? Hell, she couldn't blame him if he did.

Max put his hand over Leo's as he smiled to his lover. "I love your body, Leo, but today I truly want Adele if she's up to it."

If she was up to it? Hell yeah. That was probably one of the best things about being a woman: she knew she could come again and again and still be ready for more. Although, looking at Leo's cock, he didn't seem to have a problem getting up quickly either.

"Yes, please." She realized she wanted Max inside her like she'd had Leo earlier. She wanted to feel him fucking her with that thick, glorious cock.

Leo reached for the condoms at the side of the bed and ripped one open. Without asking, he reverently placed one on Max's cock. He tapped the tip gently before warning her.

"Go gentle on him, darlin'. He's ready to burst."

Gentle? He had to be freaking kidding. She didn't think she had much energy in her to be more than gentle.

She needn't have worried. Despite his obvious need, Max seemed as eager as her to take it slow and gentle. He eased into her, seating himself fully and not moving for a minute.

"Someday, I want to experience this without a rubber. I want to feel your walls against me, tightening as they are right now, feel your wet heat against me as we make love again."

All thoughts of a future or the meaning of his words escaped her, though, as he began to move. Slowly, he pulled out and then moved back into her just as slow. In and out he went, making love to her as though she were the most precious thing to him. The glow in his eyes as his gaze locked onto hers warmed her, even as his movements heated her to the core.

Leo lay beside her, caressing her hair, his other hand clasped with hers as Max continued to make love to her tenderly. The orgasm, when it came, rolled over her in gentle, soothing waves, bringing her to tears when she was overwhelmed by emotions and feelings.

Chapter Seven

Adele woke to a strange sensation. She was warm, very warm, but there was something else. Awareness came back to her with a snap as she realized what it was. Max and Leo were with her, cuddling her. And one of them was very aroused.

She wiggled her ass over the cock pressed against her, sure that whoever it was must still be asleep.

She was wrong.

He lifted her leg gently and slid his cock into her wet pussy as though he were sliding it home.

Adele opened her eyes and saw Max watching her as Leo fucked her from behind. The smile on his face sent shivers down her back, meeting up with the shivers the stroking cock sent up her spine.

"Good morning, beautiful."

"Mor—" Adele stopped midword as Leo thrust particularly forcefully. "Morning." She finished once she could breathe again.

Max glanced behind her. "I see you already have her going this morning, lover."

The deep chuckle that came from behind her told her Leo was extremely satisfied with himself. "Don't blame me. She started it."

A gasp of outrage escaped her lips, and Max laughed. Before she could say anything, he kissed her deeply, making her forget entirely what she had been about to say. His hand crept up to her breast and he kneaded it gently.

When he was done with the kiss, he stretched down to take her nipple in his mouth and suckle it.

Leo turned her head toward him and took his own morning kiss as he continued making love to her. She grasped the back of his head with one hand, and Max's with the other as the men showered attention on her.

Oh God, a woman could get used to this. She realized she should be sore, but she was far from it, feeling more alive and alert than she had in a long time. Her men were gentle if demanding lovers, and she'd experienced nothing but pleasure with them.

A sharp thrust by Leo pulled her attention back to the moment at hand and reminded her of what he was doing. "Ouch, darlin'. I got the distinct impression you weren't interested."

Adele smiled. "Oh no, far from it."

He must have taken that as permission to work harder, because that's exactly what he did as he grasped hold of her hips and pushed into her. Max wasn't idle. He reached down and flicked her clit in tandem with Leo's strokes.

Her body tingled and throbbed as her men continued to make love to her. Somehow they knew what buttons to push, knew how to get her revving quickly. Prickles of excitement ran over her skin in waves as the orgasm crashed through her body. Breathless and shivering, she went over, moans wrenched from her throat.

Leo pulled out of her slowly, still hard.

"But—" She started to ask him why he had pulled out, but Max once again silenced her by placing his fingers on her lips.

"Together this time, love. We want you together."

Adele's brow crinkled. They'd had her all night, together. What did they mean? And then it struck her. "I've never done anal before."

"Do you want to try? Do you trust us?"

A thought occurred to her. "Or do you want to, um, do each other? Oh, shit. I mean..." Oh God, would she ever get this straight? She was blushing so hard, she felt her face heat.

Max brushed her hair from her eyes. "We want to be inside you at the same time. But only if you're willing." Leo had wrapped his arm around her and held her tight against his chest, apparently willing to let Max speak for the both of them.

Was she willing? She'd had all kinds of fantasies fulfilled last night. Ones she hadn't even realized she'd had before. What would it be like for the two of them to be inside her at once? At the same time?

Her pussy tightened at the idea. It was so decadent and so wonderful, she knew she couldn't pass it up. And not just the act itself, the fact that it was with the two of them. The men she had come to lust after and love over the last few years.

Adele nodded, not sure her voice wouldn't crack if she said anything. Leo pulled her more tightly against him for a moment and kissed the top of her head before stretching to reach into the bedside table.

"He's getting the lube," Max assured her.

Understanding dawned on Adele and she looked down, embarrassed. This was what she wanted, but for some reason the basic mechanics of it made her close her eyes for just a minute.

Grabbing her courage in her hands and taking a deep breath, she turned her head to look into Max's smiling face. "Leo is a bit smaller than I am, beautiful, so he is gonna go in the back door this time, okay?"

"Okay."

Leo's voice came from behind her as he started to nibble on her neck. "I feel like I've been waiting a lifetime for this, Adele." He ran his tongue down the nerve at the back of her neck and continued down her spine. His breath brushed against her wet skin, forcing goose bumps to pop out and making her body squirm. She twisted away from him, giggling at the sudden sensation.

Max grasped her breasts and suckled at them as he made moans of appreciation. Her eagerness to get away from Leo's teasing licks was forgotten, her groaning matching Max's. Adele was lost as hands and lips stroked and caressed her, driving her to such a level of excitement she was ready to scream by the time Max put his mouth on her mons.

They were both excellent lovers, but Max's tongue truly was magical. He teased her clit as he dipped two fingers into her vagina. In and out he moved, scissoring them as he nipped at her clit.

Suddenly, he sat back. "Sit on my face."

"What?"

He lay on his back and pulled her over him. "Sit on my face. I want to get more of you."

This had never been one of Adele's favorite positions. She was always afraid of crushing her partner, but Leo grabbed her and helped her position herself properly. He guided her hands to the headboard and encouraged her to grab hold.

Adele looked down at Max, and his grin had her smiling and eager for what that smile promised to bring her. Carefully, she lowered herself to his face.

Oh God. What had she been missing? Damn, she was stupid. She'd never felt anything so incredible before. Max ate at her as she gazed down at him, their eyes locked together, creating a closeness entirely new to her, the love in his eyes shooting straight to her heart and back down to her core.

This position opened her up to him physically in a way she'd never been before, allowing him deeper access to her entire pussy. He closed his eyes slowly and wrapped his arms around her thighs, keeping her where he wanted her as he pleasured her.

His tongue teased her up and down, side to side, small sparks shooting through her body from his contact. Every stroke of his tongue awakened sensations she'd never felt before until her head felt like it was ready to burst.

Once again, she'd nearly forgotten about Leo until he pulled her up to meet him for a kiss. The kiss was strong and needy, forceful in its intensity as he showed her how badly he wanted her, yet again.

His mischievous grin when he pulled back made her pussy clench. He moved out of her line of sight and she began to worry what he had planned, but then her attention was pulled to Max and his tongue. She didn't know what he did, but a miniorgasm crashed through her with unexpected intensity. She rocked over his mouth, writhing in ecstasy while Max continued his ministrations, ripping moans and groans from deep within her throat. Max didn't stop, his tongue moving ceaselessly to give her continued pleasure.

Adele became aware of a noise behind her an instant before she felt the wet cold at her anus. She realized Leo had a vibrator lubed and pressed against the puckered hole. The vibrations against her rosette sent her body tingling in anticipation.

Slowly he started to press it against her, sliding it into her body bit by bit.

She inhaled sharply, but Max's tongue and fingers had her writhing on top of him, and the vibrator was in completely before she even realized it. Leo increased the speed, and Adele's insides shivered in time with it. Her attention was pulled between what Leo was doing with the vibrator and Max's actions, back and forth, unable to settle on one lover. Instead, she rolled with it until she was quickly beyond caring when pinpricks of pleasure engulfed her body. It felt as thought tiny explosions were going off under her skin. Her body trembled, and it wasn't long before her world exploded in a mind-shattering orgasm.

Barely aware of Leo turning the machine off and removing it from her body, Adele fell to the side, breathing heavily as aftershocks ran through her body. She wasn't sure if she could handle any more. But her men hadn't been satisfied, and even though she knew they would take care of each other, she wanted to do it.

Repositioning her body, she straddled Max, much lower this time. She moved against him, rubbing his cock against her lower lips. Her energy came flooding back at the sound of his moans when he grabbed her hips and rose up to meet her.

Max reached to the bedside table to get a condom, and she grabbed his hand.

"No."

"But—"

"If you are doing it for me, then don't. You've both told me you're clean, and I believe you. I'm clean too. You guys know I'm on the Pill. We don't need that, and I don't want it."

"Are you sure?"

In answer, Adele grabbed hold of his cock and slid onto it quickly. His groan of satisfaction had her smiling as she felt him slip into her core. She stayed still for a moment to allow her body to get used to having Max inside her. Then she leaned over and started to move.

As she rode Max, Leo rubbed her ass, running a lubed finger down between her cheeks before probing her back entrance. Adele whimpered when his finger entered her before he added another.

It was tight, making her feel full, but she knew it wasn't anything compared to how she would be feeling once he buried his cock in her ass. He scissored his fingers and she moaned, stopping her forward motion.

Max took her hands in his. "Are you sure you're ready for this?"

Adele closed her eyes and just felt. Felt her men with her like this and nodded. "Yes, I am." She turned her head back toward Leo. "Please, Leo. I'm ready."

Leo slowly pulled his fingers out and positioned his sheathed and lubed cock at her entrance. "Hold on to Max, darlin'."

Max's hands tightened on hers as he smiled brightly into her eyes. "Relax, love."

Adele realized she was tensing and knew it would only hurt that way, so when Max tugged her toward his mouth, she met it with abandon. She relaxed her entire body as she let herself drown in Max's kiss. Losing herself in the sensation of the moment, she was barely aware of Leo entering her from behind.

Leo slowly pushed into her tiny rosette.

"Push back," Leo directed her. Max was still distracting her with his hands and lips. Pressure. It was all she felt. No pain, but definite pressure as Leo eased inside her. She didn't have the time to decide if it was good or bad before she realized he was completely seated in her.

No one moved for a moment, allowing Adele time to get used to the feeling, and perhaps, she thought, getting used to the feeling themselves. She propped her head on Max's shoulder, reveling in it all. She decided she really liked the feel of her new lovers buried deep inside her. She felt complete and whole in a way she never had before.

A small twitch of her hips had her men moving once again. Leo moved slowly at first, making sure she was comfortable with him in her ass. Her moans must have encouraged him, because he started moving faster, pumping in and out.

Max also picked up his pace and worked in rhythm with Leo, one of them moving in, the other out, always making sure she was filled with at least one cock, pushing her, pumping her, driving her quickly toward orgasm. Her thin inner membrane was squeezed between the two as they rubbed against her and each other.

Their groans of pleasure and arousal excited her even further as they continued to make love to each other, all three of them incoherently murmuring words and sounds.

Adele couldn't decipher the feelings that were running through her body. She was filled, bursting with emotions. She felt wanted and protected, as well as desired. Sparks ran through her body from both cocks and her men's hands stroking her skin. The words they spoke, the sweet nothings, drove her further and faster until finally, with a scream, she flew over the edge into a sharp, fast orgasm.

Max shouted as he rammed into her one final time and shot his load into her pulsing canal while Leo seated himself deeply and came with a loud moan.

The three of them collapsed in a heap, breathing heavily, panting from exertion and excitement. Adele didn't think she'd be able to move for a month and, wrapped up in their arms, didn't want to.

Chapter Eight

Sunlight flickered across her eyelids, nudging her awake. Gradually she realized that she was being cuddled from behind by a warm body. She moaned and wiggled back a bit, trying to get closer and only then recognized the top of her body was draped across another very warm body.

She smiled. A girl could get used to this. And to last night. She'd lost track of how many orgasms she'd had or how many times they'd made love. With stamina like that, she wasn't sure if she could live up to their expectations. Well, if she was too tired, they had each other too.

That had to have been the sexiest thing she had ever seen, watching the two of them together, their love evident in every move they made. And that same love had shone through when they had turned their attention to her.

She'd known their love before. The love of a cherished friend, someone they'd valued in their lives. But last night had been completely different. She'd had no doubt that they loved her. The kind of love that was written about in romances, the kind of love meant to last forever.

"What are you thinking?"

Adele's eyes popped open, and she looked up the smooth chest she was lying on to meet Leo's gaze.

"How'd you know—"

"You get stiff when you're thinking about something, and that last sigh was too deep not to mean something."

"I was thinking about last night."

"You aren't regretting it, are you?"

"Why, are you?"

Max's arm tightening around her waist and the growl that reverberated against her back assured her he was awake, too. "I thought we made it clear last night that we wouldn't."

"As did I, but yet Leo still felt he had to ask."

Max sighed and Leo shook his head.

"She's right, Max. She has every right to wonder, just as we do. Just because we know our minds, doesn't mean she does."

"Okay, point made already." Max sounded irritated and annoyed. He moved away from her, but only long enough to roll her over onto her back so she could look him in the eyes. Leo adjusted his body so they were both looking down at her, now lying on her back.

"Adele, last night was incredible." He looked at Leo before turning back to her. "There was something there that we have been missing for a long time. A hole was filled that we only recently realized existed."

Adele bit her lip to help fight the smile that came unbidden at Max's wording. She knew he was trying to be romantic and sweet. And he was, but it was a horrible word choice.

"Good going, partner. You think you could have picked a better way to say it?" Leo's voice was laced with suppressed laughter.

Max's look of confusion was replaced with one of concern. "Oh God, Adele, I didn't mean that the way—"

"Sh." She reached up and placed her hand on his lips. "I know what you meant, and it was beautiful." She pulled him down for a gentle kiss that declared her love for him.

"Although my longtime lover managed to mangle that, he's right, Adele." Now Leo's voice was filled with a deeper emotion. "You fill a gap that has been empty for a long time. You complete us in a way that I don't think mere words can explain. Last night wasn't just the fulfillment of a dream for us; it was the start of a new beginning. Nothing could ever make me regret it."

Adele's gaze flickered back and forth between her two men hovering over her on the bed, assuring her of their feelings. Never in her entire life had she felt so loved or like she belonged. Her heart was flooded with emotions she found difficult to identify, in addition to the love she felt for the two of them.

Needing to sit up to say what she was feeling, she scooted her body back until she was leaning against the headboard. The sheet was wrapped around her torso, and the two of them adjusted to sit in front of her. "I don't regret last night, no matter what happens between us, but I'll be honest. I'm scared. I don't know how I should feel, what to do, or anything. I love you both with all of my heart, but this is something I never dared even dream would be possible."

Adele smiled. "Well, that's not true, I dreamed of it. Fantasized how it would be. Of you two wanting me, making love to me much as you did last night, but the dreams stopped there. I never thought about what would happen afterward. You talk about wanting a future with me. What does that mean? You two live here and I come over for an occasional roll in the hay? I'm the third whenever you need a bit of excitement in your sex life? You have my love, but what else do you want from me?"

"We want whatever you want, Adele." Leo grasped one of her hands in his, holding it tight.

"Whatever you're willing to give."

Adele shook her head. "That still doesn't answer my question."

"We want you in our lives for always," Leo tried to assure her. "As part of us. An equal partner in our relationship. Not our third, not a diversion. Our partner, our lover, our wife."

Leo and Max had always referred to each other as their husband. They never needed a piece of paper to know they belonged together. But could she live like that? With two husbands?

Was she willing to give up her townhouse, her life as it was, for them? To risk her job? Because she had no doubt, if it didn't work then she'd never be able to continue working with them. It would hurt too much to see them every day, knowing what she'd lost.

But wouldn't it be just as bad to see them now and realize she could have had more, if only she'd been a brave enough to reach for the brass ring?

She put her hand up. "I love you both, but I can't decide this right now. It's too big a change, too much of a surprise.

Like I said, I never thought past the initial act. I need some time. Please. Just give me a couple days to process all this and then we can talk again."

Max opened his mouth as though to say something, but once again Adele put up her hand to forestall him. "No. Don't say anything. I need to go home. I'll be back."

* * *

"We should have shown her the room, Leo. You shouldn't have prevaricated like that." Max leaned against the fridge, ankles crossed.

"We told her we wanted her in our lives."

"Yeah, but I don't think she got it. I don't think she understands what we mean."

"Well then, why didn't you say anything?"

Max crossed his arms and glared at his lover. "What did you want me to say? Ask her to marry me while we were still in bed? Ask her to pledge her life to both of us for all eternity? You heard her. She wasn't ready to listen. She'd already heard what you said, and didn't seem to want to hear any more."

"She's scared."

"Of what? Us?"

"No, of what others will think." Leo walked to the breakfast bar and handed Max a cup of coffee on his way.

"Scared of others? Oh, please, Leo. I think you forget the first time I ever met her."

Leo snorted. "Not likely."

The first time they'd met had been at an office party at their previous jobs. Max and Leo had heard her defending another employee from a group of women who were insulting him behind his back, despite the fact she was the newest staff member there. They'd been impressed with her right away, and that fondness had grown over the years into the love they had for her now.

Max took a swallow from his cup and sat beside his lover. "She's one of the strongest people I know, Leo. She doesn't care what other people think. Hell, even if she did, it's not like anyone at work would say anything, and her friends love her and will accept her no matter what."

"Her friends, yes."

"Oh, shit."

"You forgot what today was, didn't you?" Leo sipped his coffee, watching Max over the rim of the mug.

"She's going to brunch with her family."

Leo nodded. "Both Beverly and her father."

"You remembered, and you let her go alone?"

"What was I supposed to do, Max? She asked us weeks ago not to interfere. It's hard enough for her as it is, are we supposed to just force them to accept us?"

"She's miserable every time she sees them. We should be there for her."

Leo shook his head. "She has to do this herself. Whether she decides to stay with us or not, we can't force her to live her life the way we want her to. Adele has to make her own decisions. Set her own limits."

"Goddamn it. Every time it's the same thing. They suck her dry and break her apart."

"So we'll make sure we're there to pick up the pieces."

Chapter Nine

Adele looked at herself in the bathroom mirror and sighed. What the hell was she doing here? Who cared that Gralue's was the most expensive restaurant in town when she'd left the two people she loved more than anything or anyone else in her life to come to brunch with her father and her sister.

All they'd done since she got here was bitch and moan about her appearance, her attitude, her job. Basically her entire life. Just wait till they heard about what the guys had asked of her. Adele smiled evilly. What she wouldn't give to—"Shit."

The sound of her cell phone ringing interrupted her thoughts of making her family squirm.

"Adele? Adele! Are you there?" Sarah's voice came over the speaker and Adele had to smile again.

"Yeah, I'm here, Sarah."

"What happened, woman? Leo told me they were taking you home and teaching you a lesson and asked me not to interfere. What the hell is going on?"

"Well, it's hard to explain over the phone." Adele sighed and sat on the settee in the corner of the restroom. One thing about these upscale restaurants, they provided plenty of space to relax in, even if it was in the bathroom. "And I'm with Dad."

"Well, I know you didn't answer the phone in front of him, or I'd hear him bitching all the way across town, so that means you're alone. So give me the short version."

Adele took a deep breath and blurted it out. "The guys made love to me all night long after telling me how much they love me. They want me to be their partner. Their third, as in a triad, all three of us—lovers. I think they might even want to get married. They said something about wife. But I'm not sure."

Sarah's scream of excitement came over the phone loud and clear, only to be followed by a voice behind Adele full of scorn and disgust.

"Excuse me? What did you say?" Beverly's shrewish voice shot through Adele's head like a sharp spike. The woman never had learned the art of subtlety.

"Sarah, I gotta go." Without waiting for a response, Adele closed her phone and turned to face her sister. She should have known Beverly wouldn't give her space for any amount of time. *Hell, Dad probably sent her in here after me.* Just like her father to time her in a public bathroom.

Adele could only hope Beverly hadn't heard more than the last few seconds of her conversation with Sarah. "Whatever I said doesn't concern you. It wasn't your conversation, so you don't need to worry about it."

"Apparently I do, if you're telling our relatives that you're considering moving in with those two faggots and becoming their fuck buddy."

"Beverly! Don't be disgusting."

"Me? I'm not the one that's talking about fucking two men."

"You're repulsive." Adele shivered as the depth of Beverly's close-mindedness washed over her, leaving her cold.

"Better that than a cheap slut. Wait until I tell Daddy what you're doing."

"What I am considering or not considering doing is none of your business."

Beverly glared at her before turning and leaving the bathroom in a huff. Adele spent a few precious seconds cursing her luck, her tongue, and her sister before rushing after her. She realized she had to get out there before Beverly did anything they'd both regret.

By the time she got to the table, her father had already stood up and was demanding the check from the waiter. The look he sent her way dried up anything she wanted to say. Instead, she followed him and her sister to the parking lot.

An intimidating man at the best of times, Benjamin Waters's glowering countenance boded ill for any person who dared to cross him. And right now that person was her.

"We'll talk about this when we get home, young lady."

Adele opened her mouth to protest but closed it immediately. He was right; anything that had to be said would be better said in private.

* * *

She pulled up behind him and Beverly in his driveway and sighed deeply. Damn Beverly. Adele wasn't even sure of what she was going to do, and here her sister had probably told him all kinds of things.

Turn around. Leave now, let him calm down. Only he wouldn't calm down, he would only get angrier. Better face the music now, before it got worse.

Slowly Adele climbed out of the car and walked to the front door of the house she'd grown up in. A large Federal-style home, there were six bedrooms and five bathrooms as well as an office, library, and den. The kitchen and family room were one great room, much the same as at Leo and Max's place. Only Leo's and Max's had soul. Her father's house was too sterile to be considered a home. She and her sister had grown up in a show house, not a home.

It wasn't until she had started helping the guys with their place that she really felt the difference. She'd known it intellectually, and thought she'd succeeded in differentiating the two with her clients, but she hadn't truly experienced it personally before the two of them. It didn't matter who designed it, or what the primary style was. It was about function and feeling. Max and Leo's house welcomed her and everyone they knew. It welcomed guests to come in, make themselves comfortable, and stay awhile.

She followed them into her father's office. Growing up, they could always tell the level of trouble they were in by which room their father spoke to them in. The office had always been reserved for only the worst infractions.

"Now tell me what this is about." He sat in his personal place of power, behind his extra-large mahogany desk. From there he could rule his world without interference from anyone.

Adele debated lying, but she had never been very good at it, and he had always been able to tell. So instead, maybe some misdirection. "Beverly overheard only part of a conversation. A private conversation. What she heard was none of her business."

"If it involves you, it involves this entire family, young lady. I have worked hard over the years to make the Waters name mean something in this town, and I won't have you dragging it through the mud."

Adele forced her jaw to loosen before the grinding of her teeth became audible. She could just hear her father rambling on about how much money he'd spent on her teeth growing up. Just one more thing for him to get angry about today.

"I don't know how my friendship with two well-respected businessmen is going to drag the Waters name through the mud."

Her father scowled. He didn't like being reminded that Max and Leo weren't bums on the street. Their successful business put them on nearly the same level socially in town as he was. His status was important to him, and he relished the power it gave him, but not even he was able to deny them their success.

"I think I have tolerated it long enough. It's time you end this farce of a friendship and come home. I can get you a job in any of the better firms in town, and you can move back here where—"

"No." Her response was so low she wasn't sure he heard it. Hell, she wasn't even sure she had said it aloud.

"Excuse me?"

"I said no." Her voice was louder this time, more confident. Stronger.

"I know I didn't hear you properly, young lady." His voice was deep with threat.

"Yes, you did. I'm sorry, Daddy, but you won't have your way in this. I love Max and Leo, and they love me. I've put up with your interfering all my life. I went to the schools you wanted me to go to, I joined all the proper clubs, the right sorority. You even decided on my first job."

"I did all that to ensure you had a good life."

Adele shook her head, knowing he really had done it all for her. But that didn't change anything. "I know you did. And I appreciate it, I do. But it's my turn now. I'm thirty years old. I've never even dated anyone you haven't vetted first. Hell, I even got engaged to Nigel because of you."

"And broke the engagement against my advice." His voice rumbled across the desk to her.

"He was having sex with his secretary!"

"All men have an indiscretion or two. It's the way we are."

Adele opened her mouth to respond and changed her mind. It was an old argument and she wasn't going to let him misdirect her now. "Fine. Other than that and going to work with the guys, I have never done anything you haven't approved of, but it's over. I am going to live my life the way I want. It's my future, not yours."

"And what does that mean, exactly?" he asked. "Do you really plan on shacking up with the two of them?"

"They give me something I've never had before. Unconditional love. They love me no matter what I do, what I wear, or how much I weigh. I'm never happier than when I'm with them."

"This won't last. They'll get tired of you and throw you out."

Adele nodded. "You know, I thought of that, too. And I don't think it will happen. I know them better than I know myself, and I honestly think—no, I know this love is forever. And if something happens down the road, then so be it. I am not going to give up my chance of happiness."

Adele stood up and turned to leave.

"If you step out of that door, then you are no longer a daughter of mine. You will be disowned and stricken from my life."

She knew her father loved her, deep down. She knew he wanted only what was best for her, but her idea of what was best would never mesh with his. She loved him dearly, but she needed to live her own life.

She turned to look at her father one last time, searching for some measure of softness. "Does it make a difference when I tell you that they make me happy, Daddy? Truly happy?"

His face remained as stone-cold as it always had been.

So be it.

"Good-bye, Daddy, Beverly. I'm sorry it had to be this way. Have a nice life."

Chapter Ten

"Did you mean it?" Adele stood in the kitchen asking the most important question of her life. The men were in front of the breakfast bar, as though on their way to see who had come through the front door. She'd known where to find them and hadn't waited for them at the door. Her question was too important to wait even another second.

After leaving her father's house, she'd driven around for hours, thinking. Her response to him had been more reflexive than anything. She hadn't even thought of the repercussions before she had answered him.

When she'd gotten into her car, she realized what she had done and took the time to really think about what she had said, about why she had said it, and how she really felt about the men.

She loved Max and Leo more than anything She couldn't imagine a future without them. When she tried it looked empty and unfulfilling.

But then she balanced that with a life without her father. Because she had no doubt that her father meant it when he said she was no longer his daughter.

Her mother had been gone for ten years. Despite her addiction, she'd been a kind, gentle woman who had let Benjamin rule the house. But she'd given her girls love.

Maybe that's why Beverly was so much like her father. Although Adele had tried to fill the gap after her mother died, it hadn't been the same.

Her mother never would have given her this ultimatum. Having already lost one parent, though, Adele didn't take this loss lightly. No matter what he did and how he acted, he was still her father. But that didn't give him the right to dictate the rest of her life. She couldn't, and shouldn't, live her life for her father.

Her mother wouldn't want her to, either. "Follow your heart," she'd tell Adele whenever there was a decision to be made. Her mother had followed the dictates of society, and Adele was sure that was part of the reason for her problems. She had wanted more for her daughters. Adele owed it to both her mother and herself to be as happy as she could be.

Adele would miss her father and sister, but her obligation was to her future. And if it happened like her father predicted, then at least she'd have the knowledge she'd chosen to be happy. She wouldn't have turned her back on love.

"Your friendship means the world to me. And the thought of the two of you loving me brings to life a piece of my heart that I didn't know existed. But I'm not always the strongest of women. I need to know. Did you mean what you said earlier?"

Leo answered for the both of them. "Every word, Adele. We love you with every fiber of our beings."

"How will it work? Do you want me to move in with you? Do I keep my place? Do I sleep in the second room unless you guys want me?"

Max reached for her hand. "We have something to show you."

Adele placed her hand in his, unsure of what he wanted, but knowing he wouldn't hurt her. He led her up the stairs, Leo following behind. They walked her down the hallway and paused at the bottom of the attic stairs before turning her so she faced both of them.

Max started. "We want you to live with us, be in our bed."

"Make it our room, as in 'us,' belonging to all three of us."

Adele waited and Max continued. "You know that Leo has his private office at the back of the house. His space where he can escape when he needs to, and I have my workshop."

"Yeah." Adele nodded her head, unsure when the conversation took this strange turn.

"We created upstairs for you." Leo nodded toward the stairs behind her.

Adele shook her head, confused. "But the attic isn't done yet."

"That's what we told you because we didn't want you walking in on it half done and asking questions."

Adele furrowed her brow.

"Just come upstairs, honey." Max tugged on her hand, urging her up the stairs before them.

Adele climbed up the steps only to stop a few feet from the top. The heavy door that had been on the landing had been removed and replaced with a French door with a curtain behind it.

"You can have all the privacy you want. There's even a lock." Leo practically whispered the words, pointing out the old-fashioned key in the door.

Still confused, she slowly opened the door and stepped through, only to stop short.

The attic wasn't bare boards and floor as she had expected. Instead, it was finished as a private apartment: a large studio with various areas separated by purpose. She moved across the thick white carpet without conscious thought, as though pulled forward by some invisible string.

The main area was a large entertainment room, furnished with a television and stereo as well as overstuffed chairs and a couch. It was large enough for a small gathering of people, yet small enough to feel cozy when here alone. To the left an open door gave her a glimpse into a lavishly appointed bathroom where silver and marble gleamed in the sunlight streaming in from the skylight.

Toward the right of the main room, a section was partitioned off into two separate areas. One was a relaxation area complete with candles, yoga mat, and a daybed, while the other was set up as an office. The varied tools and supplies she'd need for her occasional work sessions at home sat on a large table that was a perfect space for her to create her designs.

A small arch led off to the northeast corner of the house and she walked through to see what awaited her. She hadn't realized it until she stepped through the doorway, but this section of the attic was directly above the master bedroom on the second floor and the library on the first. The large semicircle wall that followed the line of the turret outside was made mostly of windows with a wide, cushioned seat below them. Bookcases lined the walls on either side of the windows, mostly empty, but with a few books by her favorite authors lined up as though already waiting for her. An oversize chaise in a subdued ivory tone had a deep brown fleece throw lying across the arm, completing the picture.

Adele turned to face the men, her heart in her throat. She was so overwhelmed at what they had done for her, she was speechless.

"We want you to share our room, our bed," Max assured her softly. "When we talk about being together forever we mean in all ways, but we understand how living with two men might be overwhelming at times, so we created this sanctuary for you. Leo even insisted we include the daybed in case you really needed time away from us."

Leo smiled at Max's frown. "Although we hope nothing will ever be severe enough to drive you from the bed we will all share."

"Married people should never sleep apart when they're under the same roof." Max reached for her face and turned her to face him as he spoke. "And that's what we'll be. Married. The three of us."

Adele opened her mouth to say something, but once again wasn't given the chance.

Leo walked behind her and placed his hands on her shoulders as Max got down on one knee, holding her left hand. "Adele Waters, will you do me the honor of becoming my wife?"

Tears sprang to her eyes as she stared at the man in front of her before turning her head to see Leo's face.

She saw trust, love, and approval in his eyes before he spoke to her. "The law won't allow the three of us to marry so we were hoping you'd agree to marry Max."

Her gaze flew back to Max's face as Leo continued.

"You know he has that trust fund from his grandfather, and it's a pretty good chunk of change. This way if anything ever happened to the two of us, we'd know you'd always be taken care of."

Max's voice was low as he vowed, "I love you with all of my heart and promise to always be there for you."

Leo took her other hand and got down on his knee beside Max. "I know it won't be easy, Adele, it's a difficult thing we're asking of you. But I, too, love you from the bottom of my heart. The thought of you being part of our life forever brings such joy I feel like a little kid about to burst on Christmas morning. Will you please be our wife and help make our lives more complete?"

The sight of the two of them blurred as tears filled her eyes. Tears of joy and love. Full of the knowledge that they would always be there for her no matter what, that they truly did love her as much as they said. What kind of woman would ever be stupid enough to turn this down?

Instead, she fell to her knees in front of them, pulling their hands to her chest. "Yes. With all of my heart, yes."

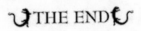

THE END

Talya Bosco

Talya is an avid fan of all forms of the printed word. She has been reading for as long as she can remember, and has dreamed of being an author for almost as long. On any given day, when she's not working, you can find her at the computer or curled up somewhere in her house writing or reading whatever has caught her fancy that week. She has been known to push the limits of her deadlines, or go to work on little to no sleep, only so she can finish a book she is reading.

Her reading habit was the bane of her family's existence while growing up, but she has found a wonderful man that shares her evil inclination. They live quietly, reading books, playing on computers, practicing martial arts and enjoying one another's company.

Talya feels all that reading has helped her to become a better author. She has devoted her professional life to writing fun, erotic stories that make you believe in second chances and happily-ever-afters.

LaVergne, TN USA
30 December 2009
168643LV00001B/185/P